"Are you ready to die?"
the piano player asked casually,
opening the top of the bench.

"If you don't find that music in the next five seconds, I'm gonna shoot you where you stand," Priest said. "One."

"You know, it seems to me like you could have picked a better reason to get yourself killed than this. 'Marching Through Georgia' isn't even that good a tune."

"What the hell are you talking about? Two," Priest said, continuing his count.

"You can't say I didn't warn you."

"Three."

Suddenly there was a loud bang. A hole appeared in the upraised lid of the piano bench and a curl of smoke arose from behind it. When the piano player lifted his right hand into view, his fingers were curled around a Colt .44.

Priest looked down in surprise at the hole the bullet had just punched in the middle of his chest. He dropped his gun and put his hand over the wound, but the blood was flowing freely and it spilled between his fingers. "You . . . you killed me." he gasped.

"Yeah, I did," Hawke said easily.

Books by Robert Vaughan

HAWKE: SHOWDOWN AT DEAD END CANYON
HAWKE: RIDE WITH THE DEVIL

HAWKE
SHOWDOWN AT DEAD END CANYON

ROBERT
VAUGHAN

HarperTorch
An Imprint of HarperCollinsPublishers

This is a work of fiction. Names, characters, places, and incidents are products of the author's imagination or are used fictitiously and are not to be construed as real. Any resemblance to actual events, locales, organizations, or persons, living or dead, is entirely coincidental.

HARPERTORCH
An Imprint of HarperCollins*Publishers*
10 East 53rd Street
New York, New York 10022-5299

Copyright © 2005 by Robert Vaughan
ISBN 0-06-072584-2

First HarperTorch paperback printing: May 2005

HarperCollins®, HarperTorch™, and ❦™ are trademarks of Harper-Collins Publishers Inc.

Printed in the United States of America

Visit HarperTorch on the World Wide Web at www.harpercollins.com

10 9 8 7 6 5 4 3 2 1

*This book
is dedicated to
Bob Robison*

HAWKE
SHOWDOWN AT DEAD END CANYON

Prologue

~◆~

THE WAR BETWEEN THE STATES WAS THE COST-
liest war in American history. From Bull Run to Franklin,
neighbor fought neighbor and brother fought brother until
half a million men lay dead on the bloody battlefields.

For all intents and purposes, it ended when Lee surren-
dered to Grant at Appomattox, Virginia, but for many veter-
ans of that terrible war, the surrender was just the beginning
of a much more personal conflict. Young men who had lived
their lives on the edge for four years found it nearly impossible to return home and take up the plow, or go back to work
in a store, repair wagons, or do any of the other things that
were the necessary part of becoming whole again.

Others found nothing to come home to. Many of the vet-
erans—especially those who had fought for the South—returned to burned-out homes, farms gone to seed or, worse,
taken for taxes. These men became the dispossessed. Unable
to settle down, they became wanderers. Many of them went
west, where there would be less civilized encroachment
upon their chosen way of life.

Some took up the outlaw trail, continuing to practice the

skills they had learned during the war. But most were innocent wanderers, with all bridges to their past burned and the paths to their future uncharted.

Mason Hawke was such a man. When he found that he had nothing to return to, he became a wandering minstrel, playing the piano in saloons and bawdy houses throughout the West. Few of those who heard him playing "Cowboy Joe" or "Buffalo Gals" realized that he had once played before the crowned heads of Europe. There were many, however, who learned to appreciate his talent, for from time to time Hawke would bring out the music at his core, playing a concert at three o'clock in the morning for the ghosts of his past. But it wasn't just the ghosts who enjoyed those midnight concerts; often, a crowd would gather silently just outside the saloon, listening to the music.

But there was another, darker side to Hawke.

The same digital dexterity that made him a great pianist also made him exceptionally good with a gun. Hawke did not openly seek trouble, but neither would he back away from it. Hotheaded hooligans would sometimes mistake the piano player for an easy mark.

It was a mistake they only made once.

Chapter 1

SECONDS EARLIER THE LUCKY DOG SALOON HAD been peaceful. A card game was in progress in one part of the room, the teases, touches, and flirtatious laughter of the bar girls were in play in another. Mason Hawke, who had only been in Buffalo Creek, Colorado, for six weeks, was at the piano, his music adding to the gaiety and celebratory atmosphere of the evening.

But all that changed in an instant when Ebenezer Priest shouted out, "By God, you'll play what I tell you to play, or I'll kill you where you sit!"

The music, conversation, and laughter stopped, the loudest sound in the saloon the ticking of the Regulator clock that stood by the door that led out to the privy. There were twelve people in the saloon, ten men and two women, and all eyes were directed toward the piano where Priest stood just behind Mason Hawke. Priest had his gun out and was aiming it at the back of Hawke's head.

Ebenezer Priest was a small, gnarled-looking man. In a world without guns, he would barely draw a second look, let alone command fear and begrudging respect. But this was a world with guns, and Priest had to be taken seriously because he had proven his skill with the pistol, and had a known propensity, almost an eagerness, to use it. He enjoyed watching bigger, stronger men quake in their boots when he addressed them. No one had ever defied him and lived.

Those thoughts were on everyone's mind now as they watched and wondered how this drama, so rapidly unfolding before them, would play itself out.

"Did you hear what I said, piano player?" Priest asked. His voice was a low, evil hiss. "I told you to play 'Marching Through Georgia.' "

"I don't know that song," Hawke replied calmly.

"You know it, you Rebel son of a bitch. All you Rebel bastards know it. I was in the Union Army, and we sang it as we marched through Georgia. Now, play it. Play it, or I'm going to splatter your blood and brains all over the front of that piano."

"Leave 'im be, Priest," the bartender called. "He ain't nothin' but a piano player. What do you want to go shucking a piano player for?"

With his left hand, Priest pointed a finger at the bartender, all the while keeping his gun pointed at Hawke's head.

"You just stay the hell out of this, Kirby. This ain't none of your concern." He turned his attention back to Hawke. "Now, start playing," he ordered.

Hawke began to play. It took but a few bars of music before Priest realized that he wasn't playing "Marching Through Georgia." He was playing "The Bonnie Blue Flag," the Confederate marching song.

The saloon patrons laughed at the joke. With a yell of rage, Priest pulled the trigger on his pistol. The laughter stopped and everyone gasped, expecting to see the back of Hawke's head blown away. What they saw instead was the destruction of a mug of beer sitting on top of the piano. The glass shattered and beer splattered. Even as people's ears were still ringing from the noise of the gunshot, they could hear the hum of the soundboard as the piano strings vibrated in resonance.

Hawke quit playing and sat quietly on the bench.

"Now, Mr. Piano Player, I'm through playing with you," Priest said in a low, menacing voice. "You had better play 'Marching Through Georgia,' or by God the next bullet is going to go through your head."

Hawke sighed. "I told you I don't know it."

Priest cocked his gun, the action making a double click as the sear engaged the cylinder and rotated a new bullet under the hammer. "You had better learn it real quick, music man."

"As I said, I don't know it, but I do have the music in my bench. I'll have to get it out."

"All right, do it. And be quick about it."

Hawke stood up, then turning around so that he was facing Priest, opened the top of the bench. As the bench lid came up, it shielded Hawke's hands from Priest's view.

"You know, it seems to me like you could have picked a better reason to get yourself killed than this," Hawke said. " 'Marching Through Georgia' isn't even that good of a tune."

"What do you mean, get myself killed?" Priest asked, confused. "You're the one that's going to get yourself killed. If you don't find that music in the next five seconds, I'm going to shoot you where you stand."

"I don't think so," Hawke said.

Priest wasn't used to anyone taking his threats so casually. And he especially didn't expect such a calm reaction from a piano player.

"One . . ." he said, beginning his count.

"Are you really this anxious to die?" Hawke asked.

"What the hell are you talking about? Two . . ." Priest said, continuing his count.

"You can't say I didn't warn you," Hawke said.

"Three . . ."

Suddenly, there was a loud bang. A hole appeared in the upraised lid of the piano bench, and a curl of smoke rose from behind it. When Hawke lifted his right hand from behind the bench, his fingers were curled around a Colt .44.

Priest looked down in surprise at the hole the bullet had just punched in the middle of his chest.

"Unh!" he grunted, taking a step back. Dropping his gun, he put his hand over the wound, but the blood was flowing freely and it spilled between his fingers. "You . . . you killed me," he gasped.

"Yeah, I did," Hawke said easily.

Priest collapsed. One of the men nearest him hurried over, then knelt beside him and put his hand on the fallen man's neck. He looked up at the others.

"He's dead," he said.

"I'll be damned! Who would've thought someone like Ebenezer Priest would ever get hisself kilt by a piano player?"

"I'm glad the son of a bitch is dead," one of the others said. "He's been ridin' roughshod over this town for nigh on to two years now."

Hawke put his gun back in the piano bench, then walked over to the bar and ordered a whiskey.

"It's on the house, Mr. Hawke," Kirby said as he poured the drink and set it in front of Hawke.

A deputy sheriff came running in then, drawn by the sound of the two gunshots. His own gun was drawn, and after a quick glance around the room, he saw Priest lying on the floor.

"Well, I'll be damned," he said, putting his pistol away. "When I heard the gunshots, I knew damn well Priest would be in the middle of it, but I figured I'd find him standin'. I never expected to see him be the one that's spread out on the floor. How bad is it?"

"He's dead," one of the patrons replied.

The deputy walked over to Priest's body and stared down at it for a moment. He kicked the body lightly, then a little bit harder. Priest did not respond. Then he kicked him so hard that it moved Priest's body slightly.

"You're right," the deputy said. "The son of a bitch is dead." There was a spattering of nervous laughter.

The deputy looked around the saloon, returning everyone's curious gaze with his own. "Who did it?" he asked.

"I did," Hawke said.

The deputy looked at the piano player and laughed. "No, I'm serious. Who killed the son of a bitch?"

"He's tellin' you the truth, Deputy," Kirby said. "He did it."

"Yeah," another saloon patron said. "Priest braced the piano player and the piano player shot 'im."

The deputy looked over at Hawke. At six feet, Hawke was a little taller than average. He was slender of build, with gunmetal-gray eyes, and his hair was light brown, almost blond. Unlike most of the other patrons, Hawke was clean-shaven, and wore a white ruffled shirt poked down into fawn-colored trousers. A blue jacket and crimson cravat completed his ensemble.

"Why, you aren't even wearing a gun," the deputy said.

Hawke nodded toward the piano. "It's over there, in the piano bench."

"And you're telling that Priest braced you, then waited for you to get your gun out of the bench?"

"Something like that," Hawke said.

The deputy walked over to the piano and looked down at the bench. He saw the bullet hole in the bench lid.

"I'll be damn," he said.

* * *

Judge Andrew Norton held the inquest two days later. The prosecuting attorney, pointing out that Hawke was an itinerant who posed a flight risk, had asked the judge to confine him to jail until the inquest. But the judge denied the motion, and Hawke upheld the judge's trust by showing up on the day of the inquest.

It was an open inquiry, with not only the witnesses to the event present, but many of the town's citizens in attendance as well.

One by one the witnesses were interviewed. The last witness was the bartender, Dwayne Kirby, and his testimony was typical.

"Ebenezer Priest was holding a cocked gun at Mr. Hawke's head," Kirby said when asked to give his version of what happened. "He shot it once, and I closed my eyes, thinkin' that when I opened 'em I'd see the piano player dead."

"But you didn't see him dead, did you?"

"No, sir, I did not."

"You didn't see him dead, because all Priest did was shoot the beer glass."

"Yes, sir, that's what he done."

"Then what happened?"

"Well, sir, Priest started in a'countin', and he told Hawke that when he got to five he was goin' to kill him."

"Hadn't he previously said that he would kill Mr. Hawke if he did not play 'Marching Through Georgia'?"

"Yes, sir, that's what he said."

"And did Mr. Hawke play 'Marching Through Georgia'?"

"No, sir, he did not. He played 'The Bonnie Blue Flag,'" Kirby said, laughing.

"I see. So, what you are telling me is, even though Priest told Hawke he would kill him if he didn't play 'Marching

Through Georgia,' he didn't do it. He shot the beer glass instead."

"That's right."

"What happened next?"

"It's just like all the others have told you." Kirby pointed toward Hawke. "Hawke turned around like as if he was goin' to get some music, and Priest commenced to countin'."

"Did Hawke say anything? Give him any warning?"

"I suppose you could say that. What Hawke said was, 'It seems to me like you could have picked a better reason to get yourself killed than this.'"

"So, in other words, Hawke threatened to kill Priest?"

"Well, I reckon they threatened each other."

"Yes, but Priest had already shown, by his earlier action, that he had no intention of killing Hawke, hadn't he?"

Kirby shook his head. "No, sir, I don't see it like that. I think Priest was plannin' on killin' him soon as he got to five. I mean, hell, he'd already killed a bunch of folks."

"We aren't talking about the people he did kill, we are talking about one that he didn't kill. We are talking about his confrontation with Mason Hawke. You said he started to count to five, but he didn't finish his count, did he?"

"No."

"Why didn't he finish his count?"

"'Cause Hawke shot him before he got there."

"And, I believe it has been testified to that Hawke shot him from behind the cover of a piano bench lid. Is that right?"

"Well, yeah, but it don't seem to me like as if he had any other—"

"Thank you, Mr. Kirby. That will be all."

"I'll tell you this—if there was ever anyone that needed killin'," Kirby said, though he'd been dismissed by the lawyer, "it was Ebenezer Priest. He was one of the sorriest bastards to ever draw a breath. He killed lots of good men for no reason at all, and he got away with it 'cause he goaded 'em into drawin' on him. Well, it didn't work with Hawke."

The gallery applauded and there were several utterances of, "Hear! Hear!"

"Thank you, Mr. Kirby," the prosecutor said again, more forcibly this time. "That will be all."

As Kirby was the final witness, the judge turned to Hawke.

"Mr. Hawke, this is an inquest, not a trial. Nevertheless, the provisions of the Fifth Amendment are just as applicable. Therefore, you cannot be forced to testify if you don't want to. On the other hand, if you wish to take the stand, now is the time to do so."

"I'll take the stand," Hawke said.

"Very well. Bailiff, would you administer the oath, please?"

The prosecutor waited until Hawke was sworn in, then stepped up to the witness chair and, hooking his thumbs in his suspenders, stared through narrowed eyes at Hawke. It was his most intimidating stare, but Hawke held the prosecutor's eyes with an unblinking stare of his own.

It was the prosecutor who broke eye contact first. Looking away, he cleared his throat before beginning his questioning.

"You understand, do you not, Mr. Hawke, that this is sworn testimony?" he asked. "If you lie during this testimony, it's the same as lying during an actual court trial. You will be subject to a charge of perjury."

Hawke, who continued his unblinking stare at the prosecutor, said nothing.

"Uh, yes," the prosecutor said, clearing his throat again. "For the record, is Mason Hawke your real name?"

"Yes."

"And, you are a piano player?"

"No."

The prosecutor was actually just getting some house-cleaning questions out of the way, and he looked up in sharp surprise when Hawke denied being a piano player.

"Wait a minute. Were you, or were you not, hired to play the piano in the Lucky Dog saloon?"

"I was."

"Well then, what would you call yourself, if not a piano player?"

"I call myself a pianist."

Several in the gallery laughed.

"Please don't play games with me, Mr. Hawke," he said. "What's the difference between a piano player and a pianist?"

"What's the difference between 'Turkey in the Straw' and Bach's Toccata and Fugue in D Minor?"

"I don't understand what you mean," the prosecutor said.

"Then you are an idiot, Mr. Prosecutor," the judge said, interrupting the dialogue. "Get on with your questioning."

Again the gallery laughed.

"Yes, Your Honor." Turning his attention back to Hawke, the prosecutor continued, "Mr. Hawke, you have heard the testimony of all the witnesses here today. Do you wish to dispute anything any of them said?"

"No."

"Just so the record is straight, did you kill Ebenezer Priest?"

"Yes."

"And how did you kill him? Was it a fair fight? Did you test your skill and courage against him in what one might reasonably call an affair of honor?"

"No. I just killed him."

"I see. And were you elated? Relieved? Did you feel a personal sense of power over having just taken a man's life?"

"No."

"Well, then, were you remorseful?"

"No."

"You felt none of those emotions?"

"No."

"Then what did you feel?"

"Killing Ebenezer Priest was like stepping on a cockroach. I felt nothing at all."

The prosecutor shook his head, then made a big show of walking away from Hawke. Standing several feet from the witness chair and looking out toward the audience, the prosecutor asked his next question in loud, well-articulated tones.

"By your own admission, your altercation with Priest was not a test of skill and courage. It was simply a killing. How can you be so cavalier about that, Mr. Hawke?"

"Have you ever killed anyone?" Hawke replied.

The prosecutor turned back. "I'm not on trial here, sir, you are," he said loudly.

"I thought this was an inquest, rather than a trial."

"All right, an inquest."

"Have you ever killed anyone?" Hawke asked again. "I'm just curious."

"All right, I'll answer your question. No, sir, I am proud to say that I have never killed anyone."

"Do you think gunfighters like Ebenezer Priest, Clay Allison, Bill Hickock, Temple Houston, and Ethan Dancer are successful killers because of their skill and courage? The answer is no. Killing is not a matter of skill and courage, it is merely a willingness to do it. The average man, the man with a soul, does not have that willingness. Even if he is faster and more skilled with a gun, he will hesitate, just for a moment, before killing someone. But men like those I just named have no soul. That's what gives them the edge."

"Like stepping on a cockroach, Mr. Hawke?" the prosecutor asked triumphantly.

"Yes," Hawke said without flinching.

"I see."

"Were you in the war, Mr. Prosecutor?"

"No, I was not."

"I was," Hawke said. "I killed many men during the war. No doubt some of them were evil, but the majority of them were decent, morally upstanding men. Each one was somebody's husband, father, son, or brother who just happened to be wearing the uniform of the other side. Do you think that if I killed good men like that, I would hesitate for one second before killing someone like Ebenezer Priest?"

"I thought you said that those who could kill without hesitation had no soul."

"Yes," Hawke said. "That is exactly what I said."

"So you are . . ."

"A man without a soul," Hawke answered.

After hearing all the evidence, the judge retired to his chambers for a short while, then returned to deliver his finding.

"On September tenth, last year, Ebenezer Priest killed William Grant. Mr. Grant was a man who, by mistake, took a drink from Priest's beer mug. Although Mr. Grant apologized, many times, Priest finally goaded him into drawing his gun, thus making it, officially, an act of self-defense. One of the ways he did this was by shooting the beer glass.

"In May of this year he goaded James Herrington into drawing his gun, by shooting his hat off his head. When Mr. Herrington went for his gun, Priest killed him. Both cases were officially ruled as justifiable homicide.

"Well, this time it did not work for him. If Mr. Hawke believed that Ebenezer Priest actually planned to kill him, then he was entirely justified in acting to save his own life. And, given Mr. Priest's history, I have no doubt that was the state of Mason Hawke's mind.

"Accordingly, I find this to be a case of justifiable homicide, and will allow no charges to be filed." Judge Norton struck the desk with his hammer. "This case is dismissed."

With the judge's ruling, those in the gallery applauded, then hurried forward to congratulate Hawke. Even the prosecutor congratulated him. "I was just doing my job," he said.

Dwayne Kirby, who was not only the bartender at the Lucky Dog, but half owner, saw this as a tremendous opportunity. He painted a sign and put it up behind the bar:

COME, MEET
MASON HAWKE.
THE MAN WHO SHOT
EBENEZER PRIEST.

He had just finished posting it when he turned around and saw Mason Hawke carrying his saddlebags over his shoulder.

"Are you going somewhere?" Kirby asked.

Hawke nodded. "It's time for me to move on."

"But why would you do that? The judge said there wouldn't be any charges against you. And think of how much money you will make in tips over the next several weeks because of this. Everybody is going to want to meet the man who shot Ebenezer Priest."

"Yes, that's exactly why I'm leaving," Hawke said. "I've no wish to meet anyone who wants to meet the man who killed Ebenezer Priest."

"But . . ." Kirby said, clearly distressed by this news. "Look, I'll tell you what. I'll cut you in for a percentage of everything wc take in for the next two months."

"Thank you," Hawke said. "That's a generous offer. But I think I'd better be moving on."

Kirby nodded, then sighed, and looked up toward his sign.

"All right," he said. "I can't keep you here. But you sure are passing up the opportunity to make a lot of money." He took the sign down.

Hawke stuck his hand across the bar. "You've been a fine man to work for, Mr. Kirby," he said. "I wish you the best."

"Same to you, Mr. Hawke," Kirby said as he morosely tore up the sign. He bent down to put the torn pieces in the trash can, and when he straightened up again, he saw Hawke stepping through the bat-wing doors.

Chapter 2

THE TOWN OF BITTER CREEK, WYOMING TERRITORY, was little more than a fly-blown speck on the Union Pacific Railroad. It had reached its peak when it was End of Track, a "hell on wheels," with enough cafés, saloons, and bawdy houses to take care of the men who were building the railroad. But as the railroad continued on its westward trek, Bitter Creek lost all of its importance and most of its population. It was gradually beginning to recover, though, and its hearty citizens hung on, waiting for the eventual bounty the railroad was sure to bring.

Two young men, passing through the town, stopped in front of the Boar's Breath saloon. Swinging down from their horses, they patted their dusters down.

"Damn me, Boomer, if you don't look like one of them dust devils," one of the men said, laughing at his friend.

"Yeah, well you ain't exactly a clean white sheet yourself, Dooley," Boomer replied. "What do you say we get us a couple of beers?"

"Sounds good to me," the other man said.

Pushing through the bat-wing doors, the two men entered

the saloon and stepped up to the bar. The saloon was relatively quiet, with only four men at one table and a fifth standing down at the far end of the bar. The four at the table were playing cards, the one at the end of the bar was nursing a drink. The man with the drink had a scar that started at his right eyebrow, came through the eye, disfiguring it, slashed down his cheek like a purple lightning bolt, then hooked into the corner of a misshapen mouth.

As the boys stepped up to the bar, the man with the scar looked over at them with an unblinking stare.

"What'll it be, gents?" the bartender asked.

One of them continued to stare back at the man standing at the end of the bar. He had never seen a face quite as disfigured.

"Dooley?" Boomer said. "The bartender asked what'll we have."

"Oh," Dooley replied. "Uh, two beers."

"Two beers it is," the bartender replied, and turned to draw them.

"And I'll have the same," Boomer added.

The bartender laughed. "You boys sound like you've got a thirst."

"Just sayin' we're thirsty don't quite get it," Dooley said. "Why, I got that much dust you could grow cotton in my mouth."

"Cotton, huh? You boys must be from the South," the bartender said as he put the two beers in front of Dooley.

"You got somethin' against the South?" Boomer challenged.

"No, Lord, no," the bartender said, chuckling. "I'm from southeast Missouri myself. I wore the gray and fought with ol' Jeff Thompson durin' the war."

"We wasn't neither one of us old enough to fight in the war," Dooley said.

"But if we had been, we woulda fought with General James Henry Lane of the Texas Fifth," Boomer said. "He's my uncle," he added proudly.

"So, you boys are from Texas, are you?"

"Yes, sir. We just rode up here."

"It's a long ride all the way up here from Texas."

"Sure is. We 'bout rode the legs offen our horses," Dooley said.

"What brings you to Wyoming Territory?"

"Well sir, we just got a little bit of the wanderin' fever, so we thought we'd come up here 'n' see what it's like," Boomer said. "We're pretty good cowhands. Do you know if any ranchers are hiring?"

"Cowhands, huh?" the man with the scar said. It was the first time he had spoken, and he snorted what might have been laughter.

"I beg your pardon?" Boomer asked.

"I'd be willing to bet that you aren't cowhands at all. More than likely, you're store clerks, out for a little adventure, and you don't know the difference between a cowhide and a buffalo turd."

"Are you hirin', mister?"

"No."

"Do you know anyone that is hirin'?"

"No."

"Well, then, whether we are cowhands or not ain't none of your business, is it?"

"Who did you say your uncle was? Some general?" the scar-faced man asked.

"I said my uncle was General Lane. General James Lane," Boomer said. He took a swallow of his beer, leaving some foam trapped in his moustache. "You got somethin' to say about that?"

"I heard of General Lane."

"Yeah? What did you hear?"

The scar-faced man poured himself another whiskey, then drank it, all the while holding Boomer in a steady gaze.

"I heard he was a cowardly son of a bitch, leadin' a pack of Texas cowards," the man replied.

"That's a hell of a thing to say," Dooley said, joining the conversation.

"Mister, I expect you'd better take that back," Boomer challenged.

The bartender leaned across the bar and said, very quietly, "You boys might want to ease up just a bit. Don't you know who that is?"

"I don't care if he is Abraham Lincoln," Boomer said. "I already don't like the son of a bitch and just met him. And if he don't shut the hell up, I may just shut him up."

"Easy, Boomer," Dooley said, reaching out for his partner. "We've come a long way from home, and we didn't come up here to get into no fight."

Boomer glared at the scar-faced man, but the expression on the man's face never changed.

"I ain't goin' to just stand by while my own kin and a bunch of brave men are being insulted by some ass-faced son of bitch who doesn't know what he's talking about," Boomer said.

"Cowboy, no!" the bartender gasped, reaching across the bar. "My God, do you really not know who this is?"

"Whoever he is, I reckon I can handle the likes of him," Boomer said.

"Boomer," Dooley said. "Come on, have your beer and leave this be."

Boomer stared at the man for a moment longer, then, with a shrug, he turned back toward the bar. "All right," he said reluctantly. "I'll let it go this time. Maybe folks up here just don't have as much sense as the folks do back in Texas."

"Texas," the scar-faced man snorted. "If it weren't for whores and their bastards, there wouldn't be anyone in the whole state but Mexicans and coyotes. You don't look like a Mexican, and you didn't come in here walking on all fours. I guess that means your mother is a whore."

"That's it, mister!" Boomer shouted in almost uncontrolled anger. "I'm going to mop the floor with your sorry hide!" He put up his fists.

The scar-faced man smiled, though it was a smile without mirth. "Well now, cowboy, if we're going to fight, why don't we make it permanent?" he asked. He stepped away from the bar and flipped his jacket back, exposing a pistol that he wore low and kicked out, in the way of a gunfighter.

"Mr. Dancer, I'm sure these boys would apologize to you if you asked them for it," the bartender said. "There's no need to carry this any further."

"Dancer?" Dooley said, his voice cracking. "Did you call him Dancer?"

"I tried to warn you boys," the bartender said. "This is Ethan Dancer."

"Boomer, back off," Dooley said. "Back off. My God, you don't want to go bracing the likes of Ethan Dancer!"

Boomer realized then that he had gotten in much deeper than he ever intended, and he stopped, then opened his fists and held his hands, palms out, in front of him.

"My friend is right," he said. "There's no need to carry things this far. This isn't worth either one of us dying over."

"Oh, it won't be *either* of us, cowboy. It'll just be you," Dancer said. He looked over at Dooley. "Both of you," he added. "You came in here together, you are going to die together."

Dooley shook his head. "No, it ain't goin' to be either one of us. 'Cause there ain' neither one of us going to draw on you," he said. "So if you shoot us, it's goin' to have to be in cold blood, in front of these witnesses."

"Oh, you'll draw all right. You'll draw first, and these witnesses will say that."

"They ain't goin' to be able to say it, 'cause we ain't goin' to draw on you," Dooley said. He looked over at the four card players, who had stopped their game to watch what was going on. "I want you all to hear this. We ain't goin' to draw on Ethan Dancer."

"Oh, I think you will," Dancer said calmly, confidently.

"Please, Mr. Dancer, we don't want any trouble," Dooley said. "Why don't you just let us apologize and we'll go on our way?"

Dancer shook his head. "I'm afraid not, gents. You brought me to this ball, now it's time to dance with the demon."

Boomer and Dooley looked at each other, then, with an imperceptible signal, they started their draw. Though the two young men were able to defend themselves in most bar fights, they were badly overmatched in this fight. They made ragged, desperate grabs for their pistols.

So bad were they that Dancer had the luxury of waiting a moment to see which of the two offered him the most competition. Deciding it was Boomer, he pulled his pistol and shot him first. Dooley, shocked at seeing his friend killed right before his eyes, released his pistol and let it fall back into his holster. He was still looking at Boomer when Dancer's second shot hit Dooley in the neck. He fell on top of Boomer.

Dancer stood there for a moment, holding the smoking gun. He put it back in his holster, poured himself another drink, then turned his back to the bar and looked at the four card players. Their faces registered shock and fear.

"Is there anyone who didn't see them draw first?" he asked.

"They drew first, I seen it," one of the card players said.

"Yes, sir, I seen it first too. They drawed first, the both of them."

"Bartender, you saw it too?"

The bartender was staring down at the two young men who, but a moment earlier, had been laughing and joking with him.

"Did you hear the question, bartender?" Dancer asked.

The bartender looked up at Dancer. His face showed more sorrow than fear.

"You goaded them into that fight, Dancer," he said. "They was just two cowboys mindin' their own business, and you goaded them into it."

"Did they draw first or didn't they?"

"They drew first," the bartender said. "But you prodded them until they did."

Dancer put a silver dollar on the bar. "Give these boys a drink on me, and have one for yourself," he said.

"A drink, yes," one of the card players said. "Damn, do I need a drink."

The four card players rushed to the bar. Dancer reached over and picked up one of the beers Dooley and Boomer had left behind.

A tall, silver-haired, dignified-looking man sat at his breakfast table reading the *London Daily Times*. Brigadier Emeritus of the Northumberland Fusiliers, Sir James Spencer Dorchester, Earl of Preston, Viscount of Davencourt, was wearing a wine-colored, silken robe. Over the left breast pocket was his coat of arms, a white shield with a blue mailed fist clutching a golden sword, placed at the intersection of a red St. Andrew's Cross.

The remnants of his breakfast, the bottom half of the shell of a soft-boiled egg, was still in its silver cup. The rind of half a grapefruit and the crust of a piece of toast were pushed to one side.

A balding, older man wearing a morning coat and striped trousers came into the room. Stepping up to the table, he raised a silver teapot.

"Would you care for more tea, sir?" Terry Wilson asked.

Wilson, Dorchester's valet, had served him for thirty years. Before that he had succeeded his own father in service to Dorchester's father. In all, the Wilsons had been "in service" to the Earls of Preston for five generations. When Dorchester got ready to leave England, he gave his valet a choice. He would either find a position for Wilson somewhere else, or Wilson could come to America with him.

Wilson could not imagine serving anyone else, so he chose to come to America. Here, even though the trappings of peerage were removed, Wilson continued to maintain a "proper" separation between them. Dorchester would have preferred a less formal relationship between them, but he honored Wilson's wishes.

"Thank you, Mr. Wilson," Dorchester said as his valet poured the tea.

"Is there anything of particular interest in the *Times* today, sir?" Wilson asked.

Dorchester took a swallow of tea as he perused the newspaper.

"It says here that Mr. Dickens may come to America to do a series of lectures," Dorchester said.

"That would be nice," Wilson replied. "It would give Americans an opportunity to meet one of our really fine authors. I'll just clear this away, sir." Wilson took the empty plates and withdrew, leaving Dorchester to read the paper.

The newspaper was actually six weeks old, having made

the journey from London to New York by ship, then from New York to Green River, Wyoming Territory, by train. The papers arrived every month in one big bundle, but Dorchester very carefully read them in chronological order, reading only one newspaper per day, and lingering over it during his breakfast.

For the one hour each morning that he devoted to his breakfast and the newspaper, he could almost feel as if he were actually back in England.

Five years ago Dorchester had been a man with a title, a 102-room manor house, and a dwindling financial base. His wife had just died, leaving him with a sixteen-year-old daughter and mounting debts. In a move that some called bold, but most called foolish, Dorchester sold everything he owned and came to America to start a cattle ranch.

Now, his ranch, Northumbria, was one of the largest in the territory, and his twenty thousand head of cattle had made him rich beyond his wildest dreams.

"Good morning, Father."

Looking up from his paper, Dorchester smiled at his daughter. Pamela was twenty-one, tall and willowy, with blue eyes and dark hair. She moved with the easy grace of someone unaware of her own beauty.

"Good morning, my dear."

"Did you sleep on it?" she asked as she took her seat. "Just toast and tea," she said to Wilson, who stepped up to the table.

"Yes, ma'am."

"Did I sleep on what?"

"Come on, Father, you mustn't tease," Pamela said. "We talked about it last night, and you said would sleep on it."

"Oh. You must be talking about your trip to Chicago."

"Yes. May I go? It's only three days by train. I'll stay no more than a week, then I'll come right back home, I promise. I'll be gone for two weeks at the most. Please, Father, may I go?"

"I've thought about it," Dorchester said with a stern expression on his face.

"And?" The expression on Pamela's face was one of concern that he was about to say no.

Suddenly, a big smile spread across her father's face. "You may go," he said.

"Oh, Father! Thank you, thank you!" Pamela said. She jumped up from her chair and hurried around the long table to kiss him in appreciation.

Poke Wheeler and Gilley Morris stood in the parlor. Neither had ever been in a house this elegant before now. In fact, it had been some time since either of them had been in a house of any kind.

"Lookie here," Poke said, running his hand over the back of one of the chairs. "You ever seen leather this soft? What kind of cow you reckon this here leather comes from?"

"I don't know," Gilley said. "Maybe they's special cows that's got skin like that."

"Ain't none that I ever seen," Poke said. "And I've saw lots of cows."

"Maybe it's from the kind of cows they got in India or China or somethin'."

Poke looked at Gilley. "That don't make no sense. Cows is cows."

"Not if they are over in China or India, or some such place," Gilley replied. "The people is different over there. I mean, look at the Chinamen with their eyes and all. Why, I reckon the cows could be different too, and maybe one of the things is, they got real soft skin."

"I'm goin' to sit down and see jus' how soft this is," Poke said.

Poke had just settled in the chair when the owner of the house came into the room.

"Don't sit anywhere, don't touch anything."

Poke jumped up quickly.

"Do you know what to do? Do you know where to go and what time to be there?"

Poke nodded. "Yeah, we know. Why are you helpin' us?"

"I have my reasons."

"And you don't want none of the money?"

"No. I don't want any of your money."

"Listen," Poke said. "Seein' as you don't want none of the money or nothin', then you must have another reason for helpin' us. That bein' the case, you reckon you could see your way clear to lend us just a little money till the job is done? I mean, maybe just enough for us to get us a good supper, and a couple of drinks before we go."

"I'll give you five dollars apiece now. But if you get drunk and fail to do your job . . . well, let's just say that I will be very disappointed."

"You don't be worryin' none about us. We'll do our job, all right."

"I'll be counting on that. Now, please leave my house. You are smelling up the place."

"Come on, Gilley," Poke said. "Let's go get us some supper."

Chapter 3

AFTER LEAVING COLORADO, HAWKE RODE UP INTO the Wyoming Territory. He was following the Green River north, not sure where it would take him and not particularly caring. The river snaked out across the gently undulating sagebrush-covered prairie before him, shining gold in the setting sun, sometimes white where it broke over rocks, other times shimmering a deep blue-green in the swirling eddies and trapped pools.

The mountains on the far northern horizon were purple and mysterious, but a closer range of wild and ragged mountains to the east of him were dotted with aspen, pine, cottonwood, and willow. There were bare spots of rock and dirt in between the trees on the mountains, then sometimes gray and sometimes red, but always distant and foreboding.

Late in the afternoon a rabbit hopped up in front of Hawke and bounded down the trail ahead of him. Hawke stopped his horse, pulled his rifle from the saddle scabbard, looped his leg around the pommel, raised the rifle to his shoulder and, resting his elbow on a knee, squeezed the trigger. He saw a puff of fur and a spray of blood fly up. The rabbit made head-first somersault, then lay perfectly still.

Stopping for the day, Hawke made camp under a growth of cottonwoods. He skinned and cleaned the rabbit, skewered it on a green willow branch and suspended it between two forked limbs over the fire. When it was golden brown, he seasoned it with his dwindling supply of salt and began eating, pulling the meat away with his teeth even when it was almost too hot to hold.

After his supper, Hawke stirred the fire, then lay down alongside it, using his saddle as a pillow. He stared into the coals, watching the red sparks ride a heated column of air high up into the night sky. There, the still-glowing red and orange sparks joined the jewel-like scattering of stars.

He had a full belly, a good fire, a good horse, and a nearby supply of water. He was content.

Dorchester accompanied his daughter to the depot in Green River, riding in a coach and four. The coach was filled with luggage, ranging from the small valise and train case she would carry on with her, to several large suitcases and trunks that were checked through and would make the trip in the baggage car.

"Now, you are sure you have enough luggage?" her father teased. "I wouldn't want you to get to Chicago and suddenly find that you didn't have a dress, a hat, a pair of shoes, or the armoire from your bedroom."

"Father, you know all of this isn't for me," she told him. "I'm taking some gifts to Carol. She will be the first of our relatives I've seen since we left England."

Dorchester chuckled. "She's your relative, my dear, not mine. She is your mother's niece."

"Nevertheless, she is the only relative I have, and I intend to enjoy my visit with her."

Dorchester leaned over and kissed his daughter on the forehead. "Of course you do, and you should. I was just teasing you a little. I want you to have a wonderful time. Give your cousin my regards."

"It's not too late for you to come with me."

Dorchester shook his head. "I had better stay with the ranch. But I do want you to send me a telegram as soon as you arrive in Chicago. I want to make certain you got there safely."

Pamela laughed. "Really, Father, do you think the train is going to be attacked by Indians? Don't worry about me. I should be worrying about you. If I'm not there to see that you eat properly, you are quite likely to forget."

"Chicago is very large, you know, not like the small towns we have here. You must watch yourself while you are there."

"Father, I will be all right."

"Board!" the conductor called.

"Oh, I must get aboard now," Pamela said. She kissed her father, then hurried to the train and stepped up onto the car vestibule. Dorchester went down to the track as well, and as the cars began to move, he walked alongside, keeping pace with the train while it pulled away from the depot.

"Remember, as soon as you arrive—"

"Send you a telegram, yes, I promise," Pamela said, calling back to him, since the train was picking up speed and opening up the space between them. "And I'll write to you in a few days to tell you what a wonderful time I'm having."

" 'Bye!" Dorchester called, waving.

" 'Bye!"

Dorchester remained on the platform, watching until the train, moving rapidly, receded in the distance. Not until it was a remote whistle and a puff of smoke in the clear, blue sky did he return to the coach. His driver was sitting on the seat, waiting patiently for him.

"Are you ready to go home now, Mr. Dorchester?"

"Yes, thank you," Dorchester replied.

As the coach pulled away from the station, he fought hard to suppress the strange sense of foreboding that was rising in his stomach.

It was late afternoon when Mason Hawke approached the little town. From his perspective and distance, the settlement looked little more inviting than any other group of the brown hummocks and hills common to that country. He stopped on a ridge and looked down at the town while removing his canteen from the saddle pommel. He took a swallow, recorked the canteen, then put back. Slapping his legs against the side of his horse, he headed the animal down the long slope of the ridge, wondering what town this was.

A small sign just on the edge of town answered the question for him:

SAGE CREEK
POPULATION 123
COME GROW WITH US.

The weathered board and faded letters indicated that the sign had been there for some time, no doubt erected when there was still some hope for the town's future. Hawke doubted there were 123 residents in the town today, and, despite the optimistic tone of the sign, that the town was still growing.

In addition to the false-fronted shanties that lined both sides of the street, there were a few sod buildings, and even some tents, straggling along for nearly a quarter of a mile. Then, just as abruptly as the town started, it quit, and the prairie began again.

Hawke knew about such towns; he had been in hundreds

of them over the last several years. He knew that in the spring the street would be a muddy mire, worked by the horses' hooves and mixed with their droppings to become a stinking, sucking, pool of ooze. In the winter it would be frozen solid, while in the summer it would bake as hard as rock.

It was summer now, and the sun was yellow and hot.

The buildings were weathered and leaning, and the painted signs on the front of the edifices were worn and hard to read. A wagon was backed up to the general store, and a couple of men were listlessly unloading it. They looked over at Hawke, curious as to who he was and what brought him to town, though neither of them were ambitious enough to speak to him.

Hawke dismounted in front of a saloon called the Brown Dirt Cowboy and went inside. Shadows made the saloon seem cooler, but that was illusory. It was nearly as hot inside as out, and without the benefit of a breath of air, even more stifling. The customers were sweating in their drinks and wiping their faces with bandannas.

As always when he entered a strange saloon, Hawke checked the place out. To one unfamiliar with what he was doing, his glance appeared to be little more than idle curiosity. But it was a studied surveillance. Who was armed? What type of guns were they carrying? How were they wearing them? Was there anyone here he knew? More important, was there anyone here who knew him, and who might take this opportunity to settle some old score, real or imagined, for himself or a friend?

It appeared that there were only workers and cowboys there. The couple of men who were armed were young; probably wearing their guns as much for show as anything, he thought. And from the way the pistols rode on their hips, he would have bet that they had never used them for anything but target practice, and not very successfully at that.

The bartender stood behind the bar. In front of him were two glasses with whiskey remaining in them, and he poured the whiskey back into a bottle, corked it, and put the bottle on the shelf behind the bar. He wiped the glasses out with his stained apron, then set them among the unused glasses. Seeing Hawke step up to the bar, the bartender moved down toward him.

"Whiskey," Hawke said.

The barman reached for the bottle he had just poured the whiskey back into, but Hawke pointed to an unopened bottle.

"That one. And a clean glass."

Shrugging, the saloonkeeper pulled the cork from the fresh bottle.

"You're new in town," the bartender said. It wasn't a question, it was a declaration.

"I'm not in town," Hawke said. "I'm just passing through. Thought I'd have a couple of drinks, eat some food that isn't trail-cooked, and maybe get a room for the night."

"What brings you to this neck of the woods?" the barkeep asked as he poured the whiskey.

"Nothing in particular," Hawke said. "I'm just wandering around."

"We don't get too many of your kind in here," one of the men at the bar said.

Hawke paid for his drink, then lifted it to his lips. Taking a swallow, he wiped his mouth with the back of his hand.

"Is there a place to eat in this town?"

"Mollie's, just down the street," the bartender said. "Nothin' fancy, but the food is good."

"Hey, mister, are you deaf?" someone at the bar said. "I said we don't get too many of your kind here."

The tone of the man's voice was more challenging than friendly, and Hawke turned to look at him. He had a bushy red beard and was wearing a dirty shirt and a sweat-stained hat.

"Oh?" Hawke replied. "And just what would my kind be?"

"I'd say you are a saddle tramp," the bushy-bearded man said.

"Barkeep," Hawke said. He nodded toward his antagonist. "Give my new friend here a drink, on me."

The bartender put a glass in front of the bearded man. "Here you go, Metzger. Compliments of the gentlemen."

Metzger picked the glass up and held it toward Hawke as if offering a toast. Hawke returned the gesture, then lifted his glass to his mouth. Metzger lifted his glass too, but he didn't drink it. Instead, with an evil smile, he turned the glass upside down and spilled the whiskey on the bar.

"I don't drink with saddle tramps like you," he said.

"Wait, let me get this straight," Hawke replied. "Is it that you don't drink with any saddle tramp? Or you just don't drink with saddle tramps like me?"

The others in the saloon laughed, and Metzger, realizing that they laughing at him, grew angry. He pointed at Hawke.

"I don't like you, mister," he said. "I don't like you at all."

"Well, maybe if you had a bath your disposition would improve. How long has it been since you had one? Two years? Three? Ten? I mean, having to smell yourself for that long is bound to get to you after a while."

Again, those in the saloon laughed.

"Metzger, looks to me like this here fella is just a little too quick for you," one of the bar patrons said.

Metzger, his face flushed red with anger and embarrassment, charged toward Hawke with a loud yell.

"Look out, mister! He has a knife!" someone shouted, and Hawke saw a silver blade flashing.

Hawke jerked to one side just in time to keep from being badly cut. At almost exactly the same time, he pulled his pistol from his holster and brought it down hard, on Metzger's head. Metzger went down like a sack of potatoes.

Hawke put his pistol back in his holster then picked up his drink.

"It can't be all that good for your business if he greets all your visitors like that," he said.

"He's a bully," the bartender said. "He has the whole town buffaloed. I reckon he figured he needed to take you down just to show everyone else that he was still the top rooster."

Hawke nodded. "That's a plan, I suppose." Finishing his drink, he put the glass down and slapped another coin on the bar beside it. "I'll have another."

"No, sir," the bartender said, pushing the coin back. "This one is on me." He used the new bottle to pour a fresh drink.

"Thanks."

"Now, I'm going to do something I should've done a long time ago," the bartender said.

Reaching under the bar, he pulled out a sawed-off, double-barrel, twelve-gauge Greener and pointed it toward Metzger's prostrate form. He handed one of the other men in the bar a glass of water. "Here, Paul. Wake the son of a bitch up."

Paul was about to pour the glass of water on Metzger, then put it back down.

"No, I've got a better idea," he said. Reaching down by the bar, he picked up the spittoon, then turned it upside down over Metzger's face.

Metzger came to, spitting and swearing. When he sat up, he saw Paul holding the spittoon.

"Why you—" he said, getting to his feet angrily. "I'm going to—"

"Leave," the bartender said.

"What?" Metzger looked at him, his face stained with tobacco juice. Little flecks of expectorated tobacco clung to his beard.

"I was just finishing your sentence for you. You were about to say that you were going to leave."

"I wasn't about to say no such thing," Metzger sputtered.

"Yes, you were." The bartender augmented his observation by pulling back both hammers of the shotgun.

"Wait a minute, you ain't the law in this town. Fact is, this town ain't got no law, so you got no right to run me out of town," Metzger said angrily.

"This says I do," the bartender said, emphasizing his statement by lifting the shotgun.

"Listen, what about you other fellas?" Metzger asked. "Are you just going to stand around and let this happen? I though we was pards."

"There's nobody here who is pards with you, Metzger," Paul said. "We've had about enough of you."

Metzger looked at the others, who, emboldened by the fact that they were all together now, stared back at him without sympathy.

"All right, all right, I'm a'goin'," Metzger said. He looked at each one of them. "But I plan to remember who was here and who didn't stand beside me. And when I come back, there's going to be a settling of accounts."

"If you come back, we'll kill you," Paul said quietly.

The anger and defiance on Metzger's face was replaced by a flicker of fear. He stood there blinking, trying unsuccessfully to regain a little of his self-respect. Finally, he ran his hand through his beard, combing out some of the bits of tobacco, and turned toward Hawke.

"You," he said. "You're the cause of this. One day me 'n' you's goin' to run across each other again."

"I look forward to the day," Hawke said easily.

"Go, now," the bartender said, coming around the bar and poking Metzger with the end of the double-barrel.

Metzger moved toward the door with the bartender behind him. Everyone but Hawke went to the door as well, and
they watched as Metzger climbed onto his horse.

"Gittup!" Metzger shouted to his horse, and a moment
later the clatter of galloping hoof beats filled the street. The
patrons of the Brown Dirt Cowboy cheered.

Chapter 4

～～～

ON THE UNION PACIFIC TRACKS, THE EASTBOUND train on which Pamela Dorchester was a passenger made a midnight stop for water. Asleep in the top berth of the Pullman car, Pamela was only vaguely aware that the stop had been made. She was too comfortable and too tired from all the packing and preparation for her visit to Chicago to pay too much attention to it.

Rolling over in bed, she pulled the covers up and listened to the bumping sounds from outside as the fireman lowered the spout from the trackside water tower and began squirting water down into the tank.

"I tell you what, Frank, we didn't stop a moment too soon," the fireman called back to the engineer. "This here tank is dry as a bone."

Pamela could hear the fireman's words. She thought of him standing out there in the elements in the middle of the night. In contrast, it made her own condition, snuggled down in the covers of her berth, seem even more comfortable. She felt herself drifting back to sleep.

* * *

Just outside the train, Poke Wheeler and Gilley Morris slipped through the shadows alongside the railroad track. The train was alive with sound; from the loud puffs of the driver relief valves venting steam, to the splash of water filling the tank, to the snapping and popping of overheated bearings and gear boxes.

The two men had been in position for nearly an hour, waiting by the tower where they knew the train would have to stop for water. Behind them, tied to a willow tree, were two horses. One of the horses was hitched to a travois.

"Which car is she on?" Poke asked.

"Well, according to what we was told, she'll be in the first Pullman behind the baggage car," Gilley answered. "First berth on the left."

Glancing up toward the tender, they saw the fireman standing there, directing the gushing water from the spout into the tank. Satisfied that his attention was diverted, the two men stepped up onto the vestibule platform. They remained there a moment to make certain they had not been discovered, and when they were sure they were safe, they pushed open the door and stepped inside.

The car was dimly lit by two low-burning gimbal-mounted lanterns, one on the front wall and the other on the rear. The aisle stretched out between two rows of closed curtains, and heavy breathing and snores assured the two men that everyone was asleep. Toward the back of the car the porter sat on a low, wooden stool. He was leaning against the wall, asleep himself.

Gilley took out a small bottle and poured liquid from the bottle onto a handkerchief. That done, he nodded to Poke, who jerked open the curtains of the berth.

Pamela, suddenly awakened when the curtains parted, turned in her bed. Before she could react, however, a hand-held handkerchief clamped down over her face. She tried to scream, tried to fight against the cloying smell, but it was a losing proposition. Within seconds she was unconscious.

Still unobserved by anyone else in the car, Poke and Gilley lifted Pamela from her berth and carried her off the train. No one noticed them putting her unconscious form on the travois.

"Let's go," Gilley said.

The two men mounted and rode off, even as the train, its tank now full of water, got underway again.

Troy Jackson was the porter for the first Pullman car. A former slave, he been a railroad porter now for five years, and he enjoyed the job.

"Best job they is for a man of color," he would tell anyone who asked. As a porter, he had traveled all over America, from New York to San Francisco, and from Chicago to New Orleans.

He took pride in his work too, which is why he was beginning to get nervous about the lady in berth number one. It was nine o'clock in the morning and her booth was the only one still not made up. He didn't want to arrive in Cheyenne without all the berths being properly made.

He had stood just outside the closed curtains of her berth a few moments earlier calling out to her, but she didn't answer. He couldn't very well stick his head in. Suppose she was just getting dressed? Finally, he stepped up to the seat of a lady passenger who was only one seat behind the still-made berth.

Bowing slightly, Troy touched the brim of his cap. "Beg pardon, ma'am, but I needs to check on the lady in this berth and it would be unseemly for me to stick my head in. I wonder could you do it for me?"

"Yes, of course," the woman replied with a smile.

Troy stood back to offer as much privacy as he could while the female passenger checked on the berth for him.

She stuck her head in, pulled it back out almost immediately and looked over at Troy.

"There's no one in the berth," she said.

"Ma'am?" Troy responded, surprised by the announcement.

"Here, have a look for yourself," the woman invited. "There's no one in the berth."

Troy looked in the berth and saw only the empty sheets. Pulling back from the berth, he lay his hand alongside his cheek.

"Oh, Lord have mercy," he said. "Where did she go?"

As soon as Troy reported to the conductor that one of his passengers was missing, the conductor turned out all the porters for a thorough search of the train. Every car was searched, to no avail.

"Are you sure you did not see Miss Dorchester leave the train at one of the stops?" the conductor asked.

"Yes, sir, I'm sure. I stood in the door at ever' stop, just like I'm s'pose to."

"What about during the water stops? Maybe she got off to stretch her legs and didn't get back on the train before it left."

"Maybe that could be. I don't stand in the door at the water stops," Troy said. "Ain' nobody ever told me to do that."

"I'm not blaming you, Troy," the conductor said. "I'm just trying to figure out what happened to her."

The conductor sighed and pinched the bridge of his nose as he shook his head. "We're goin' to have to send out telegrams to every station back along the way telling the trains to be on the lookout. Lord have mercy on her if she's wandering around out there."

"Extra! Extra! Woman disappears from train!" the newsboy shouted, hawking his papers in the café of the Cheyenne depot.

"Big mystery!" the boy shouted. "Her sleeping berth found empty! Extra, extra!"

"Boy, I'll have one of those!" a woman called.

The boy reached down into his bag to pull out one of his papers.

"Yes, ma'am, that'll be—" he started to say, but paused in mid-sentence, staring at the woman.

She was only four feet tall. He had never seen a full-grown woman this small, and he stared at her with his mouth open.

"You're going to catch flies if you leave your mouth open like that," the woman said. It was obvious that she was used to such stares.

"Yes, ma'am," the paperboy replied.

"Well, are you going to bring me the paper?"

"Oh, uh, yes, ma'am," he said. He took the paper over to her. "That'll be two cents, ma'am," he said.

"Pay him, would you, please, Mr. Dancer?"

The boy had been so mesmerized by the small woman that he hadn't even noticed the other person at her table until the man dropped two pennies in his hand. That was when he saw that the man had a terribly scarred face. But it wasn't the disfiguring scar that caused the boy to stare. It was the fact that the boy knew who he was, and that he was standing so close to a famous gunfighter.

"You're . . . you're Ethan Dancer, ain't you?" the boy asked.

Dancer didn't answer.

"You're Ethan Dancer. I know you are, 'cause I've read about you in the penny dreadfuls. You're a real famous gunfighter. What are you doin' in Cheyenne? Are you going to kill somebody?"

"Yes."

"You are? Who?" the boy asked excitedly.

"You if you don't leave," Dancer said with a growl.

The boy's eyes grew large and he turned and ran from the café, followed by Dancer's laughter.

"Ethan, shame on you," the woman said, though she allowed a smile to play across her lips.

With the boy gone, the woman and her dining companion returned to their breakfast.

Although very small, Bailey McPherson was well-proportioned for her height, and at first glance one might have compared her to a Dresden doll. But upon closer examination there was something awry about her, like an imperfection in fine crystal. One could see a disquieting edge, a hardness to the set of her mouth, and a malevolent glint in her eyes.

Individually, Bailey and Dancer drew stares. Together, they were often the subject of intense scrutiny, what with her small stature and his disfigured countenance.

"He gives me the creeps just to look at him," one of Bailey's acquaintances had told her.

What that person didn't realize was that it was exactly why she'd hired him. Because of her diminutive size, Bailey had the idea that she wasn't always taken seriously. Having Ethan Dancer as her personal bodyguard did ensure a degree of respect.

Dancer continued eating his breakfast, while Bailey read the newspaper she'd bought from the boy.

NO LEADS ON MISSING WOMAN

The fate of Miss Pamela Dorchester, daughter of a prominent Green River rancher, is still unknown. The porter on the Chicago Limited reported making her bed for her at approximately ten o'clock on the night of the 7th Instant, and then provided her with a ladder to enable her to go to bed. The next morning, when all the other berths were made and hers was still closed, he looked inside and discovered she was missing. A subsequent search of the train was conducted, but to no avail.

"We've done all we can do," Mr. Perkins, the local ticket agent, told this newspaper. "All the stations along the line have been notified and we are asking that anyone who has any information on Miss Dorchester's whereabouts to please contact my office."

"They are carrying a story in the paper about the disappearance of Pamela Dorchester," Bailey said. "That should certainly get her father's attention."

"Yes," Dancer answered as he spread jam on his biscuit.

"Wait here. I'm going to check and see if the train is on time," Bailey said, setting her newspaper aside.

"Are you going to eat your biscuit?" Dancer asked.

"No, you can have it."

Leaving the café, Bailey saw the sheriff standing in the waiting room, just beyond the door of the café.

"Good morning, Sheriff," Bailey said.

"Ma'am," the sheriff said, touching the brim of his hat. He nodded toward the dining room. "Would that be Ethan Dancer you're sittin' with?"

"It would be. Is there a problem?"

The sheriff pulled out a telegram. "I just got a telegram here, sayin' that he shot and killed two men back in Bitter Creek."

"When was that supposed to have happened?"

"According to what they say in the telegram, it happened two days ago."

Bailey shook her head. "No, that's impossible. We were on the train two days ago."

"Did that train stop for repairs in Bitter Creek?"

"Oh," Bailey gasped, putting her hand to her lips. "Oh, yes. Yes, it did, but he couldn't have—"

"Did he get off the train?"

"Yes, but only for a little while. He couldn't have been gone more than half an hour."

"That's all the time it took, ma'am. And it happened while the train was stopped for repairs."

"Oh, my. What happened?"

"Accordin' to the telegram, the two men drew on him. They're sayin' it was a fair fight."

"It was a fair fight?"

"That's what they're saying."

"I see. Do you intend to arrest him?"

"That is my intention, yes, ma'am," the sheriff answered.

"Why?"

"I told you, ma'am, he killed two men yesterday."

"But you also said the other men drew first, did you not?"

The sheriff nodded. "That's what the witnesses are all sayin'."

"If that is the case, wouldn't it be classified as justifiable homicide?"

"Justifiable homicide?"

"Self-defense," Bailey explained.

"Yes, ma'am, I reckon a body could call it self-defense. But that's not for me to decide. It is up to a judge and prosecutor to decide whether or not they want to charge him and bring him to trial."

"You and I both know that when they hear the witnesses' testimony, they are going to rule it was self-defense," Bailey said. "So, there's really no need to arrest him, is there? Couldn't you just parole him to my care? I promise to be responsible for him."

The sheriff chuckled. "You promise to be responsible for

him?" he asked. "Excuse me, ma'am, but you must know how strange it sounds that you, a . . . woman"—though he didn't say small woman, he implied it by the break in his words—"could be responsible for Ethan Dancer?"

"Sheriff, you have to understand that Mr. Dancer does what I tell him to do. *Exactly* what I tell him to do," she added pointedly.

The sheriff stroked his jaw for a moment. He obviously didn't want to face Dancer. Finally, he nodded.

"What is your name?"

"My name is Bailey McPherson. I'm sure that even the most rudimentary check as to who I am would satisfy you that I can do what I say."

"And you want me to parole him to you?"

Bailey smiled up at him. "I do."

"You'll make certain he is present for the trial?"

"If a trial is necessary, I will make certain that he is present," Bailey promised. "But for now, I have business that I must attend to in Green River. And I shall require Mr. Dancer to accompany me."

"If you don't mind my askin', what would he be accompanyin' you for?"

"If you must know, he is my bodyguard. I frequently carry large sums of money, and I feel safe when he is with me."

"Yes, ma'am, well, I reckon I can see that all right. Is there a way to get hold of you, Miss McPherson? I mean, if I need you for anything."

"Yes. You can always send a telegram to Bailey McPherson Enterprises, Green River. The telegrapher will get the message to me."

"All right, I'll parole him to you," the sheriff said, clearly pleased that he would not have to attempt to arrest Dancer.

"You've made a good decision, Sheriff," Bailey said.

Leaving him, Bailey walked up to the ticket counter to

check on the train. She could barely see over the counter.

"Excuse me," she said.

The ticket clerk turned around. For a moment he was confused as to where the voice had come from.

"I'm down here," Bailey said.

Looking down, the clerk saw her. "Yes, may I help you?" he asked.

"What is your latest information on the westbound train? Will it be on time?"

"We received a telegram from Bushnell a short time ago," the clerk replied. "It left the depot on time."

"Thank you."

As Bailey returned to the depot dining room, she thought of what the sheriff had told her. Although Dancer had said nothing about killing the two men, they had been in Bitter Creek two days earlier and the train had spent an hour in the depot there while some repair work was being done. Bailey stayed on the train, but Dancer left to go to the saloon. He returned in time for the train to leave, then sat in the overstuffed chair of the parlor car and went to sleep.

He had said nothing at all about an encounter at the saloon.

Bailey wasn't really surprised, either that it happened or that he had said nothing about it. Employing a man like Ethan Dancer was a little like staring into the abyss. She found it frightening, but at the same time strangely erotic.

"I just spoke with the ticket agent. The train is on time," she said to Dancer when she returned to the table they were sharing.

Dancer nodded but said nothing.

"I spoke to the sheriff too."

"Did you?" It was Dancer's only response.

"Mr. Dancer, when the train stopped in Bitter Creek the other day, did anything happen?"

"Why do you ask?" Dancer replied.

"The sheriff says you killed two men."

"I did."

"God in heaven, man!" Bailey burst out. "You killed two men just in the period of time that we were in Bitter Creek, and you didn't even think it was important enough to mention?"

"I figured you had read about it," Dancer said.

"Read about it?"

Dancer picked up the paper and pointed to a story that was on the front page in the lower right-hand corner.

"It's no secret," he said.

Bailey looked at the article he pointed out.

TWO MEN KILLED

Thursday night last, a terrible shooting affair occurred at the Boar's Breath saloon in Bitter Creek. Two Texans, at this point known only as Boomer and Dooley, arrived in Bitter Creek, ostensibly to look for employment as cowboys.

An altercation developed between the two cowboys and Ethan Dancer. It is not known why Ethan Dancer was in Bitter Creek, as this small town is not a normal part of his "haunts." It is believed, however, that he was on the eastbound train, which remained in town longer than normal due to a mechanical problem.

Apparently, the cowboys did not recognize Ethan Dancer, despite his distinctive appearance. As tempers grew hotter, angry words were exchanged, and the two cowboys went for their guns. Although no witness can recall what caused the altercation, all are in agreement that the cowboys drew first.

It is not known how many rash men, attempting to try their hand at besting Ethan Dancer, have fallen under his guns. It is not

certain that even Dancer knows. But let all who
would challenge him be warned. He is as deadly
as a rattlesnake, and as quick as thought.

A collection was made to purchase two coffins
and the cowboys are buried in a common grave
under a single grave marker with the following
inscription:

> Here Lie Boomer and Dooley
> Two cowboys from the South.
> They would still be alive
> If they had not opened their mouth.

Bailey read the article, then looked up. "Mr. Dancer, what
is it like?" she asked.

"What is what like?" Dancer replied.

"What is it like to kill a man? What does it feel like?"

Dancer was surprised by the expression on Bailey's face
and the intense look of excitement in her eyes. He realized
then that, instead of being distressed by the fact that he had
killed two men, she was actually intrigued by it. She was
more than intrigued, she was fascinated, even excited.

"It's a good feeling," Dancer said.

"A good feeling, how?"

"A good feeling like when I have a woman and—"

"No!" Bailey said. "That's enough. I had no business asking such a question."

Bailey shivered in what could only be sexual excitation,
and yet she knew it was not because of any attraction to
Dancer, whose badly scarred face repulsed her. The sexual
excitation came from the act of killing itself.

She cleared her throat, then closed the newspaper.

"They'll be here soon," she said.

* * *

Addison Ford, Administrative Assistant to the Honorable Columbus Delano, Secretary of the Interior, was traveling at government expense, on government business. The trip from Washington had been long and tiring. But because their accommodations were first class all the way, it had not been what he would have called an exhausting trip.

It was almost as if Ford, his wife Mary, his son-in-law Jason White, and his daughter Lucy were traveling by private accommodations, because they were the only passengers in the parlor car, and had been since leaving Omaha.

Ford was carrying a letter from Secretary Delano granting him full power of attorney to act on behalf of the Secretary of Interior. Ostensibly, he was making the trip as one of exploration to determine whether the application to build the Sweetwater Railroad should be favorably considered.

"There have been too many railroads built for no other purpose than to provide the railroad builder with free land," Delano told his assistant before he left Washington. "I place full trust and confidence in you to make the correct decision, then to act upon that decision."

"I will not betray your trust and confidence," Ford had replied. Even as Ford made that statement, he was holding a bank draft for $10,000, an inducement he had personally received from the Sweetwater Railroad. It had been loosely described as an offset against any expenses incurred while investigating the application, but it was a bribe, pure and simple.

The money was good, but Addison Ford wanted much more than $10,000, and he was certain that in head-to-head negotiations with the person who had paid him this bribe, he would be able to secure a larger piece of the pie.

Chapter 5

WHEN THE *WESTERN FLYER* ARRIVED, BAILEY AND Dancer boarded the train, then were shown to their first-class accommodations in the parlor car. Before the train got underway, though, Bailey stepped into the next parlor car, in which there were only two men and two women. They looked up when she entered and looked at her for a moment longer than was courteous, but Bailey said nothing.

Seeing that she wasn't going to leave the car, the older of the two men stood up.

"Is there something I can help you with, madam?" he inquired.

"Are you Addison Ford?" Bailey asked.

"I am."

"I'm McPherson," Bailey said.

When the expression of Ford's face didn't change, she said, "Bailey McPherson? I believe we have been doing some business together."

"Bailey McPherson? You're a woman?"

Bailey laughed. "Yes, I am."

"I thought . . ."

"I know what you thought," Bailey said. "And I apologize if I let you think that, but it was by design. It was my belief that we would be able to negotiate our arrangement better if you thought I was a man."

"Yes, well . . . Miss . . . McPherson, it is a pleasure to meet you at last. And I assure you, your gender will have no bearing on our arrangement." He stuck his hand out.

"The pleasure is all mine," Bailey said, shaking.

"Let me introduce my traveling companions," Ford said. "This is my wife, Mary; my daughter, Lucy White; and her husband, Jason. Jason is the civil engineer who will be doing the surveying for us."

Bailey shook hands with all of them, then said to Ford, "Secretary of Interior Delano is with us on this?"

Ford smiled. "I have with me full power of attorney to act for the Secretary. He isn't the one you need to please. I am."

"Oh?" Bailey said. "Tell me, Mr. Ford, are you suggesting that you were not pleased by the, uh . . . inducement I sent you to ensure your cooperation?"

"Oh, I was very pleased with it," Ford replied. "As a good-will gesture," he added pointedly.

"A goodwill gesture?" Bailey asked.

"Yes, to —as they say —ensure tranquility between us."

"I see."

Ford cleared his throat. "Miss McPherson, surely you understand all of the intricacies and details I must arrange. There are other agencies to bring on board, congressmen to convince, and expenses to incur. All of that will have to be funded. And of course, we both know that you stand to make a great deal of money from this operation. A great deal of money. As the only person who can bring all this to fruition for you, I don't think it is at all unreasonable to expect to be generously compensated."

"Very well, Mr. Ford," Bailey agreed. "We'll have an organizational meeting first thing after we reach Green River."

"I look forward to it," Ford said.

The engineer blew two short blasts on the whistle, and, with a series of jerks, the train started forward.

"I'll be getting back to my car," Bailey said. "We'll postpone any further business discussion until later. In the meantime, please enjoy your trip."

It was now two days since Poke and Gilley brought Pamela to the little cabin, and she had been tied up the whole time. Her back and legs were cramped and the ropes were beginning to rub blisters on her wrists. She had no idea where she was, nor did she know how she got here, though she was vaguely aware of being awakened in her berth to the smell of the chloroform-soaked handkerchief.

"You want some jerky?" Poke asked.

"No, thank you," she replied.

"Here, take a piece," Poke said, offering her a piece of the dried meat.

Pamela shook her head. "I don't want it."

"You got to eat something. You ain't et a bite since we brung you here."

"I'm not hungry."

"How can you not be hungry?"

"It stinks in here," Pamela said. "You stink. How can I have an appetite under such conditions?"

Gilley laughed. "Poke, I done tol' you that you smelled somethin' awful. By God, man, your stink would gag a maggot on the gut wagon."

"You ain't no bed of roses yourself," Poke replied angrily. He looked back at Pamela, who was still in her nightgown. "Look, if you don't want to eat, I ain't goin' to beg you. It ain't no skin off my ass, that's for sure," he said. He put the proffered piece in his own mouth and tore a chunk off with his crooked yellow teeth.

"She's got to eat sometime," Gilley said. "We ain't goin' to get nothin' from her pa if she starves herself to death."

"You aren't going to get anything from him anyway," Pamela said.

"That's what you think, girlie. This has all done been thunk out for us," Poke said.

Despite her condition and situation, Pamela chuckled. "It would have to have been thought out for you by someone else," she said.

"Hey, Poke. Someone's comin'!" Gilley said.

"Who is it?"

"I don't know. Maybe it's somebody come lookin' for the woman."

"Better get a gag on her so's she can't yell out none," Poke said.

Less than an hour earlier the sky had been clear and blue, but now dark rolling clouds darkened the day and sent jagged bolts of lightning streaking to the ground. The change in the weather had occurred quickly, the way it often did on the plains. But fortunately the rain had not yet started when Hawke saw the little cabin. Smiling at his good luck, he headed toward it.

He saw a flash of light at the window and heard the report of a rifle shot. The bullet struck his horse in the head, making a thocking sound, like a hammer hitting a block of wood. The horse went down and Hawke went down with it. His impact with the ground caused the Colt .44 to pop out of his holster and slide away from him. Worse, the horse fell on his leg, pinning him beneath the animal and leaving the .44 about three feet beyond his grasp.

Hawke was still reaching for his pistol when he saw two men leave the cabin then disappear behind a large boulder. A moment later they reappeared, mounted now, and rode up slowly, confidently, arrogantly. The boulder had hidden their horses, contributing to Hawke's belief that the cabin was unoccupied.

"Well now, Poke, what do we have here?" the smaller of the two men asked when they reached Hawke. He was narrow-faced, hook-nosed, and with one eye that didn't quite track with the other one.

Poke's laugh was high-pitched, a cackle. The larger of the two, his most prominent feature was a mouth full of crooked yellow teeth.

"I'll tell you what we got us here, Gilley. We got us a rabbit, all staked out on the ground, waitin' to get his ass killed."

The two men, still mounted, looked down at Hawke. Their drawn pistols were pointed at him.

"You got 'ny last words before we kill you, mister?" Poke asked.

"Yeah. Why did you shoot at me?"

"You come ridin' in here like the cavalry gallopin' in to save the settlers," Poke said. He looked over at Gilley. "I'll bet he was already countin' his reward money."

"I don't know what you're talking about," Hawke said. "All I was doing was looking for a place to get out of the rain."

"Yeah, well, in a minute you ain't goin' to be worryin' about the rain," Gilley said.

"I still don't know what you're talking about."

"Then I'll make it easy for you," Poke said. "We shot you 'cause you was here."

"Well hell, mister, everyone has to be somewhere," Hawke said.

Poke laughed again. "Everyone has to be somewhere," he repeated. "You know what, Gilley? This here is a funny man. Too bad we have to kill him."

"Then don't do it. What do you say that the three of us go into town and have a few drinks? You'll find out that I'm just a barrel of laughs," Hawke said.

He was playing for time by keeping the conversation going for as long as he could. All the time he was talking, he was also working his rifle out of its saddle sheath. But like his leg, the saddle sheath was held down by the weight of the horse, making it difficult for him to extract the weapon. On the other hand, the fact that the horse was lying on the rifle managed to cover his efforts, so neither of the two men realized what he was doing.

"Yeah, well we ain't likely to be havin' no drinks together," Poke said. "'Cause you see, we'll be busy and you'll be dead."

Laughing at his own joke, Poke and Gilley raised their pistols to fire.

At that moment Hawke managed to yank his rifle free. He knew he had no time to aim. All he could do was jack a round into the chamber and fire. His bullet hit Poke's horse just before Poke pulled the trigger. As the horse went down, it caused Poke to twist around as he fired, and because he was out of position, his bullet shattered the knee on the right foreleg of Gilley's horse. That left Gilley on a collapsing horse, and like Poke, his shot was also wild.

Using the rifle barrel as a lever, Hawke managed to get enough space to pull his leg out. He rolled away just as Poke and Gilley, both unseated now, fired a second time. Their bullets kicked up dirt where a split second earlier he had been lying.

As Hawke rolled away he passed over his pistol. Grabbing it, he came out of the roll on his stomach and thrust his gun hand forward.

"What the hell! Poke, he's got—"

That was as far as Gilley got with his warning, because

Hawke pulled the trigger and his shot caught Gilley in the Adam's apple. Poke fired a third time, but again Hawke managed to roll away. Hawke's second shot was as deadly as his first, and Poke went down as well.

Still wary of his two would-be assailants, Hawke got to his feet, gun in hand. His leg, which had been pinned under his horse, bothered him a bit as he limped over to have a closer look at the two men. It didn't take much of an examination to see that both men were dead. There was a hole in Poke's forehead, and Gilley's eyes were open but opaque, staring off in two directions, even in death.

He was still puzzled as to who his attackers were and why they had opened fire on him. What did they mean when they said he had ridden in like the cavalry rescuing settlers? And what reward were they talking about? Hawke looked at the three horses. His and Poke's were dead. The third horse, Gilley's, had managed to stand up again, but was wobbling around on a shattered and bloody knee. Hawke sighed, then limped over and embraced the horse's head. He looked into the creature's big, liquid brown eyes and saw intense pain and confusion.

"I'm sorry, fella," he said to the horse. "It wasn't your fault that your rider was such a sorry-assed bastard. It breaks my heart to do this, but believe me, it's better for you."

Hawke shot the horse between the eyes, then shook his head as he realized that he was in the middle of nowhere without a mount.

"Damnit!" he shouted in anger. "Who the hell were you two? And why did you shoot at me?"

The dark sky and ominous clouds chose that moment to deliver on their threat. The rain came down in large, heavy drops. The lightning, sporadic until then, increased in frequency until it was almost one sustained lightning flash, a new bolt striking before the previous one left. The thunder boomed in a continuous roar, not unlike the artillery bombardments Hawke could remember from the war.

Pulling his saddle and saddlebags from his horse, he hurried through the rain toward the shelter of the small cabin. He was about to step inside when he thought of the two men lying in the dirt a hundred yards behind him and realized there might be another one waiting for him. Pulling his pistol, he kicked open the door then fell to the floor inside, rolling away from the door with his gun at the ready.

No one came toward him.

Hawke lay on the floor for a moment, making a slow, thorough sweep of the cabin. Convinced that the cabin was empty, he stood and returned his pistol to the holster.

That was when he heard the bump.

Drawing quickly, he spun toward the sound, gun in hand again, eyes narrowed and ready.

He heard another bump, accompanied this time by a squeaking sound.

Curious, and cautious, Hawke moved carefully toward the sound. It was coming from the back of an overturned table. Looking around the table, he was startled by what he saw.

A pair of wide-open, blue, frightened eyes stared back at him. The eyes belonged to a woman, obviously the source of the squeaking he'd heard. She was making the only sound she could, because there was a gag around her mouth. In addition to the gag, she was bound, head and foot, by ropes, and Hawke was surprised to see that she was wearing a nightgown.

After one more quick perusal to make certain nobody was using the girl as bait, he knelt beside her and removed her gag.

"There were two outside," he said. "Are there any more?"

"Not that I have seen," the woman answered. "Please, don't let them come back."

"They won't be coming back."

"How can you be so sure?"

"I killed them," Hawke said.

The woman nodded. "Good. I'm glad you killed them."

"Who were those men, do you know?" Hawke asked.

"Other than the fact that they called each other Poke and Gilley, I have no idea."

The woman spoke with a cultured accent that Hawke recognized as British.

"Are you all right? Did they do anything to you?"

"What sort of question is that? Of course they did something to me. They kidnapped me, then they tied me up and gagged me. You don't think I came here of my own accord, do you?"

"No, I mean did they do anything . . . else?"

"I wasn't raped, if that is what you mean."

By now Hawke had pulled a knife from his belt and was cutting through the ropes that bound her ankles. After that, he cut the ropes from her wrists.

"Did my father send you?" the girl asked as she gingerly rubbed her wrists. "I was sure that he wouldn't pay the ransom. It's not the money, it's the principle of the thing. And my father is nothing if he is not a man of principle."

Finished with her wrists, she leaned forward and began massaging her rope-burned ankles.

"Your father didn't send me," Hawke said.

The girl looked up in surprise. "He didn't?" Her resultant laughter was genuine, and totally unexpected. "No doubt he will be amused to learn that one solitary knight dressed, not in shining armor, but blue jeans and a red and green plaid shirt, succeeded where his army failed."

"Army?"

"Figuratively speaking," the woman said. "I'm sure that the moment he learned I was missing, he dispatched a veritable army of his employees in the field, looking for me."

"Could I ask you a question?"

"You've just saved my life. That certainly should earn you the right to ask a question."

"Why are wearing a nightgown?"

"I'm wearing a nightgown because I was asleep in my berth on the train when they took me."

"The train? You were taken from a train?"

"I can't believe that news of my capture wasn't in all the papers."

"It may well have been," Hawke replied. "I've been on the trail for some time. I'm afraid I haven't read many papers lately."

"I'm sorry. I know that was very vain of me."

"Do you have any other clothes with you?"

The girl shook her head. "This is it, I'm afraid."

Sighing, Hawke opened his saddle bag, removed a waterproof pouch, and took a pair of jeans and a gray flannel shirt from it.

"These will be too big for you," he said. "But it will be better than wearing a nightgown."

"Thank you," Pamela said. "Might I inquire as to your name, sir?"

"The name is Hawke. Mason Hawke."

"I'm exceptionally pleased to meet you, Mr. Mason Hawke. My name is Pamela Dorchester."

"It is good to meet you, Miss Dorchester."

"The name Dorchester doesn't mean anything to you?"

"No, I don't think I've ever heard of it."

"I must say, Mr. Hawke, meeting you has certainly been ego-deflating."

"I'm sorry, I don't intend to be."

"Nonsense, don't be sorry. I'm sure it's quite good for me . . . character building or some such thing."

Pamela made a circular motion with her fingers. "Would you please present me with your backside, Mr. Hawke?"

"I beg your pardon?"

"Turn around, please, so that I may have some privacy while I get dressed." In the way of the British, she used the short *i* when she said the word privacy.

"Oh, yes, all right," Hawke said, complying with her request. "Do you have any shoes?"

"No."

"I'll make you some."

"You are going to make me some shoes?"

"Moccasins, anyway," Hawke said.

"How are you going to do that?"

"I'll look around until I find something," Hawke said, and poked through the cabin until he found some saddlebags. "This will do," he told her, still keeping his back turned.

He dumped the contents out—a couple of dirty shirts and even dirtier socks—then, using his knife, he began to carve out the components of a pair of moccasins.

Meanwhile, Pamela put on the clothes he'd given her. "You can look now," she said.

Hawke turned around and smiled. The bottom of the pants legs were rolled up several turns. "You look better in my clothes than I do," he said. "Even if they are too big. Hold up your foot."

"I beg your pardon?"

"Hold up your foot, I need an idea of how big it is."

Pamela held up her foot, and Hawke measured it by making a fist then extending his thumb and little finger. Satisfied, he went back to work.

"Oh, my," Pamela said, pointing to the clothes Hawke had dumped. "I must say, you keep cleaner clothes in your satchel than they did."

"I like to keep a clean change of clothes all the time," he replied. Looking up, he smiled at her. "After all, you never can tell when you might run into a pretty young woman."

"And tell me, Mr. Hawke, do you put your clothes on every woman that you meet?"

"No," Hawke replied. "On the other hand, I don't run into that many women who are wearing only their sleeping gown."

"Touché," Pamela said.

"Give me your foot," Hawke said.

"I beg your pardon?"

"Give me your foot. I want to see if this will work."

"Oh. Yes, of course."

Pamela extended her foot, and Hawke slipped the moccasin on and tied it in place with a strip of rawhide cut from the saddlebag.

"How does that feel?"

"Quite comfortable, actually."

"I'll have the other one done in a couple of minutes."

Resuming work, he said, "You say these two men actually took you off the train?"

"Yes, in the middle of the night, when we were stopped to take on water."

"That sounds like a well-thought-out operation. I wouldn't have given those two credit for that much intelligence."

"Oh, they didn't come up with it by themselves."

Hawke looked up. "They didn't?"

"According to Poke, it was all 'thunk up' for them."

"Do you have any idea who that would be? Who would be behind such a thing?" Hawke asked.

"No. Oh!" she said suddenly. "If there is someone else, they may be coming here."

"That's true."

"Then we must get out of here. Mr. Hawke, would you

please take me back to Northumbria? I'm sure my father would be quite generous with his reward."

"Northumbria? Is that a town near here?"

"Northumbria is my father's estate . . . uh, ranch. It's near Green River."

"I'm not familiar with this area. How far is Green River?"

"It's about forty miles, I would think."

"I'll get you home, Miss Dorchester, but I'm afraid it's going to take a few days."

"Why is that?"

Hawke took his hat off and ran his hand through his trail-length ash-blond hair. "Unfortunately, the horses are dead."

Pamela looked at him incredulously. "The horses are dead? All of them?"

"They shot my horse and I shot both of theirs."

"That seems unnecessarily cruel of you," she said. "Those poor beasts certainly had nothing to do with any of this."

"It was an accident," Hawke explained. "I didn't intend to shoot them. Here. Put this on."

"Oh, so then it becomes less a matter of cruelty and more a matter of extreme clumsiness," she said as she put the second moccasin on, tying it down just as Hawke had. She laughed. "Heavens, I don't know which is the more discomfiting thought."

"Yes, well, whatever the reason, the horses are dead, so the only way we have of reaching Green River is by shank's mare."

"Shank's mare?"

"Walking."

"You Americans and your quaint expressions." Pamela sighed. "Very well. If we are going to go 'shank's mare,' as you call it, then it might be better to walk to the railroad."

"How far are we from the railroad?"

"I don't know exactly how far, but I'm sure it's much

closer than Green River. As I said, Poke and Gilley took me off the train when we stopped for water."

"You should've screamed or something. They would never have gone through with it if anyone on the train had been alerted."

"I couldn't scream, I couldn't talk, I couldn't do anything. It was all I could do to breathe. They put something over my mouth and nose, and the next thing I knew, I was waking up here."

"My guess is they used chloroform," Hawke said.

"Yes, well, the problem is, I was unconscious when they took me, so I don't know if we are north of the railroad or south. And if we start out in the wrong direction, we could wander around for who knows how long."

"We're south of the railroad," Hawke said.

"How do you know we're south? I thought you said you were new here."

"I came up from the south and I haven't crossed it," he explained. "You think your feet will hold out for nine or ten miles? The moccasins will keep the rocks and stickers out, but they won't give your feet much support."

"They'll be fine," Pamela insisted.

"All right, we'll head for the railroad. We'll start as soon as the rain stops."

Chapter 6

HEADING TOWARD THE BRILLIANT SCARLET AND gold sunset beneath the darkening vaulted sky, the *Western Flyer* made its way west across the Wyoming landscape. Inside the Baldwin 440 locomotive the engineer worked the throttle while his fireman threw chunks of wood into the roaring flames of the firebox. The train was exactly on schedule, passing a milepost every 180 seconds.

Behind the engine and tender was a string of coach cars, inside of which the passengers were getting down to the business of eating their supper. Although America liked to call itself a classless society, nowhere were classes more evident than on a transcontinental passenger train.

The third-class passengers were the immigrants seeking better opportunities out West than they had found in the East. The immigrant cars were filled with exotic smells such as smoked sausages, strong cheeses, and fermented cabbage.

The second-class passengers were those in the day coach. Often, these were not transcontinental passengers, but merely people traveling from one city or town to another along the route. Most of them were eating their dinner from the boxed meals they had bought for twenty-five cents at the previous stop.

The more affluent, first-class passengers occupied the parlor cars, and they took their meals in the dining car at linen-covered tables set with gleaming china and sparkling silverware. They made their meal selections from expansive menus that could compete with the finest restaurants in the country.

One of the diners stopped the conductor as he passed by the table. "I say, how long until we reach Green River?"

The conductor was wearing a watchfob, chain, and watch across his vest. With an elaborate show, he pulled the watch out and opened it.

"We shall be there in exactly two hours and forty-seven minutes," he said. "Barring any unforeseen stops."

To his relief, Hawke discovered that as he walked, his leg felt better, and after a while he lost the limp altogether. When he and Pamela Dorchester reached the railroad, Hawke dropped his saddle with a sigh of relief, then climbed up the little rise to stand on the tracks.

Before him the empty railroad tracks stretched like black ribbons across the bleak landscape, from horizon to horizon. The tracks gave as little comfort as the barren sand, rocks, and low-lying scrub brush of the great empty plains, but Hawke was certain that a train would be coming through before sundown.

"Oh," Pamela said. "I don't believe I have ever walked this far in my entire life."

"You did well," Hawke said.

"Well? Ha! That's because you don't see the bruises and blisters I have on my feet now."

"No, I mean you did well because you didn't complain all the way here," Hawke said. "You're a strong woman, Miss Dorchester."

"It's the Brit in me," Pamela said. "And the fact that my father would have it no other way." She sat down and gingerly unlaced her moccasins.

"Your father must be quite a man."

"Brigadier Emeritus of the Northumberland Fusiliers, Sir James Spencer Dorchester, Earl of Preston, Viscount of Davencourt," Pamela said as she rubbed her feet.

"That's quite a mouthful."

"Of course, here in America he is simply Mr. Dorchester. He gave up his title and his holdings when we left England."

"And your title too," Hawke said.

"I beg your pardon?"

"You would be Lady Dorchester. No, that's not right, it's your father's title, not your husband's, so it would be Lady Pamela."

Pamela tilted her head and looked up at Hawke with a quizzical expression. "Oh, my, I'm very impressed, Mr. Hawke. How is it that you know such a thing?"

"I picked it up somewhere," he replied.

"I'm beginning to suspect that you are not quite the itinerant you appear to be."

Hawke chuckled. "Thanks. I think."

"I don't suppose you have a watch?"

"As a matter of fact I do," he said, and pulled his watch from his pocket. "It is lacking fifteen minutes of seven."

"Ah, very good. We shall have no more than a fifteen minute wait."

"You carry a timetable in your head, do you?"

"In a manner of speaking. The westbound train reaches Green River at nine P.M. every day. We are forty miles from Green River, and the train proceeds at a velocity of twenty miles each hour. Therefore, it will be here at seven o'clock."

"I can't argue with that logic."

As Pamela had predicted, fifteen minutes later they saw a train approaching. Hawke knew that it was running at a respectable enough speed, but because of the vastness of the prairie, it appeared to be barely moving. Against the great panorama of the wide open spaces, the train seemed very small, and even the smoke that poured from its stack made but a tiny mark on the big, empty sky.

He could hear the train quite easily now, the sound of its puffing engine reaching him across the wide flat ground the way sound travels across water. He stepped up onto the track and began waving. When he heard the steam valve close and the train began braking, he knew that the engineer had spotted him and was going to stop. As the engine approached, it gave some perspective as to just how large the prairie really was. The train that had appeared so tiny before was now a behemoth, blocking out the sky. It ground to a reluctant halt, its stack puffing black smoke and its driver wheels wreathed in tendrils of white steam that purpled as they drifted away in the fading light.

"Perhaps you had better stay down here until I call you," Hawke cautioned.

"That's all right by me," Pamela agreed. "I don't feel like walking, or even standing up, until I have to."

The engineer's face appeared in the window, backlit by the orange light of the cab lamps. Hawke felt a prickly sensation and realized that someone was holding a gun on him. He couldn't see it, but he knew that whoever it was—probably the fireman—had to be hiding in the tender.

"What do you want, mister? Why did you stop us?" the engineer asked.

Hawke knew that his appearance was not all that reassuring.

"My horse went down," he explained without going into detail. "I need a ride."

"You'll have to take that up with the conductor," the engineer said.

Even as the engineer was talking, the conductor came walking up alongside the train to see why they had made an unscheduled stop. He was holding an open watch in his hand.

"Smitty, what's going on? Why are we stopped?" he asked. "We've got a schedule to keep."

"This here fella wants a ride," the engineer replied. "His horse went down."

The conductor studied Hawke, obviously put off by his trail-worn appearance. He shook his head no and waved his hand dismissively.

"We don't pick up drifters," the conductor said to Hawke.

"Are you saying you'd leave a man stranded out here?" Hawke asked.

"When we reach the next stop, I will inform someone that you are out here," the conductor replied.

"Well now, that certainly isn't very Christian of you, Mr. Marshal," Pamela said, coming up from her place of seclusion.

The conductor gasped. "Miss Dorchester! My Lord, what are you doing out here in the middle of nowhere? Did you know the whole line has been looking for you? What happened? Did you fall from the train?"

"I was kidnapped," Pamela said.

"Kidnapped? What do you mean, kidnapped?"

"I mean that when the train stopped for water, someone came on board and kidnapped me."

"Oh, heavens!"

"This gentleman saved my life. Now we are trying to get back to Green River. That is, unless you plan to make us rely on shank's mare." Pamela looked over at Hawke and smiled, calling his attention to the fact that she had acquired the Americanism for her own.

"No, of course I would never do anything like that," the conductor said, falling all over himself now to please her. "I can find accommodations in one of the first-class cars for you, and your friend can ride—"

"In the first-class car, with me," Pamela said, interrupting the conductor.

The conductor cleared his throat. "Uh, yes, ma'am. Yes, of course, he can ride with you as well."

"I appreciate that," Hawke replied. "Oh, and by the way—Smitty, is it?" Hawke called up to the engineer.

"That's what folks call me. My real name is Malcolm Smith."

"Well, Mr. Malcolm Smith, you can tell your fireman to take his gun off me? I'm just another passenger now."

"Billy," the engineer called. "Come on out."

There was a rustling sound as the fireman climbed out of the pile of wood. He leaned the shotgun against the edge of the tender, then began brushing himself off.

"How'd you know he was there?" Pamela asked.

"He had to be somewhere," Hawke said. "It takes two men to drive a train, and Mr. Smith was the only one in the cab."

"Billy, you were pointing your gun at me?" Pamela asked.

"No, ma'am, not you," Billy replied. "I was just pointin' it at him." He nodded toward Hawke. "Hope you didn't take no offense at it, mister," he added.

"No offense taken," Hawke replied. "Under the circumstances, it was the prudent thing to do."

"This way, please," the conductor said, starting toward the rear of the train.

"Do have someone bring us some food from the dining

car, would you?" Pamela said. "I haven't eaten for some time now, and I am famished."

"Oh, that won't be possible, I'm afraid. The dining car is closed," the conductor replied.

"Open it."

"Yes, ma'am."

Hawke followed Pamela onto the train, dropping his saddle on the platform deck just before they went into the car. There were two men and two women in the car, all sitting in overstuffed, comfortable chairs. They were well-dressed, as befit their station, and they looked up in curiosity and ill-concealed irritation as Hawke and Pamela invaded their domain.

"Good evening," Pamela said, smiling brightly at the others in the car. No one returned her greeting, and a moment later Hawke overheard one of the men grumbling to the others.

"I'm all for picking up unfortunate souls who may be wandering around in the desert. But to put them in the car with us is unconscionable."

Hawke glanced over toward Pamela to see if she heard, but she had taken her seat and was looking through the window. It was getting dark outside, and because it was well-lighted inside the car, Hawke could see her reflection in the window. Her face expressed no reaction to the comment.

Shortly after the train got underway, the conductor came into the car, accompanied by two dining car stewards. Each of the stewards carried a silver-covered serving dish. A table was set up between them and the meal served.

"Oh heavens," one of the women in the car said. "Now they are going to eat here. Well, I say, this is just too much."

"Indeed it is," the older of the two men said. "And I shall certainly complain to the railroad, you can rest assured of that."

"Anything else I can do for you, madam?" the conductor asked as, with a flourish, the two stewards unfolded white napkins and gave them to Pamela and Hawke.

"Yes," Pamela said. "Our fellow passengers seem to resent our presence. Perhaps you could find other accommodations."

"Well now, that's decent of you, madam," the older of the two men said. "I have nothing against you personally, you understand. I have nothing but compassion for those who are down on their luck. But I'm sure you can see our position."

"Other accommodations?" the conductor asked.

"For them," Pamela said as she picked up a fresh asparagus spear and took a bite.

"Yes, ma'am," the conductor replied. Looking toward the other passengers, he held up his hand. "I'm afraid I'm going to have to ask all of you to leave this car," he said.

"What?" the older man replied in loud disbelief. "Do you know who I am? I am Addison Ford, Administrative Assistant to Secretary of Interior Columbus Delano! And I am undertaking the journey on official cabinet business. You might even say that I represent the President of the United States! How dare you ask us to leave!"

"Yes, Mr. Ford, I know who you are. But don't worry, I'm sure I can find accommodations on one of the other parlor cars that are just as nice as these."

"See here, I will not be put out of this car. I paid good money for my passage."

"Indeed you did, sir," the conductor replied. "But it has come to my attention that you would prefer not to share this car with Miss Dorchester and her guest. Therefore I am sure you will be more comfortable in one of the other cars. Come along, please."

"Well, I never!" one of the women said. "Addison, do something."

"What would you have me do, my dear? Wrestle them off the car?" Addison replied.

Grumbling and complaining, the four passengers left the car, glaring at Hawke and Pamela as they passed the table where the two were eating. Neither Hawke nor Pamela glanced up at them.

"You seem to have some influence with the conductor," Hawke said after everyone was gone.

"I think the conductor feels beholden to me because my father owns some stock in the railroad," Pamela replied as she carved into her piece of ham. "Is the food satisfactory?"

Hawke smiled. "I'm sure if it wasn't, you would find some way to make it right. It's quite good, thank you."

When Addison Ford and his party came into the second parlor car, they were greeted by Bailey McPherson.

"Addison," she said with a smile. "How nice to have you join us."

"It wasn't by choice, Miss McPherson."

"Oh?"

Addison stammered. "I didn't mean it that way," he said. "What I meant was, the conductor threw us out of our car in favor of the two people that we just picked up when the train stopped."

"And two more unkempt and disagreeable people you've never seen," Mary Ford said. "They are filthy, and dressed in rags."

"And with the most boorish manners," Lucy White said. "Why, do you know that she is actually wearing men's clothes?"

Bailey McPherson looked questioningly at the conductor. "Is that right, Mr. Marshal? You threw Mr. Ford and his party out of the car to accommodate a couple of indigents?"

"It is Miss Pamela Dorchester, Miss McPherson," the conductor said. "As I'm sure you know, she disappeared from the *Chicago Limited* a few nights ago."

"Yes, I read about it in the paper. Well, how delightful that she has been found safe and sound. She is all right, isn't she?"

Marshal sighed. "I assure you, Miss McPherson, she is quite all right."

"Well, in that case, Addison, Mary, you, and your son-in-law and daughter are certainly welcome to join Mr. Dancer and me. Isn't that right, Mr. Dancer?"

Ethan Dancer made no direct response.

"I, uh, thank you for the invitation," Addison said.

"Do make yourselves at home," Bailey invited. "But I ask you to excuse me for a few minutes while I go pay my respects to Miss Dorchester."

"I can't believe you are actually going to go speak to that horrid woman," Mary Ford said.

"My dear, that 'horrid woman' is Pamela Dorchester."

"Should that mean something to me?"

"Well, for one thing, her father owns one hundred thousand shares of this railroad, as well as six hundred thousand acres of land. You might have heard of his ranch, Mr. Ford. He calls it Northumbria."

"Northumbria?" Addison said. "You mean, the eminent domain section?"

"That is exactly what I mean."

Addison smiled. "Well, I'll be damned. It's almost worth getting thrown out of the car for that."

"I thought you might appreciate the irony."

Hawke and Pamela were just finishing their meal when Pamela looked up to see the small woman come into the car.

"Bailey," Pamela said. "What a . . . surprise."

"Yes, isn't it?" Bailey McPherson replied. "Ever since we heard you disappeared from the train to Chicago we have been worried to death about you."

Hawke had stood when Bailey came into the car, and when she approached the table, he towered over her.

"I'm sure you were. But as you can clearly see, I'm fine," Pamela said.

"I am so relieved." Bailey looked up at Hawke. "Aren't you going to introduce me to your handsome gentleman friend?"

"Bailey McPherson, this is Mason Hawke. Mr. Hawke is my knight in shining armor."

"So, I take it we have you to thank for Pamela's rescue."

"Nothing heroic," Hawke said. "I just happened to stumble into the cabin where she was."

"Oh, it was much more than that," Pamela said. "He killed the two desperadoes who kidnapped me."

"Killed them?" Bailey said with a gasp. She turned toward Hawke. "Oh, my, you must be very brave to take on two men in a fierce gun battle."

Hawke chuckled. "It wasn't like I had a choice," he replied. "They forced the fight on me."

"Yes, I'm sure they did."

Bailey turned toward Pamela again.

"How fortunate you were to have this gentleman come to your rescue. Well, you will have a story to tell to your grandchildren, won't you, my dear?"

"I will indeed," Pamela said. "Won't you join us for tea?"

"No, thank you, but I have people waiting for me in the other car." She laughed. "In fact, they happen to be the very people you displaced from this car."

"Oh. Do you mean Mr. Addison Ford, Administrative Assistant to Secretary of Interior Columbus Delano?"

"Then I see that you do know who he is."

"He informed us of his identity. He was quite put out, I'm afraid."

"Never mind about Mr. Ford. I will do what I can to soothe his ruffled spirits," Bailey promised. "I'm glad you survived your ordeal. And, Mr. Hawke, it was a pleasure meeting you."

"The pleasure is all mine," Hawke said with a slight nod. He waited until she had left the car before he sat down again.

"What did you think of her?" Pamela asked.

"Your friend is rather small," Hawke said. He could think of nothing else to say.

Pamela laughed out loud. "She is small. But I would hardly call her my friend. She is a scheming opportunist who doesn't let a little thing like ethics stand in the way of her goal."

"Oh," Hawke said. "Well, you can understand my confusion, I'm sure, but you two were carrying on like best friends."

"Women aren't like men, Mr. Hawke, anxious to settle differences with fisticuffs. We can hide our most bitter disagreements behind disingenuous smiles."

"So I see," Hawke said.

Chapter 7

HAWKE WAS ASLEEP WHEN PAMELA SHOOK HIM gently by the shoulder. Opening his eyes, he saw her smiling down at him.

"Have you always been able to fall asleep so quickly?" she asked.

"Yes," Hawke said. He yawned, then rubbed his eyes. Feeling the train's speed diminishing, he asked, "Where are we?"

"We are coming into Green River," she said. "This is where I get off."

"I guess I'll get off here as well."

"You needn't detrain unless you wish to. I've made arrangements with the conductor. You can travel all the way through to California if you want."

"Thank you, but this is good enough."

Hawke looked out the window. There was nothing to see but a black, seemingly empty maw, interspersed with low-lying brush that grew alongside the track, illuminated for a brief moment by light cast from the windows of the train, then disappearing back into the darkness. Not until the train had slowed considerably did he see any indication of life, a few low-slung unpainted wooden buildings of such mean construction that, had he not seen dim lights shining from within, he would have thought unoccupied.

With a rattling of couplings and a squeal of brakes, the train gradually began to slow. Still looking through the window, Hawke saw a brick building with a small black-on-white sign that read: GREEN RIVER, WYOMING TERRITORY.

"So this is Green River," he said.

"Yes. It doesn't look like much at night, but it's really quite a growing little town," Pamela said. She laughed. "Listen to me, English born and bred, extolling the virtues of a tiny town in the American West. But it has become my home and I feel a sense of proprietorship toward it now."

"I'm sure the town has no better advocate than you," Hawke said. "It has been a pleasure meeting you, Miss Dorchester."

Nodding good-bye to Pamela, he went out to the car platform to pick up his saddle, then stepped down even before the train had come to a complete halt.

The depot was crowded with scores of people. Trains connected the three thousand citizens of Green River with family, friends, and memories. They also brought visitors, returning citizens, mail, and the latest goods and services. It was no mystery, then, that at the arrival of each train the depot was the liveliest place in town.

Hawke picked his way through the crowd, went into the depot, then stepped up to the freight window. A sign on it read: SHIPPING CLERK. In the little office behind the window, the shipping clerk himself, a thin man wearing a striped shirt with garters around each sleeve, was sitting at a desk. Under the light of a kerosene lantern, he was busily making entries into an open ledger book. Sensing Hawke's presence, he looked up.

"Yes, sir, somethin' I can do for you?" he asked.

"I wonder if I could store my saddle here for a while," Hawke said.

"You sure can, but it'll cost you ten cents a day."

Hawke pulled out a dollar and handed it to the clerk. "Here's ten days worth," he said.

The clerk took the dollar then nodded toward a door with his head. "You can stash it in there," he said. "Go on in and find a place for it."

"Thanks."

Hawke went into the room the clerk had pointed out. It was dimly lit by a wall-mounted lantern, but there was enough light to allow him to walk around without stumbling over anything. He found a spot by the wall for his saddle and dropped it there.

As he was turning away he saw a piano—not the beer-stained, cigarette-burned, spur-scarred upright of most saloons, but a Steinway Concert Square.

Hawke walked over and ran his hand across the smooth, ebonized rosewood. Pulling the bench out, he sat down between the carved cabriole legs, then lifted the lid and supported it with the fretwork music rack.

It had been a long time since he'd touched such a fine piano. He hit a few keys and was rewarded with a rich, mellow tone. As he began playing, Hawke felt himself slipping away from the dark, depot storeroom in a small western town. He was at another time and another place.

Fifteen hundred people filled the Crystal Palace in London, England, to hear the latest musical sensation from America. When the curtain opened, the audience applauded as Mason Hawke walked out onto the stage, flipped the tails back from his swallow coat, then took his seat at the piano.

The auditorium grew quiet, and Mason began to play Beethoven's Concerto Number Five in E Flat Major. The mu-

sic filled the concert hall and caressed the collective soul of the audience. A music critic, writing of the concert in the London Times, *said:*

"*It was something magical. The brilliant young American pianist managed, with his playing, to resurrect the genius of the composer so that, to the listening audience, Mason Hawke and Ludwig Beethoven were one and the same.*"

"I say, my good man, who is that playing the piano?"

The shipping clerk looked up to see a tall, white-haired, distinguished-looking man.

"Oh, Mr. Dorchester! I'm sorry," the shipping clerk said. "I don't know just what the hell that fella thinks he's doin' in there."

The shipping clerk got up from his desk and went around the counter, heading for the storage area. "I'll put a stop to it at once."

"No wait," Dorchester said, holding up his hand. "I'll see to it myself."

"I thought you were going to find Mr. Hawke and thank him," Pamela said.

"I will, my dear, I will," Dorchester replied. "But listen to that music. I have not heard anything so beautiful since we left England. I must see who it is."

Dorchester and his daughter stepped into the dimly lit storeroom. The man playing the piano was practically in the dark, but even in the shadows of the dingy and crowded room, he projected a commanding presence as he sat on the bench dipping, moving, and swaying to the powerful movements of the allegro.

"It can't be," Pamela said in a shocked tone of voice.

"It can't be what?" Dorchester asked.

"It's him!" Pamela said quietly. "This is the man I told you about! Father, he is the one who rescued me."

"This can't be possible," Dorchester whispered.

"Father, it is him. I swear it is."

Dorchester held out his hand as if to quiet his daughter, then, seeing a box and a stool nearby, motioned that they should be seated.

When Hawke finished the piece, he sat there for a moment, listening to the last fading echo of the music. It wasn't until then that he heard two people applauding him. Turning, he saw Pamela and a tall, white-haired man that he knew must be her father.

"I am sure that, for as long as I own that piano, I will never hear it played more beautifully," Dorchester said.

"Father, this is Mason Hawke, my knight in shining armor," Pamela said.

"This is your piano, Mr. Dorchester?" Hawke asked.

"Yes, it arrived last week. I'm waiting to have it delivered to my house."

"I'm sorry. I had no right—" Hawke began, but Dorchester interrupted him.

"That is nonsense. Who, I ask, has more right to play any piano than Sir Mason Hawke, Knight of the British Empire? You are that person, are you not? You were knighted by Queen Victoria during your triumphant concert tour of Britain and the Continent?"

Hawke waved his hand in dismissal. "As you have learned, Mr. Dorchester, there are no titles in America. The knighthood was strictly honorary, and of no practical use."

"Of course it was honorary, but in my opinion, an honor well deserved, for your music truly is inspiring."

"Well, I'll be," Pamela said. "When I said you were my knight, I wasn't just talking, was I?"

Hawke smiled and bowed. "What knight, real or honorary,

would pass up the opportunity to rescue such a lovely damsel in distress?" he asked.

Pamela smiled. "Mr. Hawke, you truly are an amazing man. Wouldn't you say so, Father?"

"I would indeed," Dorchester said. "Mr. Hawke, I obviously cannot place a price on my daughter's life. But I would like to reward you in some way."

"No reward is necessary," Hawke replied. "I just happened to discover your daughter's predicament. Anyone else in the same situation would have done the same thing I did."

"Yes, but it wasn't anyone else. It was you," Dorchester said. "And I truly would like some tangible way of expressing my appreciation for what you did. Tell me what you want."

Hawke smiled and stroked his chin. "Well, if you happen to have any influence with one of the local saloon owners, I could use a job playing a piano."

"In a saloon? You would play a piano in a saloon?"

Hawke nodded. "It's how I've been making my living for the last several years."

"But, God in heaven, man, you could play in any concert hall in America. In the world. Why would you lower yourself to playing in a saloon?"

"It's a long story," Hawke said.

Dorchester stared at Hawke for a long moment, as if stupefied by what he had just heard. Then, shaking his head as if to clear it of such distressful information, he sighed.

"Very well, sir. I will respect your privacy." Abruptly he smiled. "Wait a minute. You want a job playing the piano, do you?"

"Yes."

"Let me look around a bit. I may be able to come up with something for you. In the meantime, I would like to invite you to my home on Saturday next. I should have the piano in place by then. You would honor me, greatly, by attending?"

"And playing the piano for you?"

Dorchester chuckled. "Of course I would be thrilled if you would play for us." He held up his hand. "But the invitation is for you, personally, not for someone to entertain me. Whether you choose to play or not will be up to you."

"I'm sorry, it was rude of me to suggest that you had that in mind," Hawke said. "Please forgive me for that insolence. I would be glad to come."

Dorchester smiled happily. "Good, good. And maybe by then I will have something for you."

Hawke took a room in the Morning Star Hotel. When he awoke the next morning, he heard the ringing sound of a blacksmith's hammer. Because the blacksmith's shop was at the far end of the street, the hammering, though audible, was not particularly intrusive. He could also hear the scrape of a broom as the storekeeper next door swept his front porch.

The blacksmith's hammer fell in measured blows, so that after each ring of the hammer, he could hear the scratch of the broom. *Ring, scratch, scratch. Ring, scratch, scratch.*

As a counter melody, the hotel sign, which was suspended from the overhanging porch roof just below Hawke's window, was squeaking in the morning breeze, while across the street in the wagon yard, someone was using a sledgehammer to set a wheel. The result, in Hawke's musical mind, was a symphony of sound. *Ring, scratch, scratch, sqeak, thump. Ring, scratch, scratch, squeak, thump.*

Hawke lay in bed for a full minute until the storekeeper stopped sweeping, thus breaking up the composition. Then he finally got up, stretched, and walked to the window to look out over the street of the town he had thus far seen only at night.

Directly across the street from the hotel was the saloon,

advertised by a huge wooden sign. On the left side of the sign was a painted mug of golden beer, over which was a large 5¢. Across the center of the sign, in large red letters, was the name: ROYAL FLUSH SALOON. On the right side of the sign was a painted hand of cards, a royal flush in spades.

A single-story office building was next to the saloon. The sign in front read: MCPHERSON ENTERPRISES. Next to that was the wagon yard. The wheel, now set, was being packed with grease. Beyond the wagon yard he saw an apothecary, a hardware store, and, finally, a Chinese laundry. The depot and railroad were at one end of the street, a church at the other end. On his own side of the street, he couldn't see all the buildings.

When he'd taken the room last night, he paid an extra quarter to be able to take a bath. Now, he decided to avail himself of that luxury.

Across the street in the McPherson Enterprises' office, as Hawke was taking his bath, Bailey McPherson was standing in the front room with Addison Ford. In the back room, Ethan Dancer and Jason White were sitting at a large conference table.

"Must Ethan Dancer attend this meeting?" Addison asked quietly.

"Mr. Dancer is my personal bodyguard," Bailey replied. "He goes everywhere I go."

"But the way he looks, that terrible scar. He makes me feel uneasy."

"Good! That is what makes him so effective as a body-guard." She laughed. "That, and his skill with a pistol."

"But surely you don't think you need a bodyguard with me?"

"He goes where I go, Mr. Ford. If you are going to do business with me, I suggest you get used to that."

The front door opened then and two men came in. One of them was carrying a bag, and as far as Addison was concerned, that was about the only way to differentiate the two. Both men needed a shave, and the clothes they wore looked as if they had come from an odds and ends charity barrel. The fact that they also needed a bath was immediately apparent to Addison, who had to turn away from the smell. Amazingly, neither their appearance nor the odor they exuded seemed to bother Bailey.

"Ah, Luke, Percy, come in," she said. "We've been waiting for you." She led them back into the conference room, where she took a seat next to Dancer. Addison sat next to Jason White.

There were no chairs around the table for Luke and Percy, and Bailey made no offer to provide any. Instead, she got right into the purpose of the meeting.

"Gentlemen," she said, by inference addressing only those who were seated, "this is Luke Rawlings and Percy Sheridan. These two men have been doing some . . . prospecting of late, and I invited them here this morning to give us their report. Suppose we begin, Luke, by you telling us what you have in the bag?"

Luke, who had blotchy red skin, reached down into the bag and pulled out a fist-sized, irregular-shaped rock. He handed it to Bailey.

"Take a gander at that," he said, revealing that he had no upper teeth.

Bailey examined the rock for a moment, then looked up. "I don't see anything."

"Turn it around and look up in the crevice. Hold it up to the light and you'll see it."

Bailey did so, and saw a glitter just where she was told it would be.

"Oh, yes, I see it now," she said.

"That's gold," Luke said, a broad smile spreading across his face.

"Where did this rock come from?"

"The Little Sandy River in the Sweetwater Mountains," he answered.

"How many rocks like this are there?"

"They's quite a few of 'em around, ain't they, Percy?"

His partner, who had been quiet so far, now said, "Yeah. They's a lot of these here rocks up there."

"Just lying around on the ground to be picked up?" Bailey asked.

"Oh, no ma'am, they ain't like that," Percy said. "You can't just go up there 'n' start pickin' up rocks thinkin' ever' one of 'em is goin' to show color. A fella is goin' to have to hunt around some."

Bailey turned her attention back to the rock. "Did you get an assay report?"

"Yes, ma'am," Luke said. "It will prove out at eighty dollars per ton."

"Well, now, gentlemen, what do you think of those numbers?" Bailey asked.

"Eighty dollars a ton is going to start a rush like the one they had in California," Jason White said.

"Is that good enough for you, Mr. Ford?" Bailey asked.

"It's more than good enough," Addison said. "I will telegraph the Secretary of Interior tomorrow that I have approved your application for operational status under the provisions of the Railroad Land Grant Act of 1862."

"Mr. White, how soon can you start the survey?"

"Right away," he replied.

"Gentleman," Bailey said, "the Sweetwater Railroad is in business.

* * *

The piano player in the Royal Flush saloon was bad. The only thing worse was the piano he was playing. Though in a way, Hawke thought, the fact that the piano was so badly out of tune might be a blessing in disguise. It made it difficult for the average person to be able to differentiate from a discordant note badly played and the harsh dissonance of the sound-board.

Hawke stepped up to the bar and ordered a beer.

"Ain't seen you around," the bartender said as he held a mug under the beer spigot.

"I haven't been around."

"Well, welcome to the Royal Flush." The bartender set the beer in front of Hawke. "My name is Jake."

"Good to meet you, Jake. My name is Hawke." Hawke put a nickel on the bar, but the bartender slid it back and shook his head.

"No sir, the first beer is on the house. That's the owner's rule."

"Really?"

"Yes, sir. The reason is, Mr. Peabody won this-here saloon in a game of cards. Fact is, he was holdin' this very hand," he said, pointing to a glass-encased box. There, fanned out for display, was a royal flush, exactly like the one depicted on the sign out front. "That's how come he came to change the name of the saloon from Red's Place to the Royal Flush. And to show his gratitude, well, first time anyone comes into the saloon, their first drink is on the house."

"That's very generous of Mr. Peabody."

At that moment the piano player hit a note that was so discordant it raised the hackles on the back of Hawke's neck, like chalk squeaking on a blackboard.

"Where did you get your piano player?" he asked, nodding toward the bald, sweating man who was pounding away at the keyboard.

"That there is Aaron Peabody," the barkeep replied.

"Peabody? The owner?"

The barkeep shook his head. "The owner lives back in Cheyenne. Aaron is his younger brother."

That was all the information Hawke needed. The guy could be playing with his elbows, but if he was the owner's brother, his position was secure.

In the mirror behind the bar Hawke saw someone come into the saloon. The man moved quickly away from the door, then backed up against the wall, standing there for a long moment while he surveyed the room.

Hawke noticed this because he had made the same kind of entrance a few moments earlier. It was the entrance of a man who lived by his wits, and often by his guns. It was the move of a man who had made enemies, some of whom he didn't even know.

Hawke had never met Ethan Dancer, but he had heard him described, and from the way this man looked and acted, he would bet that this was the gunfighter. Even as he was thinking about it, Jake bore out his musings.

"Donnie," Jake said to a young man who was sweeping the floor. "Mr. Dancer is here. Go into the back room and get his special bottle."

"All right," Donnie said. He bent down to pick up the little pile of trash he had swept up.

"Quickly, man, quickly," Jake said. "Never mind that."

Dancer walked over to an empty table. By the time he sat down, Donnie had returned with the special bottle, and he handed it to Jake. The barkeeper poured a glass, then took it and the bottle to the table.

"Here you go, Mr. Dancer," he said obsequiously.

Dancer said nothing. He just nodded and took the glass as Jake set the bottle in front of him.

"Call me if you need me, Mr. Dancer," Jake said, wiping his hands on his apron.

Again Dancer just nodded.

Jake returned to the bar, then, seeing that Hawke's beer was nearly empty, slid down the bar to talk to him.

"Do you know who that is?"

"I heard you say his name was Dancer."

"Yes. Ethan Dancer. I reckon you have heard of him, haven't you?"

"I've heard of him."

"They say he's kilt hisself more'n fourteen men," Jake said, not to be denied the opportunity to impart the information.

"Fourteen, huh?" Hawke replied.

"Yes, sir, at least that many. And truth to tell, they don't nobody really know just how many he's kilt. He mighta kilt a lot more'n that."

"You don't say," Hawke said. "That's quite a reputation to be carrying around."

"Yes, sir, I reckon it is," Jake said.

For the next few minutes Hawke just stared at Dancer's reflection in the mirror. After a while Dancer sensed that he was being stared at and glanced up. The two men's eyes caught and locked in the mirror.

Dancer stared back at the man in the mirror, and was surprised to see his stare returned with a similar unblinking gaze. There were very few men who could meet his gaze without turning away, whether in revulsion from his looks or out of fear of his reputation.

Dancer continued to glare at the image in the mirror, giving him his "killing" expression. It was a glare had made men soil their pants, but it looked to him as if the man at the bar actually found the moment amusing.

"Hey, you," Dancer called, his words challenging.

All conversation in the saloon stopped and everyone looked at Dancer.

Hawke did not turn around.

"You, at the bar," Dancer said. "Quit looking at me in that mirror."

This time Hawke did turn, still with a bemused expression on his face.

"Do you know who I am?" Dancer asked.

"I heard the bartender say your name was Ethan Dancer," Hawke replied.

"Does that name mean anything to you?"

"I've heard of you," Hawke said easily.

"If you've heard of me, then you know I'm not a man to be riled."

Hawke smiled and lifted his beer. "I'll try to remember not to rile you," he said.

This wasn't going the way it should, Dancer thought, finding the situation disquieting. Clearly, this man knew who he was . . . and clearly, he wasn't frightened. He wasn't used to that.

"Ya hoo!" someone shouted, coming into the saloon then. He was holding a rock in one hand and his pistol in the other. He fired the pistol into the ceiling.

The others in the saloon were startled by the unexpected pistol shot.

"Luke! What the hell are you doin', coming in here shootin' up the place?" Jake scolded.

"Gold!" Luke replied. "Me 'n' Percy's done discovered gold!"

"What? Did you say gold?" one of the other customers asked.

"That's what I said all right. Gold, and a lot of it too. Why, they's enough gold up there to make ever' man in Green River rich as a king!"

"Up where?" Jake asked. "Where is this gold?"

"Yeah, where is it?" another asked.

"Up in the Sweetwater," Luke said. He waved the rock around. "I done had this assayed. Eighty dollars a ton, boys! Eighty dollars a ton!"

By now everyone in the saloon, including Jake, was crowding around Luke, trying to get more information from him. Where, exactly, in the Sweetwater Range was the gold? How did he find it? Did anyone else know about it yet?

As the discussion of gold was taking place, Hawke continued to stare at Dancer, who had quit returning the gaze and was now staring pointedly into his glass of whiskey.

One of the patrons slipped out of the saloon, and a second later those inside could hear the clatter of hoofbeats as he rode away.

"Hey, boys, some have already started. If we don't get up there now, we're goin' to be left suckin' hind tit!" someone shouted, which started a rush for the door. Within moments nobody was left in the saloon but Jake, the piano player, Hawke, and Dancer.

Hawke picked up his beer and turned his back to the bar. He lifted his mug to his lips as he studied Dancer.

"You ain't goin' after the gold?" Jake asked Hawke.

"No."

"I'd be out there with them right now if I didn't have this here job," Jake said.

"The man who discovered gold . . . I think you called him Luke?"

"Yes sir. Luke Rawlings is his name."

"Why do you think Luke came in here like that?"

"Well, wouldn't you be excited if you'd discovered gold?"

"Yes," Hawke said. "But I don't think I'd be telling everyone exactly where I found it."

"I'll be damned. I never thought about that. Why do you reckon he did tell?"

"I don't know," Hawke replied. "It is puzzling."

Chapter 8

ON SATURDAY AFTERNOON HAWKE PICKED UP HIS clothes from the Chinese laundry. For his dinner engagement with the Dorchesters, he changed from the jeans and plaid shirt into something he considered more appropriate.

For many men such a drastic change in apparel would make them uncomfortable. Hawke felt at ease in his formal attire, having donned such clothes many times for his piano performances. He told himself it was his last connection with the genteel life that he had so long ago abandoned.

Shortly before he left his hotel room there was a knock. Hawke pulled his gun and stepped up to the door.

"Who is it?"

"Mr. Hawke, my name is Joey," a young-sounding voice said from the other side. "I work down at the livery stable."

Curious as to why someone from the livery would be calling on him, Hawke opened the door. The boy in the hall looked to be about fourteen.

"Are you Mr. Hawke?" he asked.

"Yes."

"Your horse is tied up in front of the hotel."

"My horse? I don't have a horse."

"Yes, sir, you do. Mr. Dorchester come down to see me, and asked me to come out to his place to pick out the finest horse I could find and bring him in to you. You want to see him?"

"Yes," Hawke said.

Hawke followed the boy downstairs, then out the front door. There, tied to the hitching rail in front of the hotel, was one of the best-looking horses Hawke had ever seen. It was a buckskin stallion standing about seventeen hands high with a long neck, a sloping shoulder, a short strong back, a deep heart girth, and a long sloping hip. His musculature was smooth and well-defined. Hawke noticed that his saddle was on the horse.

"How'd my saddle get there?" he asked.

"I knowed you'd left it down to the depot, so I went down and got it. Do you like the horse?" Joey asked.

"Yes, he's a magnificent animal."

"I picked 'im out my ownself," Joey said proudly. "I figured I pick 'im out as iffen I was pickin' 'im out for me."

Hawke pulled out a silver dollar and gave it to the boy. "Well, you did a good job, Joey," he said. "Yes, sir, a fine job."

"Gee, thanks, Mr. Hawke!" the boy said, excited over the dollar.

Dorchester's ranch, Northumbria, was about five miles north of Green River. Once out of town, Hawke urged the horse, and it responded instantly, going from a walk to a full gallop in a heartbeat. Hawke leaned forward, encouraging the horse to give him all it had. The ground flashed by in a blur, and he had the irrational sensation that if he went any faster, he would fly.

Hawke held the gallop for about two minutes, then eased back and let the horse cool down with a trot, then a brisk walk. Almost before he knew it, he was at the southern boundary of Dorchester's ranch, indicated by an arched gate with the word NORTHUMBRIA worked in metal across the top.

It was another mile up the road from the entry gate before the house came into view. When Hawke saw the house for the first time, he stopped just to take it in. It was huge, with cupolas and dormers and so many windows that the setting sun flashed back in such brilliance that it looked almost as if the house were on fire.

The edifice reminded him of a wedding cake, white and tiered. But the tiers did not end with the house. Even the surrounding lawn was built up in a series of beautifully landscaped terraces that worked up from the road to the base of the house itself.

A large white-graveled driveway made a U in front of the house where a coach and four sat at the ready, its highly polished paint job glistening in the setting sun. A crest of some sort was on the door of the coach.

Hawke had started toward the broad steps leading up to the front porch when Pamela and her father came out to meet him. Seeing Pamela, Hawke couldn't hold back a gasp of surprise. He would have been hard pressed to identify her as the same bedraggled-looking young woman he last saw wearing his rolled-up jeans and flannel shirt.

The woman who greeted him now looked as if she had just stepped down from a fine oil painting. She was wearing an off-the-shoulder dress with a neckline that plunged low enough to show the top of her breasts, though a red silk rose strategically placed at the cleavage helped preserve some modesty. The dress itself was clinging yellow silk, overlaid with lace. Her coiffure featured a pile of curls on top and a French roll that hung down her neck.

The intensity of Hawke's gaze made Pamela uneasy. With a nervous laugh she touched her hair.

"Have I gone green?" she asked.

"What?"

"You are staring with such concentration," she said.

"Oh, I'm sorry," Hawke apologized. "It's just that . . . well, you must admit, this is quite a change from the way I last saw you."

"Well, I would hope so," Pamela said. "And speaking of changes, I must say that you do look more like a knight now than when you rode to my rescue. Oh, wait, you didn't exactly ride to my rescue, did you? As I recall, you had clumsily killed all the horses."

Hawke laughed as well. "I had indeed," he agreed. "And speaking of horses, I want to thank you, Mr. Dorchester, for the loan of the horse tonight. He is certainly a fine animal."

"It isn't a loan," Dorchester said.

"I beg your pardon?"

"It isn't a loan," Dorchester repeated. "It is a gift. I have the bill of sale inside."

Hawke held out his hand in protest. "Oh, no, Mr. Dorchester, I could never accept such a gift."

"Why not? Do you think Pamela isn't worth a horse?"

"What? No, no, I didn't mean to imply anything like that."

"Then prove it by accepting this gift."

Hawke was about to protest again but stopped, sighed, then chuckled. "All right, Mr. Dorchester. I'll be glad to accept the horse, and I offer you my sincerest thanks for it."

"You are welcome," Dorchester replied.

"Good," Pamela said. "Now that that is all settled, shall we go inside?"

"Show him around a bit, would you, Pamela?" her father said. "I'll check on our dinner."

"Your arm, sir?" Pamela said, reaching for Hawke.

He held his arm out and she took it, then led him inside. She was so close to him, her body pressed against his, that he could feel the warmth of her curves. There was a suggestion of perfume—heady, but not overpowering.

They walked down a long, wide hall, on a floor so highly polished that it reflected the items of furniture standing on it as clearly as if it were a mirror. Along the way, as if standing guard, were several polished suits of armor and painted shields. All the shields were decorated with the same crest: Against a white background, a blue mailed fist clutched a golden sword, placed at the intersection of a red St. Andrew's Cross.

"Your father's coat of arms?" Hawke asked, nodding toward one of the shields.

"That's the coat of arms of the Earldom of Preston. I am told, by the way, that a distant ancestor of mine, the first Earl of Preston, wore this very suit of armor in the Battle of Agincourt," she added, pointing to one of the iron suits.

Hawke stepped up to the suit of armor, his larger size notable.

"Hmm," Pamela said. "I don't think you would fit."

He laughed. "No, I don't think I would. You're sure your ancestor was a full-grown man?"

Pamela laughed. "Oh, yes. But the Battle of Agincourt happened over four hundred years ago, and I believe people were smaller then."

"Four hundred years?" Hawke said, shaking his head. "I find it amazing that people can keep track of their ancestors for so long."

"That is an important date in our family, for that was when Geoffery Dorchester was invested with the Earldom of Preston," Pamela explained.

After a tour of the rest of the house, Pamela escorted Hawke to the dining room, where Dorchester met them at the door. He had changed clothes since Hawke arrived, and was now wearing a white uniform of some sort, with a red sash running diagonally across his chest, gold-fringed epaulets on his shoulders, and a splash of medals on his breast.

"Well, are you ready to eat?" Dorchester asked.

"If you knew me well enough, you'd know that is a question you never have to ask," Hawke replied. "I'm always ready to eat."

Dorchester led them into the large room with polished oak wainscoting running halfway up the walls, flocked cream and green wallpaper finishing it off. At strategic spots, large portraits hung by wires from the picture rail. One of them was of James Spencer Dorchester astride a horse, wearing the same uniform he wore now. Another was of a beautiful woman. For a moment Hawke thought it was a portrait of Pamela. Upon a closer examination, however, he realized that the young girl standing beside the woman was Pamela.

"That was my mother," Pamela said, seeing his interest. "She died the year before we left England."

"She was very beautiful."

"Yes, she was," Dorchester agreed.

"I see that you are wearing the same uniform now that you wore for that painting," Hawke remarked.

"Yes," Dorchester said. "I still hold a brigadier's commission in the Royal Reserves, though I seriously doubt that the Queen will ever call me to active service."

"My father fought in the Crimean War," Pamela said. "He was at Balaklava as a leftenant in the Light Brigade. You may have heard of the famous poem written by Tennyson, 'Theirs not to make reply/Theirs not to reason why . . . '"

"'Theirs but to do and die,'" Hawke continued, taking over the poem. "'Into the Valley of Death rode the six hundred. . . .' yes, I have heard of it."

"You never cease to impress me, Mr. Hawke," Pamela said.

"I was always impressed by the bravery of those soldiers," he replied. "It's an honor to actually meet one of them."

"I was young and imprudent," Dorchester said. "It was a foolish battle in a war fought with honor but no sense. Of the six hundred troops we committed to the charge, four hundred were killed. But then, I needn't tell you about such things. Your country has recently come through its own war, with battles just as foolish, just as deadly, and just as honorable. And, unless I miss my guess, you were there."

"I was there," Hawke said without elaboration.

"Let's change the subject, shall we?" Pamela said. "War is so distressing."

"Of course, my dear," Dorchester replied. He pointed to the center of the dining room, at a long table covered with a damask tablecloth and set with crystal candelabra, silver chargers, and glistening china. "Won't you be seated?" he invited.

The meal was brought to the table in various courses. The main course was a pastry-wrapped beef.

"Beef Wellington," Dorchester explained. "It is said that distant cousin, Arthur Wellesley, Duke of Wellington, came up with the recipe. I doubt that is true, but this magnificent dish does bear his name."

After the meal, Dorchester invited Hawke into his library. Here, twenty-foot-tall bookshelves lined the walls, and books of various sizes and colors filled the shelves. Dorchester gestured toward the leather chairs. Brandy was served and Pamela offered them cigars. When the offer was accepted, she trimmed the ends, ran her tongue down the length of each side, lit each of them, then sat down as well.

"I hope you find them satisfactory," Dorchester said. "They are from Cuba."

Hawke took the cigar out of his mouth and examined the burning tip. "It is an excellent cigar."

"I suppose you heard about the gold strike up in the Sweetwater Range?" Dorchester said.

"Yes, it's all anyone has been talking about, almost ever since I arrived in town."

"By now it's gone out by telegraph and the whole country knows about it. No doubt we are about to have a rush."

"I imagine so," Hawke said.

"Will you be going up there?"

"What, to hunt for gold?"

"Yes."

Hawke shook his head and squinted through the wreath of cigar smoke. "No, sir. I'm not one for chasing rainbows. Even if there is gold up there, there won't be one in a hundred who will benefit from it."

"You have a wise head on your shoulders," Dorchester said. "I just hope I don't lose all my cowboys."

"Lose your cowboys?"

"Three have already left, and I hear talk that more soon will."

"The cowboys who are leaving aren't our biggest problem, Father, and you know it," Pamela said.

"I think you may be making a mountain out of a molehill," Dorchester told her, then explained the situation to Hawke: "The most logical access to the Sweetwater Range is through Northumbria."

"Can you imagine all those people tramping out across our rangeland?" Pamela asked. "At best, they are going to be in the way. And at worst, they are going to get hungry and start stealing our cattle."

"Oh, surely it won't be all that bad," Dorchester said. "And we have twenty thousand head. We could afford to lose one every now and then if that is all that stands between a man living and a man starving to death."

"If that's all there is to it, we'll be lucky," Pamela said.

"And you know who is probably chortling with glee over our situation? Bailey McPherson. Bailey and that scar-faced ogre of hers."

Hawke squinted at Pamela through the aromatic cloud of cigar smoke. "Scar-faced ogre? Are you talking about Ethan Dancer?"

"That's exactly who I'm talking about," Pamela said. She frowned. "Good heavens, Hawke, don't tell me you know that loathsome creature?"

Hawke shook his head. "No, although I did see him in the saloon the other day. What does he have to do with Bailey McPherson?"

"He is her bodyguard. She probably needs one. Nobody can be as conniving and as manipulative as she is without making enemies. But why she chose a cold-blooded killer like Dancer, I'll never understand."

"Yes, well, enough discussion about that unpleasant fellow," Dorchester said. "Mr. Hawke—"

Hawke held up his finger. "Couldn't you just call me Hawke?"

"You prefer to be addressed by your surname, as opposed to your Christian name?"

"I'm used to it," Hawke said.

"Very well, Hawke. You said you wanted to play the piano. I have something that may interest you."

"I'm listening."

"How would you like to go to Chicago?"

"Chicago?"

"To play the piano."

"Mr. Dorchester, for reasons I'd rather not go into, I have no desire to go back on the concert tour."

Dorchester laughed. "If you accept this job, you'll be touring, all right. But not at all the way you think."

"I must confess that you do have me curious," Hawke said.

"Hawke," Pamela interjected. "Before you and father get into all that, would you play the piano for us?"

Dorchester reached out to touch his daughter on the arm. "Now dear, I promised Hawke that he would not be expected to play for his supper like a performing monkey."

Hawke chuckled. "That's all right," he said. "I would like to play your new piano for you. You should see some of the things that pass for a piano that I've had to play over the last few years."

"I can imagine," Dorchester said. "You're sure it would be no imposition to have you play?"

"None at all," Hawke replied.

The piano was in the corner of the parlor, and Hawke walked over to it. He stared down and ran his hand over it. "Do you play, Mr. Dorchester?" he asked.

"Heavens no," Dorchester said. "I leave that up to Pamela."

"You play, Pamela?"

"No. Not very well."

"Nonsense, my dear. You are an excellent pianist," Dorchester insisted. "Of course, you aren't as good as Hawke, but few are." Then, to Hawke, he added, "She is just intimidated by you, that's all."

Hawke saw a piece of music on the music fret: Mozart's Piano Concerto Number 21.

"You've been playing this?"

"Yes."

Hawke sat on the piano bench, then moved to the left and patted the bench beside him. "Let's play it together," he suggested.

Pamela smiled, nodded, and joined him. "What part will I play?" she asked.

"Just play the music as it is written," Hawke said. "I'll fill in around the edges."

"All right," she replied hesitantly. She put her hands on the keyboard, paused for a second, then began to play. Hawke began playing as well, providing counter melodies and trills, filling the parlor with such music that it almost seemed that an orchestra was playing.

Terry Wilson, Dorchester's valet, came to the door of the parlor and stood in the hallway to listen to the music. Then one by one others came as well. Seeing this, Dorchester motioned for them to come on so they could better hear the music. Hesitantly, quietly, they did so.

Hawke was pleased to learn that Pamela was actually quite skilled. She was so good, in fact, that he was pressed to match her with his improvised chording. But he did so, and at the conclusion of the piece, Dorchester and the servants who had come into the room applauded. So did several cowboys, who had gathered on the porch outside.

"Bravisimo," Dorchester said with a broad smile. "The two of you were magnificent!"

"You played very well," Hawke said to Pamela.

"Oh, I've never enjoyed playing as much," she replied. Spontaneously, she kissed him, quickly, on the lips.

"You'd better watch that, young man, or I shall start inquiring as to your intentions," Dorchester teased. He laughed, and, because Hawke didn't know what to say in response, he laughed with him.

"Now," Dorchester said, "let me tell you about Chicago."

Chapter 9

HAWKE HAD BEEN IN CHICAGO FOR THREE DAYS, and though he had neither the desire or intention to remain much longer, he'd found his time there enjoyable. He had attended a play and a concert, visited a couple of art museums, and enjoyed the cuisine of some of the city's finer restaurants.

It was just after sunset, and he was walking down State Street when he heard a woman cry out.

"No! Please, don't hit me again! Please, don't hit me again!"

Looking up an alley, he saw a man shove a woman, hard, into a brick wall.

"You're holdin' back on me, whore," the man growled.

"No, I'm not. I swear I'm not."

Hawke hurried up the alley toward the two. "What's going on here?" he called.

The man who had pushed the woman against the wall turned toward him. He was tall and broad-shouldered. He wore a low-crown, wide-brimmed hat, and his waxed moustache curled up at each end like the horns of a steer.

"Get the hell out of here, mister, this is none of your business," the man warned.

Hawke saw that one of the woman's eyes was black and puffed shut. Her lip was swollen and bleeding.

"Get away from her," Hawke said.

The man laughed. "What did you say to me, you dandified little piece of shit?"

Hawke, who was wearing a suit with a vest, flipped his jacket to one side, showing his pistol.

The big man just laughed and, reaching around behind him, pulled out a knife. "Mister, you think you can scare me by showing me a pistol? Why, if you actually shot it, you would be so afraid that you would probably piss in your pants." He bent forward at the waist and held his knife hand in front of him, palm up. He moved the knife around in little circles. "Now I aim to carve off your ears, just for the fun of it."

"Wrong," Hawke said. In a lightning fast move, he drew his pistol and fired, the bullet clipping the big man's right elbow. The man dropped his knife and grabbed his elbow. Hawke put his pistol back in his holster. "Now, like I said, get away from the woman."

"Why, you bastard, I'm going to gut you like a fish!" the man shouted. He bent down to retrieve his knife, and Hawke shot again. This time, his bullet hit the knife and sent it sliding down the alley.

"This is the last time I am going to ask you," Hawke said. "Leave the woman alone."

The man glared hatred at Hawke, who pulled the hammer back and pointed the gun between the man's eyes.

"I just nicked you the first time," he said. "If you don't go away and leave this woman alone, I'm going to kill you," he said coldly.

The man turned and started up the alley, walking at first, then breaking into a run.

Hawke looked at the woman. "Are you all right, ma'am?" he asked.

"Are you crazy?" the woman replied angrily. "Now you've made him really mad." She turned and yelled at the retreating man. "Johnny! Johnny, wait! I'm sorry! I'm so sorry!"

Hawke watched in surprise as she chased after him. Shaking his head in disbelief, he left the alley and returned to the Palmer House Hotel for his last night in Chicago. Tomorrow he would take the train back West.

Hawke sat in the waiting room of Chicago's Union Station, reading the *Chicago Tribune*. His attention was particularly drawn to one article.

SPECIAL TO THE *TRIBUNE*:

Green River, in the Territory of Wyoming, could well be called one of the wonders of the world. Its growth has been rapid. But a brief time ago, there was not a house here. Now the houses can be numbered by hundreds, and its inhabitants by thousands, although there is a large floating population, which undoubtedly will grow much larger as news of the recent gold strike reaches the greater public.

There is a great deal of excitement in regard to the Sweetwater mines, about ninety miles north of here. We are constantly receiving fabulous news concerning their richness. Already a gold rush is underway, and more treasure hunters are expected.

Plans have recently been announced for the building of the Sweetwater Railroad. The railroad, when completed, will run from Green River to the goldfields in the Sweetwater Mountains.

The Sweetwater mines are said to be confined to gold-bearing leads, and those who go to that country in search of mines will find that, by obtaining possession of good leads and thoroughly developing them, they will realize a ready demand and good prices for their endeavor. Fortunes will be made in that country, as they have been made in others.

The building of the Sweetwater Railroad will ensure that provisions and equipment can be delivered promptly and at low costs. No doubt exists that in another year Sweetwater will be one of the most extensive mining districts in the United States.

More than a dozen trains were backed into the car shed of the Union Pacific depot. The engines were maintaining their steam, and as a result the sounds of venting pressures echoed and reechoed throughout the station. In addition, at any given time there was at least one train departing and one arriving, the rolling sounds of steel wheels on steel tracks adding to the din.

The cavernous shed smelled of smoke and steam-wilted clothing. Arriving and departing passengers hurried along the extended narrow boarding platforms between the trains. Vendors were peddling their wares: everything from amazing apple peelers to aromatic lunches in boxes.

Hawke walked along the platform behind the trains, examining the paper in his hand and comparing it with the large numbers that were mounted on poles at the head of each track. He was looking for track number seven, and had just located it when a baggage handler came by, pulling a large cart filled with luggage.

"Make way! Make way, sir! Make way!" the baggage handler was saying over and over.

Hawke stepped aside to let him pass.

"Careful, baggage handler, don't let that top bag fall," an attractive woman called. She was holding onto the arm of a man who was nattily dressed, including a silk cravat and a diamond stickpin.

"Don' you worry none, Mrs. Dupree. I ain't goin' to let nothin' fall."

"Libby, will you quit worrying and let the man do his job? I'm sure he knows what he is doing."

"Oh, but Jay, I've got a bottle of very expensive perfume in that bag. It would be awful if it got broken, to say nothing of spreading the fragrance on all the clothes."

"It seems to me like having your clothes doctored with perfume would eliminate you having to put it on," Dupree said with a chuckle.

"Some of your clothes are in that bag," the woman replied. "I know you are somewhat the dandy, but do you really want to smell like a Parisian fancy woman?"

Dupree laughed out loud, then raised his hand and called toward the baggage handler, "Careful with those bags."

Libby laughed as well, then took his arm with both hands.

As they passed Hawke, Dupree saw him studying the paper in his hand.

"Are you looking for the transcontinental train?" Dupree asked. "Because if you are, you're at the right place."

"Yes, thank you, I do appear to be," Hawke said, folding the paper and putting it into his inside jacket pocket.

"I'm Jay Dupree, sir. This beautiful young lady is Libby St. Cyr."

"St. Cyr?" Hawke looked toward the baggage handler, who was well down the length of the train by now.

Dupree, noticing the expression on Hawke's face and his glance toward the baggage handler, chuckled.

"Miss St. Cyr is my employee. If people draw the wrong

assumption about us, I have found that it is better to let them think as they will. And you are?"

"Mason Hawke."

"Well, Mr. Hawke, would you care to walk with us as we board the train?"

"I would be glad to," Hawke said.

As they walked along the length of the train, Hawke could see, through the windows, those passengers who were already in the cars. They sat in their seats, reading newspapers or carrying on conversations, a world apart from the hustle and bustle outside the train.

"Where are you headed, Mr. Hawke?" Dupree asked.

"You can drop the 'Mister.' Most folks just call me Hawke. And I'm not headed anywhere in particular. I'm just going to be on the train."

Libby looked at him in surprise. "You are going to be taking a trip to the Far West, but you've no idea where?"

"It isn't the destination, it's the trip," Hawke replied.

"I don't understand."

"If you come into the palace car at any time during the trip, you will understand," Hawke said. "I'm a pianist, and the Union Pacific Railroad has hired me to play the piano on this train."

"Oh, how wonderful," Libby said, smiling and clapping her hands in delight. "Well, I'm sure we will be stopping in to hear you play from time to time."

"Have you heard about the gold strike in the Wyoming Territory?" Dupree asked.

"Yes, I was just reading about it in the local paper."

"I believe some enterprising people are going to make a lot of money," Dupree said. "And I intend to get my share."

Hawke shook his head. "If you don't mind my saying so, Mr. Dupree, you don't have the looks of a gold hunter."

Dupree laughed. "It depends on where you are looking for the gold," he said.

"I beg your pardon?"

"My . . . associates and I plan to open a social club there. I think men who have been working hard in the hills, prospecting for gold, would appreciate a place to come for a few drinks, the companionship of an attractive woman, and some relaxation."

Dupree stopped, then checked the paper in his hand. "Ah, here we are, my dear. Our accommodations are in this car."

A beautiful young blond-haired woman stuck her head out the window of the car, joined a few seconds later by a second, this one a redhead, just as pretty as the first.

"Jay, Libby, where have you been? Lulu and I have been on the car for just hours, waiting for you," the blonde said.

Dupree laughed. "I doubt that you have been here hours, Sue. The train itself hasn't been here that long."

"Sue is right," Lulu said. "It has been a long time. What kept you two?"

"Someone had to take care of the luggage," Libby replied.

"These two ladies will be traveling with us as well," Dupree said. "Sue, Lulu, meet Mr. Hawke."

Both girls flashed broad smiles and stuck their hands out.

"Pleased to meet you," they said at the same time.

"Like Libby, they are my associates."

"Yes, I see. And I think I understand the nature of your business now," Hawke said.

"Surely, Mr. Hawke, you aren't a prude?" Libby asked. "An urbane gentleman like you?"

Hawke laughed. "I've been called a lot of things, Miss St. Cyr. I'm quite sure I've never been called a prude."

"I wouldn't think so. You don't have that look about you," Libby said.

"Have a pleasant journey," Hawke said, touching the brim of his hat as Dupree and Libby stepped up into their car.

"Thank you, and the same to you, sir. We'll see each other frequently, I'm sure," Dupree replied.

Hawke continued until he reached the car he had been told to board. A porter was standing in the car door.

"Beg your pardon, sir, but this here be the crew car," the porter said.

"My name is Mason Hawke, and I believe this is the car I'm supposed to be on. I've signed on to play the piano on this trip."

"Oh, now that will be fine," the porter said. "On these long trips, the passengers do enjoy the music."

"I expect the conductor will be wanting to talk to me after a while. When he's not too busy, perhaps you could tell him where I am."

"Yes, sir, I'll do that. And welcome aboard."

"Thank you."

Hawke settled in a seat near a window, put his long legs forward, folded his arms across his chest, then pulled his hat down over his eyes. Within a few moments he was sound asleep.

Chapter 10

~~~

THE ANGRY BUZZ OF BULLETS COULD BE HEARD *even above the rattle of musketry, the heavy thump of cannon fire, and the explosive burst of artillery rounds. Men were screaming, some in defiance, some in fear, and many in agony.*

By now the blood was pooling in the rocks and boulders of Devil's Den, but still the fighting continued. Mason Hawke had taken shelter in those rocks, and from his position was engaged in long distance shooting, killing Yankee soldiers from five hundred to a thousand yards away. He shot until the hexagon barrel of his Sharps breechloader was so hot that he could no longer touch it, so he took off his shirt to use as a pad to allow him to hold the rifle and continue his killing. He lost count of how many men he had killed, but knew that one of his victims was a brigadier general.

Around him, sixty-five of his fellow soldiers had already fallen victim to the Yankee Sharpshooters under the command of Colonel Hiram Berdan.

"This ain't never going to stop!" a private next to him

shouted in horror. "We're just goin' to keep on a'killin' each other till ever' last one of us is dead."

Hawke turned to answer him, to assure him that this battle, like all the others they had been in, would end. But before he could say a word, a minié ball slammed into the private's head. The man's blood, brains, and tiny fragments of bone splinters sprayed into Hawke's face.

Hawke didn't even bother to wipe off the detritus as he selected his next target.

"Hawke, we've got to get out of here!" one of the others shouted.

"Hawke!"

"Hawke!"

"Mr. Hawke!"

"Mr. Hawke?"

The sound of gunfire faded away, replaced by the sound of a train in motion.

"Mr. Hawke?"

Hawke was fully awake now, and already this dream of the hell of Gettysburg, like many before it, was mercifully slipping from his memory. He could feel the gentle sway of the train in motion, and when he pushed his hat up and looked through the window, he saw that they were well out of the city. They were passing a farm, and on the other side of the field he saw a man walking behind a mule and plow.

"Mr. Hawke."

The tone grew more insistent.

Hawke turned to see who was addressing him and saw a man wearing a blue uniform jacket and billed cap.

"Yes?" Hawke replied

"My name is McCutcheon, Mr. Hawke. I am the conductor. If you would come with me, I'll show you to the palace car where you will be playing."

"All right," Hawke said.

"I don't know what you have been told as to what your duties are," the conductor said, "but let me go over my rules with you."

"Your rules?"

"Yes, Mr. Hawke, my rules. As the conductor of this train, I am the man in charge, the captain, so to speak, of this ship. Do you have a problem with that?"

"No problem."

"Very good. First of all, I shall expect absolute courtesy to all the passengers. Some may get a little out of hand from time to time, but if they do, I want you to remember that we are here to serve them.

"Secondly, I will require you to be present in the palace car until midnight, every night, until we have completed our journey. You will be allowed one hour off for your meals, and you may take your meals in the dining car."

Hawke was following the conductor now, and as they passed between the cars, it was necessary to step across a gap of some two feet from the platform of one car to the platform of the next. Looking down through the gap, Hawke could see the ballast and railroad ties slipping by rapidly. Also, out here there was a breath of hot wind and the smell of smoke.

With the train in motion, there was a great deal of independent movement in the sway and roll of the individual cars, though they were connected. Because of that, it was not possible to step from one car to the next without paying attention to what you were doing. Despite the conductor's haughty attitude, Hawke had to give him grudging respect for the ease with which he negotiated the transit from car to car.

As they passed through one of the parlor cars, Hawke saw Jay Dupree and Libby St. Cyr.

"Well, we meet again, I see," Libby said. "Are you going to play now?"

"Yes."

"Good. I'll be in to listen, shortly."

When they stepped onto the rear platform of this car, Mc-Cutcheon held up his hand to stop Hawke.

"Another thing," he said. "There is to be absolutely no fraternization between employees of Union Pacific and passengers."

When Jason White entered Bailey McPherson's office in Green River, he was carrying a large, rolled-up document.

"Miss McPherson, I have the preliminary surveys here, if you would like to see them."

"Yes, of course I want to see them," Bailey said. "Spread your map out here on the table."

Jason unrolled the map, and Bailey began finding ways to hold down the corners. She put an ink bottle on one corner, a book on a second corner, and a lantern on the third. When the fourth corner attempted to roll up, she looked at Dancer.

"Ethan, put your gun on that corner," she said.

Dancer hesitated a moment, then took his gun from the holster and put it where she directed.

"Now, show me the route," she said to Jason.

He used his finger to trace along the drawn railroad tracks.

"We will follow the Green River northwest until we reach the conflux of the Green and the Big Sandy. We turn north along the Big Sandy until we reach the Little Sandy River. We will follow the Little Sandy almost due north until we arrive at its terminus at South Pass."

"And the entire route is along the rivers?" Bailey asked.

"Yes. Of course, you do realize, don't you, that by routing your railroad this way, instead of going straight to South Pass, you are increasing the length by some thirty miles. That's almost half again what a straight route would be."

"Yes, I know that," Bailey said.

"What will we tell the railroad commission? They will question why you aren't going by the shortest route."

"You don't worry about that," Bailey said. "Addison has already taken care of it. All you need to do now is submit the surveys for compensation. According to the Railroad Land Grant Act of 1862, we are entitled to a four-hundred-foot right of way, and ten square miles of property for every one mile of route."

"Good Lord! That gives you a five-mile-wide swath of land from here to the Sweetwater!" Jason did some quick figuring. "That's over a quarter of a million acres!"

"A quarter of a million acres of the best range land in the entire territory," Bailey said. "With sweet water and green grass."

"That's a lot of land."

"Yes, it is. It challenges Northumbria in size." Bailey looked up with shining, beady eyes. "And, if I play my cards right, I'll own Northumbria as well."

Hawke had been on the train for two days, playing the piano in the palace car. Dupree and the three women with him—Libby, Lulu, and Sue—were his most faithful listeners. The women were young, attractive, and very flirtatious. If Hawke had had any question as to the purpose of Dupree's social club, spending some time around these women answered it for him.

The first night out, after departing Chicago, Hawke played mostly classical music. But as the train got farther west and picked up new passengers, the demographics of his audience changed. Mechanics, farmhands, and ultimately cowboys now outnumbered the wealthy eastern businessmen by a substantial number, and their music tastes were more rural. As a result of these changing dynamics, the music was now little different from the kind of music he played in the saloons.

Just west of Cheyenne, a young cowboy in chaps and silver spurs and rowels got on the train. He had a bottle with him, and Hawke was just finishing a song as he stepped into the palace car.

Hawke's audience applauded him, and the cowboy, though he had not heard Hawke, tucked the bottle of whiskey under his arm so he could pointedly join the applause.

"Well now," he said loudly. "Ain't this a little bit of fancy drawers? We got us a piano player."

"Yes, and he has been playing beautifully too," Lulu said.

"Is that the truth? Well now, tell me Mr. Fancy Pants piano player. Is this here little lady tellin' the truth? Have you been playing . . . beautifully?" He sat the word apart, mocking Lulu. "Or does this little filly have her cap set for you?"

"Sir, if you would please find a seat and be quiet so the others can enjoy the music, I will continue to play," Hawke said as politely as he could.

"Oh, yeah, I should be quiet," the cowboy said. Standing in the middle of the car, he turned to everyone, making an exaggerated show of putting his finger across his lips in the symbol of shushing. "All right, I'll be quiet."

"Thanks, I would appreciate that," Hawke said as he turned back to the piano.

It wasn't a second later before the cowboy spoke up again.

"Hey, piano player!" he shouted in a loud and belligerent voice. "Play 'My Dog Is Dead.' "

Over the last several years of playing piano in saloons from Beaumont, Texas, to Denver, Colorado, Hawke had played just about every cowboy ditty ever written. But he had never heard of the song "My Dog Is Dead."

"Sorry, I don't know it," he said.

Hawke moved into another song, but out of the corner of his

eye he saw the cowboy move to sit next to Lulu. She moved a couple of times, but each time she did so, he moved with her.

"Hey! Piano player! Play 'My Dog Is Dead'!" the cowboy shouted again. Laughing, he turned the bottle up to his lips and took several, Adam's-apple bobbing swallows. Lowering the bottle, he wiped his mouth with the back of his hand and extended the bottle, by way of offer, to Lulu. She shook her head no.

"You sure?" he asked. "It's not bad whiskey."

"No, thank you," Lulu said quietly.

Several of the others in the car made shushing sounds.

"Oh, yeah, I'm s'posed to be quiet so Mr. Fancy Pants piano player can play," the cowboy said.

Hawke began playing.

"Hey! Piano player! Play 'My Dog Is Dead'!" the cowboy shouted one more time.

By now the others in the car were getting fed up with him, and one of the men asked him to leave.

"I'll leave when I damn well want to leave," the cowboy said. "Unless there is someone in here who is man enough to make me leave."

The cowboy's belligerence and implied threat quieted everyone.

"Hey, ladies, you all turn your heads now and don't peek," he said, laughing. "'Cause ol' Johnny is goin' to go out on the platform and take a leak."

"Well, I never!" one woman gasped.

"Hey, that rhymes," Johnny said. "Did you hear that? Turn your heads and don't peek, 'cause ol' Johnny is goin' to take a leak. Listen here, Mr. Fancy Pants piano player, when I come back, maybe me 'n' you could get together and write that up as a song."

Laughing, Johnny stepped out of the car, onto the vestibule platform.

"Ladies and gentlemen, would you please excuse me for a moment?" Hawke said just after the cowboy left. He got up from the piano and went outside behind the young cowboy. Johnny was standing on the edge, unbuttoning his pants.

"No, no, no," Johnny said in a singsong voice. He didn't bother to look around. "I told you ladies not to take a peak."

"I promise not to look," Hawke said.

"What?" Johnny replied, turning around when he heard a man's voice.

Hawke grabbed the cowboy by his collar and belt, then tossed him over the side, pitching him far enough to make certain he cleared the cars.

"Hey, what the hell!" the cowboy yelled, though it was in Doppler effect because as the train proceeded, his voice receded.

When Hawke returned to the palace car, he was roundly applauded by everyone there. Bowing, he took his seat then played a piece by Chopin.

"That was beautiful!" Libby said. "What was it?"

"It was Waltz in D flat, Opus 64, Number 1. Sometimes called the Minute Waltz."

"The Minute Waltz? Why do they call it that?"

Hawke chuckled. "I never have figured that out, because it takes a minute and forty-five seconds to play it."

Those in the car laughed.

"It's dinnertime, Mr. Hawke," Dupree said. "Would you care to join the ladies and me this evening?"

"Thank you," Hawke replied. "I believe I will."

As the dining car was just one car in front of the palace car, it was a short walk to dinner. They were met by one of the stewards who, showed them to a table.

"Mr. Hawke will be joining us for dinner tonight, Adam."

"But sir, the table will only seat four," the black steward replied.

"You can put these two ladies at the table just across from us," he said, pointing to Lulu and Sue.

"Very good, sir."

The dining car was set up so that tables on one side would seat four, while on the other side the tables sat only two. Lulu and Sue were put at the table for two.

Outside the window the bare, featureless seascape that had been their vista yesterday while still in Nebraska had turned to yellow and gray foothills climbing up to red buttes, guarded by ring-tailed hawks that sailed along the walls, their sharp eyes searching for prey.

The steward returned with the menus.

The main choice tonight seemed to be between steak and salmon. Hawke and Dupree chose steak. Libby, Lulu, and Sue selected salmon.

"So, what do you think you will do when this trip is over?" Dupree asked as the steward left with their order. "Will you continue to play piano for the Union Pacific?"

"Well I—" Hawke began, but was interrupted by the conductor, who came storming into the car, his face red and twisted in rage.

"Mr. Hawke! I have been told that you threw a passenger from the train. Is this true?"

Hawke chuckled. "I wondered how long it would be before you heard about it."

"It is no laughing matter, Mr. Hawke," McCutcheon said with barely controlled anger.

"Look, Mr. Conductor," Dupree said, "if Mr. Hawke hadn't thrown that unpleasant gentleman from the train, I would have done it myself. And if not me, someone else would have. Either that or someone would have shot him. He was one of the most obnoxious people I've ever met."

"Nevertheless," McCutcheon said, addressing himself to Hawke, "you can't just go about tossing disagreeable passengers off the train. Especially when it is moving, and especially in the middle of the desert."

"I'll be more careful where I throw him next time," Hawke said.

"In addition to throwing a paying passenger from the train, you are in blatant violation of my specific orders not to fraternize with the passengers. You don't have to worry about being more careful next time, because there won't be a next time. Your employment with Union Pacific is hereby terminated."

Literally spinning on his heel, McCutcheon turned and left the dining car. For a moment the five sat in silence, with the women staring at their plates in embarrassment.

"I believe you asked if I intended to stay with the railroad?" Hawke said.

"I did ask that, yes."

"I think I can safely say that I will not be playing piano for the Union Pacific Railroad."

Dupree laughed, and Hawke laughed with him. Then the three women laughed as well, and when the conductor happened to glance through the door and saw them all laughing, he turned away, angry and confused as to why Hawke would find it so amusing that he had just been fired.

"So, what are you going to do now?" Dupree asked.

At that moment, their meal was delivered and Hawke waited until the steward withdrew before he answered.

"I don't know. I guess I'll go looking for a saloon that needs a pianist."

"Have you ever considered playing the piano in a whorehouse?"

"Jay!" Libby said.

"Well, let's face it, dear, what we will be running is a whorehouse, no matter what fancy title we give it. And if Mr. Hawke accepts the invitation, he will have to know what's going on upstairs."

Hawke smiled. "I've not only considered playing in such an establishment, I've actually done it. At many of the saloons where I've worked, a rather brisk business was being conducted upstairs."

"Then you have nothing, in principle, against the profession? You might come to work for us?"

"I have absolutely nothing in principle against playing the piano in a whorehouse," Hawke said. "But I'm going to say no, because I don't want to commit myself to anything right now. I do thank you for the job offer, though."

"I understand," Dupree said. "But I do want you to know that if you ever change your mind, the invitation still stands."

Chapter 11

ALTHOUGH HAWKE HAD BEEN GONE LESS THAN two weeks, he almost didn't recognize Green River when he returned. There were at least twice as many people as when he'd left. The new arrivals had come from all over the country: longshoremen from New York, coal miners from Pennsylvania, farmers from Missouri, and gamblers from New Orleans.

Their accents were different, their clothing different, their backgrounds different, but in one respect they were all the same. All were there in response to the news that had spread throughout the country about the gold discovered in the Sweetwater Mountains. And everyone was there to make their fortune.

Just exactly how they were going to do that differed among the individuals. Some planned to strike it rich in the goldfield. Others started new businesses to take advantage of the rush. In fact, the businesses were so new that most of them didn't even have permanent buildings, but were working out of tents.

An outfitter was selling picks, shovels, tents, ponchos, canteens, knives, boots, everything a prospector would need to get started. A brand new wagon outfit, with the ambitious and optimistic name of Gold Nugget Haulers, was in business, providing both freighting and passenger service up to the Sweetwater Range.

One enterprising huckster was selling "Maps to the Goldfields," purporting to show the best places to dig to guarantee success.

Jay Dupree and his girls planned to make their fortune by catering to the prurient interests of all, prospector and businessman alike.

"Well, now," Dupree said, rubbing his hands together in glee as he eyed the crowded streets of Green River. "Ladies, I do believe we have already discovered gold."

Not all the gold seekers were recent arrivals. Practically every ranch in the valley suffered losses, as cowboys left to search for gold. Northumbria was no exception. Three of Dorchester's hands had left with the initial news of the discovery, now seven more, including his foreman, had come to see him.

Rob Dealey was at the head of the group, and he and the others stood on the front porch of the building the cowboys referred to as the "Big House," holding their hats in their hands. Most of them couldn't meet the gaze of the man who had kept them on year round, even during the slack season when all the other ranchers let their cowboys go.

"So, that's the way it is, Mr. Dorchester," Dealey said as he rolled the brim of the hat around in his hands. "Me 'n' some of the boys figured that, well, if there is gold up there just lyin' around waitin' to be picked up, we'd like to try and get our hands on some of it."

"All right," Dorchester replied. "I certainly can't force you to stay here."

"So, what we was thinkin'," Dealey went on, "that is, what the men wanted me to ask you was, uh, that is, if . . ."

"You are wanting to be paid out, is that it, Mr. Dealey?"

Dealey nodded. "Yes, sir, if you don't mind. I mean, the thing is, you owe us the money up until now, so . . ."

"That's not entirely correct," Dorchester said. "The agreement is that I will pay you once a month, for a month's work. If you haven't done a month's work, you haven't completed your part of the agreement."

The men looked at each other in disappointment and concern.

"But don't worry," Dorchester said with a dismissive wave of his hand. "I fully intend to pay you, even though I am not legally bound to do so. I just wanted you to know the way it really was."

"You're a good man, Mr. Dorchester," Dealey said. "Ever'body says you are the best rancher they ever worked for."

"But not good enough to keep you away from the goldfields, right?

Nobody answered.

"That's all right," Dorchester said. "I've no doubt but that if I were a young man, I would go up there myself. Wait here, I'll get the money."

"Hey, Eddie, what you goin' to do with your money when you get rich?" one of the cowboys asked another.

"I don't know. Maybe buy all the horehound candy they got in the store. Oh, and send my mama some money," the young cowboy answered.

The others laughed.

"What about you, Win? What will you do?"

"If I get just a little bit rich, I'll prob'ly go someplace like San Francisco or Denver and spend it all on a good time. But if I was to get really rich, why I reckon I'd come back here and buy this ranch," Win said.

All the cowboys laughed again.

"What makes you think Mr. Dorchester would sell it?" Eddie asked.

"I'd give him so much money he'd have to sell it. Then I'd let him and his daughter stay with me in the Big House."

"Oh, I'm sure they would love that," one of the others said, to more laughter.

Dorchester had overheard the last bit of conversation and chuckled to himself as he came back out onto the porch with his money box. He walked over to sit at the table he used on pay day, opened the box and took out a ledger book.

"Mr. Dorchester, if it don't work out up there for us . . . uh, that is, if we don't find nothin', can we come back and work for you?" one of the cowboys asked.

"Well, now, I don't know about that," Dorchester replied. "If I find it necessary to hire more men while you are gone, then I'm afraid there won't be a place for you."

"I reckon that's only right," one of them said. "I mean, what with us runnin' off on you an' all."

"I will take you back if I have a place for you," Dorchester said. "But, Mr. Dealey, if you come back and I am able to re hire you, you must understand that I won't be able to give you your job as foreman back. I will have to replace you as soon as I can."

"Yes, sir," Dealey said. "But I don't reckon I'll be comin' back. If there's gold up there, I aim to find it, and if I do, and get rich, I won't be doin' no more ranchin'."

"Very well, as long as you understand. All right, gentlemen, as you know, I keep my book in chronological and not alphabetical order. So line up according to how long you have been working at Northumbria."

The men lined up accordingly.

"Mr. Rob Dealey," Dorchester said. "Forty-five dollars per month is a dollar and a half per day. At twenty-two days that comes to thirty-three dollars."

Dorchester counted the money out and Dealey picked it up, thanked him, then stepped aside for the next person.

"Win Woodruff, thirty dollars per month is a dollar a day. Twenty-two days is twenty-two dollars."

The cowboy who was going to strike it rich and then come back to buy Northumbria picked up his money with a mumbled thanks.

"Eddie Taylor, thirty dollars per month is a dollar a day. Twenty-two days is twenty-two dollars."

Eddie took his money then joined Win, who was waiting for him on the steps.

"First thing we've got to do," Win said as they walked away while, behind them, the other cowboys were getting paid, "is get into town and get some of the tools and stuff that we need."

"Are we goin' to be partners, or look for gold for ourselves?" Eddie asked.

"I don't know. Why do you ask?"

"'Cause if we are goin' to be partners, we wouldn't both of us have to buy every piece of equipment. We could share equipment and it would be a lot less expensive gettin' started."

"Good idea!" Win said. He stuck out his hand. "All right, we're partners."

In the back room of her office, Bailey McPherson pulled a chair over and climbed up on it to get a closer look at the large map that Jason White had tacked up on the wall.

The map covered the southwestern corner of Wyoming Territory from the Continental Divide in the east to the territorial line in the west, and from the territorial line in the south to the Wind River Range and Sweetwater Mountains in the north.

A wide, cross-hatched swath ran from Green River City, along Green River to the Big Sandy, up the Big Sandy to the Little Sandy River, and up the Little Sandy to South Pass.

"That's a lot of territory," Addison Ford said, standing beside her, looking at the same map. Even though Bailey was standing on the chair, her head was only slightly higher than Ford's head.

"Yes, it is," she said. "And since it controls all of the water, once we get our hands on this land, we'll be able to squeeze the others out."

"In order to do that, you will have to dam off the rivers and creeks," Ford said.

"I've already started."

"You've already started?" Ford replied, surprised. "How can you have already started? We haven't served any papers on anyone yet."

"Well, you and the government have your schedule, Mr. Ford, and I have mine."

"You must be very careful about this," Ford said. "As it stands now, we have the law on our side. So far, everything we are doing is legal. Step over the bounds, just a little bit, and everything could fall apart."

"Do you have the papers drawn up yet?" Bailey asked

"I do. It's just a matter of where to serve the first one."

Bailey looked back at the map, then put her hand on the Little Sandy, way up top.

"We may as well start here and work our way down," she said. "Serve them there."

Ford nervously cleared his throat. "You want me to serve them? Personally?"

"Yes. You are the one who represents the U.S. government, are you not?" she asked.

"Well, yes, I am. But that doesn't mean that I want to—or even have to—serve them personally," Ford said.

"Given the rewards, I'd think you would be more than willing to serve the papers," Bailey said.

"I haven't been out here very long," Ford said, "but I have

lived here long enough to know that if you tell a rancher you are taking his land away from him, you'd better get back out of the way. He may not take it all that well. In fact he could get, uh . . ."

"Dangerous?" Bailey suggested.

"Yes."

"In other words, you are afraid to serve the papers." It wasn't a question, it was a statement.

"Yes," Ford replied. "I'm a government official, I'm not a lawman. I wouldn't know how to handle it if someone decided to put up a fight."

"Don't worry," Bailey said. "I'll have Mr. Dancer serve the papers."

"Dancer, yes," Ford replied. "He would be just the one to serve them."

From the *Green River Journal*:

GREEN RIVER A BOOMTOWN

From the beginning, the town of Green River could have been classified as hardworking, fairly sober, and almost always conscientious. But recently it has turned into a rip-snorting, hell-raising town, bent upon divesting every citizen who arrives of his poke in the quickest manner possible.

What has caused this usually mild and law-abiding town to undergo such a change? It is the discovery of gold in the Sweetwater Mountains to our north, and the desire of all to make their fortune.

And who has come to town, to flood our streets and fill our saloons, cafés, and gambling houses? Those selfsame fortune seekers. There

are a good many people here now. Broad-
brimmed and spurred Texas cowboys, Nebraska farmers, keen businessmen from
Chicago, St. Louis, and even New York, real estate agents, land seekers, hungry lawyers, gamblers, women with white sun bonnets and
modest dress, painted women with colorful ribbons and scandalous dress, express wagons going pell-mell, prairie schooners and farm
wagons, all rushing after the almighty dollar.

Already a struggle has begun for control of
the soul of our fair town, between the preach-
ers who have come to save us and the gamblers
and harlots who have come to drag us into
their parlors of sin.

Green River has many characteristics that
prevent its being classified as a town of strictly
moral ideas and principles, notwithstanding it
is supplied with a church, a courthouse, and a
jail. Other institutions counterbalance the good
works supposed to emanate from the first men-
tioned. Like many other frontier towns of this
modern day, fast men and fast women are
around by the score, seeking whom they may
devour, hunting for a soft target, and taking
him in for cash. Many is the would-be gold
seeker who can testify as to the abilities of
these charlatans to successfully follow the call-
ings they have embraced in quest of money.

Hawke folded the newspaper and put it to one side, then
picked up his beer and looked around the saloon. Aaron
Peabody was pounding away on the piano, but fortunately
there was so much noise in the saloon that his cacophonous
efforts could scarcely be heard.

Libby St. Cyr came into the saloon. She was wearing a low-cut dress that showed a generous spill of breasts at the neckline. The dress clung to her body until just below the flare of her hips, where it became fuller. When she saw Hawke standing at the bar, she walked over to talk to him.

"That should be you playing the piano," she said.

Hawke shook his head. "No, I think not. Not that piano," he said.

Peabody hit another sour note.

"Oh, my, is he that bad, or is it the piano?"

"Yes," Hawke replied, and it took Libby a second to understand his answer.

When she did understand it, she laughed.

"Could I buy you a drink, Miss St. Cyr?" he asked.

"Yes, thank you."

"From a good bottle," Hawke said to Jake, holding up a finger.

Jake poured whiskey into a clean glass and gave it to Libby.

"Miss, are you looking for work?" he asked.

"No," she said, lifting the drink. She smiled at Hawke, then tossed it down quickly. "Why do you ask?" she asked, turning back to Jake.

"Well, uh, the way you look, uh, I mean . . ."

"Oh?" Libby said, pouting. "You don't like the way I look?"

"No, ma'am, I didn't say nothin' like that."

"You are teasing him, Miss St. Cyr," Hawke said.

"I suppose I am."

"But I am as curious as the bartender. Why are you in here? I thought you were going up north."

"We are leaving tomorrow morning," Libby said. "But today I'm on my own, so I thought I would come over here and see if I could find a good poker game."

"There's always one going," Hawke said. "And if you can't find one, I'm sure you can start one."

"Good idea," she said. She stepped out onto the floor and held up a deck of cards. "Gentlemen," she called. "I'm looking for three men who aren't afraid to play cards with a woman. I'll be at that table right over there."

Chapter 12

BY THE TIME LIBBY REACHED THE TABLE, THERE WERE three men sitting there, waiting patiently.

Chuckling, Hawke turned back to the bar and ordered another drink. He had just finished it when one of the players got up.

"I've got to make my rounds," he said. He chuckled. "And it's a good thing too. If I stayed here any longer, I'd lose a month's pay."

"Why, Deputy Hagen, if you had paid more attention to your cards and less attention to my, uh . . . breasts, perhaps you would have done better," Libby teased, and the others laughed.

"You fellas better watch her," the deputy called back good-naturedly as he left.

"Well now, Deputy, that's the problem. We all have been watchin' her, and not the cards," one of the other players said, and again everyone laughed.

"Mr. Hawke," Libby called. "There is a seat open at the table, if you would care to join us."

"Thanks," Hawke said. "Maybe I will."

Hawke joined the game.

"Gentlemen, new player, new deck," Libby said. She picked up a box, broke the seal, then dumped the cards onto the table. They were clean, stiff, and shining. She pulled out the joker, then began shuffling the deck. The stiff new pasteboards clicked sharply. Her hands moved swiftly, folding the cards in and out until the law of random numbers became king. She shoved the deck across the table.

"Cut?" she invited Hawke. Leaning over the table, she showed a generous amount of cleavage.

Hawke cut the deck, then pushed them back. He tried to focus on her hands, though it was difficult because she kept finding ways to position herself to draw his eyes toward her more interesting parts. When he looked around the table, he saw that the other players were having the same problem.

"You aren't having trouble concentrating, are you, Mr. Hawke?" Libby teased.

"Not at all," Hawke replied with a laugh. "Not at all."

After a few more hands one of the other players left and a new player joined. He was a big man with red hair and a bushy beard. Hawke recognized him at once as the man he had encountered several weeks ago at the saloon in Sage Creek.

"Hello, Metzger," he said.

Metzger squinted his eyes at Hawke. "How do you know my name?" he asked.

Hawke studied Metzger for a moment, wondering if Metzger really didn't know who he was or if he was just pretending not to know. Whichever it was, he decided not to pursue it.

"I must've heard someone say it," Hawke said.

"Yeah, that must be it, 'cause me 'n' you have never met before," Metzger said.

Hawke knew then, by the way Metzger was so specific

about their never having met, that he was lying. He could also tell by the little twitch in Metzger's left eye and the sound of his voice. He just didn't know why.

"The game is five card," Libby said, then paused and looked directly at Hawke before saying the next word. "Stud," she added pointedly.

"Fine," Hawke answered.

Hawke won fifteen dollars on the first hand, and a couple of hands later was ahead by a little over thirty dollars. The other players were taking Hawke's good luck in stride, but Metzger began complaining.

"Somethin kinda fishy is goin' on here," he said.

"Fishy, Mr. Metzger?" Libby replied sweetly.

Metzger looked at Libby, then nodded toward Hawke. "You're dealin' him winnin' hands," he said.

"How can you say that?" Libby asked. "The deal has passed around the table, and Mr. Hawke has been winning no matter who is dealing."

"Are you trying to tell me his winnin' is just dumb luck?"

"No, it's not just luck, and there's nothing dumb about it," Hawke said. "There's a degree of skill involved in knowing when to hold and when to fold. You obviously haven't learned that."

"Is that a fact?" Metzger asked. He stared across the table through narrowed eyes. "Suppose you and I have a go by ourselves? Showdown for twenty-five dollars."

"Showdown?" Hawke chuckled. "All right, I see you're trying to even up the odds a bit by taking the skill out. But I'll go with you."

Metzger reached for the cards, but Hawke stuck his hand out to stop him. "You don't think I'm going to let you deal, do you? We'll let the lady deal."

"Uh-uh," Metzger said, shaking his head. He nodded toward one of the other players. "We'll let him deal."

"All right," Hawke agreed.

The man Metzger selected dealt five cards to each of them. Hawke took the pot with a pair of twos.

Metzger laughed. "Not exactly a big hand, was it? How about another?"

Hawke won that hand with a jack high.

"Want another one?" Hawke asked.

"Yes," Metzger replied. "You can't possibly win three in a row."

Hawke did win the third, with a pair of tens, and Metzger threw his cards on the table in disgust. He slid the rest of his money to the center of the table. "I've thirty-six dollars here," he said. "High card."

Hawke covered his bet, then the dealer fanned the cards out.

"You draw first," Metzger said.

Hawke started to reach for a card, but just as he touched it, Metzger stopped him. "No, I changed my mind," he said. "I'll draw first." Metzger smiled triumphantly, then flipped over the card Hawke was about to draw. It was a three of hearts.

"What the—" Metzger shouted in anger. "You cheated me, you son of a bitch! You knew I was going to do that so you reached for the low card!"

"How was I supposed to know that was a low card?" Hawke asked. "The cards are facedown on the table." Hawke turned over a seven of diamonds, then reached for the money.

Metzger stuck his hand down into his pocket and pulled out a "pepperbox"—a small, palm-sized pistol.

"Mister, I ain't givin' up my money to a cheater," Metzger said. "I'll thank you to slide that money back across the table."

"How the hell was he cheating, mister?" the dealer said. "I'm the one who was dealing the cards."

"I ain't figured that out yet." Metzger smiled. "But it don't make no difference now, 'cause I'm about to put things right." He motioned with his other hand. "Push the money over here to me."

"I don't think so," Hawke replied.

"What do you mean, you don't think so? I'm holdin' a gun on you, or ain't you noticed?"

"So you are," Hawke said. "And I'm holding one on you," he added. "It's pointed at your belly right now."

Metzger started to sweat and his hand began to shake. Glancing down, he saw Hawke's pistol in his holster.

"No you ain't," he said. "Your gun is right there in your holster. I can see it."

"You think you're the only one with a holdout gun?" Hawke asked. "The difference is . . ." From under the table came a distinct sound, like the sound of a gun being cocked. ". . . mine is already cocked, and yours isn't."

Glancing down toward his pepperbox, Metzger saw that he had not yet pulled the hammer back. He moved his thumb toward the hammer.

"I wouldn't do that if I were you," Hawke cautioned, smiling and shaking his head slowly. "You start to come back on that hammer and I'll blow a hole in your chest big enough to stick my fist into."

Slowly, and with a trembling hand, Metzger put the pistol down on the table. Hawke reached over to pick it up, then handed it to Libby.

"Break it open and empty the charges," he said.

Libby pushed the hinged barrel down and shook out all the cartridges.

"Now, perhaps we can get on with our game," Hawke suggested, and he brought his other hand up to the top of the table. He was holding a pocketknife. With his thumb, he flipped the blade open and closed, making a sound exactly like that of a gun being cocked.

"You . . . you didn't even have a gun in your hand!" Metzger sputtered angrily.

"No, I didn't," Hawke replied easily.

Everyone laughed.

Metzger stood up and pointed at Hawke. "One of these days, mister, you're going to try something like that, and it's going to blow up right in your face."

"I suppose there is always that chance," Hawke agreed. "But then, that's what makes life worth livin'."

Metzger stormed out of the saloon, chased out by the laughter of everyone present.

Hawke played a few more hands before he excused himself and stepped over to the bar. After a couple of drinks and a few flirtatious exchanges with one of the bar girls, he took a walk around town, then returned to his hotel.

One of the things he liked most about this hotel was that it had a bathing room, complete with a large bathtub, as well as a water-holding tank and a small wood-burning stove to heat the water. Hawke started the fire, then went back to his room to wait for the water to heat. Standing at the window, he looked out over the town, watching the commerce for a few minutes. He saw Libby coming into the hotel downstairs and chuckled over the way she used her obvious charms to distract the men who played cards with her. He wondered how much money she'd won.

He didn't begrudge her her winnings, because, thanks to Metzger, he had done pretty well himself.

Leaving the window, Hawke lay down on his bed for about fifteen minutes, until he was sure the water would be warm enough for a bath. Then, taking a change of clothes, a bar of soap, and a towel, he walked down the hall to the bathing room.

A woman was just getting into the tub when he opened the door. She stood there a moment, so surprised by his unex-

pected appearance that she made no effort to cover herself.
She was totally nude, and Hawke breathed in a quick gasp of
appreciation for her beauty.

"Mr. Hawke, as you can readily see, this room is occupied," Libby said calmly.

Hawke smiled. "So I see," he replied. He pointed to the
little stove. "I'm sorry, I had built the fire for my own bath,
but I see you beat me to it."

"Oh, then I have you to thank?" she said. "I thought that
was a service of the hotel."

"No, lighting the fire is the responsibility of the guest."

"I see," Libby said. "You are staring, Mr. Hawke."

"I suppose I am. On the other hand, you have made no effort to deny me the view."

Libby laughed, then sat down in the water, restoring a bit
of modesty, if not dignity, to the situation.

"You really should have knocked, you know," she said.

"You should have locked," Hawke replied.

"But I did lock the door," Libby said, pointing to a door at
the rear of the room. "I came through that door. I didn't realize this door had been unlocked."

"No harm done," Hawke said. "I'll wait until you are finished."

"That's very . . . decent . . . of you," Libby said.

Hawke opened his eyes. Something had awakened him, and
he lay very still. The doorknob turned and he was up, reaching for the gun that lay on a table by his bed. He moved as
quietly as a cat, stepping to the side of the door and cocking
his Colt .44. Nearly naked, he felt the night air on his skin.
His senses were alert, and his body was alive with readiness.

He could hear someone breathing on the other side of the
door. A thin shaft of hall light shone underneath. He took a

deep breath, smelled lilacs, then smiled. He had smelled this same perfume earlier.

"Libby?" he called.

"Are you awake?" the visitor replied.

Like the scent, the voice belonged to Libby. It was low and husky, with just a hint of rawness to it.

Hawke eased the hammer down on the pistol, then opened the door to let a wide bar of light spill into the room. Libby was standing in the doorway, the hall lantern backlighting the thin cotton robe she wore. He could see her body in shadow behind the cloth.

"Come on in," Hawke invited, moving back to let her step inside. He closed the door and crossed over to light the lantern on his table. A bubble of light illuminated the room.

"Oh, my. You aren't wearing much, are you?" Libby said.

"Would you prefer that I get dressed?"

"Why bother?" Libby asked. "You'll just have to get undressed again." Crossing over to him, she put her arms around his neck and pulled him to her for a kiss. When she pulled her lips away from his, the very action of pulling her head back pressed her pelvis more tightly against his groin. His reaction was instantaneous.

"I just came to tell you good-bye," she said. "Jay has gotten everything together for our trip up to the Sweetwater Mountains, so we are leaving tomorrow."

She stepped back from him, then opened her robe and let it fall from her shoulders. As he had already surmised, she was nude underneath, and her body shined golden in the soft light from the table lantern. "I thought I would give you another look, just in case you forgot everything you saw this afternoon."

"I haven't forgotten a thing," Hawke said. "But I would enjoy another look."

They moved over to the iron-stead bed. The covers were already turned back, and the springs squealed in protest as Libby lay down.

"As you can see, the bed squeaks," Hawke said.

"Good," Libby said. She moved up and down, making the springs squeak more loudly. "You played the piano for me on the train. Now I'll play a concert for you."

Chapter 13

METZGER WAS BROKE, HAVING LOST ALL HIS money in the card game the other night. He told himself that if he could just raise a stake— not a large stake, just enough to get the bare necessities—he would go up to the Sweetwater Mountains and look for gold like everyone else was doing.

But he couldn't do that without a stake.

He stole four dollars from the poor box at the church, figuring that since he was poor, it was rightly his anyway.

Four dollars got him some bacon and beans, and a couple of drinks, but it wasn't enough to outfit him for gold hunting.

He was in the Royal Flush saloon having his supper when Luke Rawlings came in. Luke was wearing a new suit and hat, and everyone rushed over to talk to him about his gold find.

"How much have you pulled out, Luke?" someone asked.

"I don't rightly know how much," Luke said, hooking his thumbs under his armpits. "But as you can see, I'm all decked out in new duds. If I was you boys, I'd be up there lookin' for gold right now."

"I'm goin' up there first thing tomorrow," one cowboy said.

"What about your job out at Lazy Q?" someone asked the cowboy.

"Ah, to hell with that job," the cowboy said with a dismissive wave of his hand. "Most of the hands has done quit anyway."

"From what I hear, there ain't a ranch anywhere in the valley but what half or more of the cowboys is quit," another said.

"Well hell, who wants to work for wages when you can go up to Sweetwater and just pick gold up, right off the ground?" Luke asked.

"That settles it. I'm goin' up first thing tomorrow," another cowboy said.

"Me too."

"You boys can all wait till tomorrow if you want to, but I'm goin' up right now," someone else said, and when he left the saloon, he was followed by at least half a dozen others. The rush left the saloon half empty.

"I tell you what, Luke," Jake said. "I wish to hell you had stayed up there."

"Is that so?"

"Yeah."

"Why?"

"Well look around the place. You sure ain't doin' much good for the saloon business."

Luke chuckled. "Well, what the hell do you care? It ain't your saloon anyway."

"I know it ain't. It belongs to Mr. Peabody, but I work for him, and my wages is based on the business we do."

Luke bought a beer, then turned around and leaned back against the bar, looking out over the rest of the saloon as he lifted his beer to his mouth. That was when he saw Metzger raking his biscuit through what was left of a plate of bacon and beans.

"Metzger?" he called. "Leon Metzger?"

Metzger looked up. At first he didn't recognize Luke, because he had never seen him so finely dressed.

"Luke?" he said in surprise when he figured out who it was.

"Yeah, it's me," Luke said. He held out his arms. "What do you think of the duds?"

"You look like a whorehouse dandy," Metzger said.

Luke laughed. "Yeah, I do, don't I? I seen me a whorehouse dandy oncet, and I said right then that if I ever got enough money, I was goin' to buy me some duds just like the ones he was a'wearin'." Luke turned back toward the bartender. "Draw me another beer for my friend, there."

Luke carried the beer over to the table, then put the mug in front of Metzger.

"Here, have a beer on me. You look like you could use a drink," he said.

"Yeah, well, what I could use is some money."

"Want a job?" Luke asked.

Metzger picked up the mug and took a long drink, then sat it back down. Beer foam hung in his moustache and beard, and he wiped it away before he answered.

"Who would I be workin' for? You?"

"No, not me. You'd be workin' for a woman that I know."

"Workin' for a woman?" Metzger shook his head. "No, I'm not sure I could do that. Work for a woman, I mean."

"Why not? I work for her."

"You do? I thought you was rich because of findin' gold."

"Yeah, well, things ain't always what they look like," Luke said. "Me 'n' Percy both work for her."

"Percy Sheridan?"

"Yep. And Poke and Gilley . . . they worked for her too."

"What kind of a job?"

"The kind where you make a lot of money without doin' too much work."

"And you say you are workin' for her?"

"Yes. Been workin' for her 'bout a month now, ever since I quit the Lazy Q."

"I don't know. Don't seem to me like no real man would want to work for a woman, no matter how much he's gettin' paid."

"You want to tell Ethan Dancer that? He's working for her."

"Ethan Dancer? You mean the gunman, Ethan Dancer?"

"Yeah, the gunman Ethan Dancer," Luke said. "You want to tell him that no real man would work for a woman?"

"No, I don't reckon I'd care to do that."

"I didn't think so."

Metzger stroked his beard for a moment, then nodded. "All right," he said. "All right, I'll work for this woman."

"You mean you'll see if she'll hire you," Luke said.

"Well, maybe if you'll put in a good word for me," Metzger suggested.

Luke shook his head. "No, I ain't goin' to stick my neck out for you. If you don't work out, and I'm the one recommended you, why, she's likely to come down on me. And I got myself too good a thing goin' here to take a chance on you gettin' her pissed at me. So, if you want to work for her, you gotta do it yourself."

"All right," Metzger said. "Where do I find her?"

"More'n likely she'll be in her office now."

"Where's her office at?"

"Can you read?"

"Yeah, I can read."

"Well, her office is right next door. The sign out front says McPherson Enterprises. Her name is Bailey McPherson."

"Bailey? She's a woman and her name is Bailey?"

"Yeah."

"What does she look like?"

Luke laughed. "You mean you've never even heard of her?"

"No. Should I have?"

"I guess not."

"So, what does she look like?"

"You'll find out soon enough."

A little bell was attached to the front door of the office of McPherson Enterprises, and it rang when Metzger pushed it open. At first he didn't see anyone, so he stood there for a moment, just inside the door.

"You here to see Miss McPherson?"

Metzger looked toward the sound of the voice and saw a man sitting in a chair. He hadn't noticed him when he came in.

The chair was tipped back against the wall, and the man was peeling an apple.

"Uh, yes," Metzger said. "Is she here?"

The man looked up then, and Metzger saw his face, which had been somewhat shielded by his wide-brimmed hat.

The face was badly scarred; one eye and his mouth were disfigured. Metzger knew immediately that this was Ethan Dancer. He had never seen the gunfighter before, but had heard him described.

"She'll be right out," Dancer said, returning to the task of peeling the apple.

"Yes, can I help you?" a woman's voice asked.

Metzger looked toward the sound of the voice, but saw nothing but the counter that separated the front of the building from the rear.

"Hello?" he called tentatively.

"May I help you?" Bailey asked again, coming around the corner of the counter so she could be seen. Metzger stared at her in complete shock. She wasn't even tall enough to come up to the top of the counter. He had never seen an adult this small, male or female.

"Uh, yes," Metzger said, finding his voice. "A pard of mine, Luke Rawlings, said you might be lookin' to hirin' me," he said.

"Oh?" the woman replied, arching her eyebrow. "And why would I be looking to hiring you?"

"Well, uh . . ." Metzger cleared his throat. "I don't mean just me, I mean, not like it sounded. What I meant was, he said that maybe you was interested in doin' some hirin'. And if that's so, why, I reckon I'd like to work for you."

"You would like to work for me?"

"Yes."

"Yes, ma'am," Bailey said.

"What?" Metzger asked.

"When you speak to me, you will say ma'am," Bailey said pointedly.

Metzger cleared his throat again. He could crush this little woman with one hand, yet here she was, telling him that he had to hem and haw in front of her, and say yes ma'am to her.

He glanced over at Dancer. Dancer had quit peeling his apple and was now looking at him.

Well, how hard would it be to say ma'am? Metzger wondered. On the one hand, he did not need to make Dancer mad, while on the other hand, he did need the job.

"Yes ma'am, I meant to say yes ma'am," he said. "I just forgot."

"Don't forget again."

"No ma'am, I won't forget again. Uh, so, would you be interested in hirin' me?"

"I might be," Bailey replied. "What can you do?"

"What kind of work you got in mind?"

"That's not what I asked. I asked, what can you do?"

"Uh, look here, Luke told me that you once hired another couple of my pards, Poke Wheeler and Gilley Morris, to do some work for you. Do them two names come to mind?"

"Yes, I recognize the names."

"The kind of things you hired them to do for you? That's more like the kind of things I can do too. Me 'n' Poke 'n' Gilley used to run together."

"I hope you are more efficient than they were," Bailey said. "They were unable to do the simplest job, and they got themselves killed while doing it."

"Kilt?" Metzger replied in surprise. "Wait a minute. Are you tellin' me that Poke and Gilley is dead?"

"Yes."

Metzger shook his head. "I'll be damn. I don't know. Luke didn't tell me that. How did they get theirselves kilt?"

"By being totally incompetent."

"In comp what?"

"It means they had shit for brains," Bailey said caustically. "I hope you don't suffer from the same malady."

"I used to run with 'em, but I'm better'n they was."

"All right, you're hired," Bailey said. "You'll be working for Mr. Dancer."

Again Metzger glanced toward Dancer. All during the conversation, except when Dancer had paused to stare at him, he had continued peeling the apple. Now, a long unbroken peel hung from the apple to the floor, and again Dancer looked up at him.

"I'm goin' to be workin' with Dancer?" Metzger asked.

"Yes," Bailey said. "Do you have a problem with that?"

"No," Metzger replied, wiping the back of his hand across his mouth. "I mean, no ma'am, I ain't got no problem with that."

"All right, you're hired."

"You got a horse?" Dancer asked.

"Yeah, I got a horse."

"Be ready in half an hour. We got a long ride ahead of us."

"All right," Metzger said. "I'll be ready."

Chapter 14

IT TOOK TWO DAYS OF RIDING FOR METZGER AND Dancer to reach the Hilliard ranch. Dancer wasn't much of a talker, so after a few frustrated attempts to get a conversation started, Metzger gave up.

They had made a cold camp the night before, eating jerky and drinking water. Once, when Metzger suggested that they ought to build a fire and brew some coffee, Dancer glared at him, but said nothing in reply. They spread out their bedrolls just after sunset, and within minutes Dancer was asleep. Metzger did not sleep soundly.

In most of Metzger's relationships he had been the dominant person, the one who, because of strength and size, intimidated the others. In fact, he was bigger and stronger than Dancer, and in any kind of street brawl could easily have beat him. But Metzger knew that any confrontation with the gunman would be permanent, so he held his belligerence in check. It wasn't something he would admit to anyone, but the truth was, Dancer scared him.

* * *

During the late war, Roy Hilliard had been a prisoner of war in the Confederate prisoner of war camp at Andersonville, Georgia. He spent eighteen months in that hellhole, emerging from the ordeal at just a little over one hundred pounds. When he went back home to Pennsylvania, he found his old job gone and no prospects for anything new. So he and his wife Cindy left home and went west.

It was a gamble, and some of his family tried to talk him out of it. But, luckily, the gamble had paid off, and now Hilliard was the proud owner of a small but thriving ranch. Last year he had not only managed to support his family, but actually turned a profit, and now he was thinking about taking on a few hands to help him run the place.

Yesterday had been his son's eighth birthday, and he and Mary had a little party for him. He was looking forward to the day Roy Jr. would be old enough to become a full partner in the operation of the ranch.

Hilliard pumped water into the basin, worked up lather from a bar of lye soap, then washed his hands and face. The cold well water was bracing, and he reached for a towel and began drying off, thinking about the pork chops Cindy had cooked for their supper. He had worked hard today, and the enticing aroma was already causing his stomach to growl.

Sometimes when he got hungry he would recall those days in the Andersonville prison, when starvation was a way of life, and the leading cause of death. He had been one of the lucky few who survived the ordeal. And he considered himself even luckier to have found a woman like Mary.

Hilliard had the towel over his face when he sensed a presence nearby. Dropping the towel, he was surprised to see two mounted men looking down at him. Where had they come from? He had neither seen nor heard them approach.

One of the men was big and unkempt, with a bushy red beard. The other man had a large, puffy, purple scar.

"Where the hell did you men come from?" he asked. They made him uneasy, and though just the appearance of the man with the scar was enough to unnerve anyone, it wasn't what he looked like that bothered Hilliard. There was something about him and the other man appearing as suddenly as they had that left him with a troublesome and unsettled feeling in the pit of his stomach.

"Are you Roy Hilliard?" the man with the scar asked.

"Yeah, I'm Roy Hilliard." He twisted the towel in his hand, wishing it were shotgun. "What can I do for you?"

"Hilliard, you've got twenty-four hours to get off this property."

"What?" Hilliard gasped. "Now just why in the hell would I do that?"

"Your ranch has been confiscated by the United States government."

"What are you talking about? I have clear title to this land. I don't owe one cent."

"Show him the paper, Metzger," the man with the scar said.

The big, bushy-bearded man dismounted and took a paper over to show to Hilliard.

"Can you read?" the man with the scar asked.

"Yes."

"Then read that."

Hilliard took the document and began to read, growing angrier as he did.

United States Government
Department of the Interior
Federal Order to all concerned:
To wit:

In a vote of Congress, the Railroad Land Grant Act was passed 1862. Under this act, land will be given to qualified companies for the purposes of building a new railroad. The Sweetwater Railroad Company, having met that requirement, is therefore granted all land encompassed within the longitudinal boundaries 32 degrees 30 minutes east to 32 degrees 40 minutes west, and latitudinal boundaries 41 degrees 40 minutes south to 42 degrees 20 minutes north. Privately owned land currently situated within the aforementioned boundaries are hereby seized, set aside, and declared to be the property of the United States Government under the code of eminent domain.

All who reside within said boundaries are instructed, directed, and ordered to quit their habitation and vacate the area within 24 hours of said notification. All buildings, fences, wells, and other such stationary improvements will remain with the property. Livestock, rolling stock, and all such items as may be easily transported may be taken. Application for recompense must be submitted, in person, to the nearest U.S. land office within two weeks of vacating the property.

Signed: Addison Ford, Assistant to the Secretary of Interior, Columbus Delano

Hilliard finished reading the document and, without a word, handed it back to the man who had been called Metzger by the one with the scar.

"We will expect you to be off this property by noon tomorrow," Dancer said.

"Mister, I've got five hundred head of cattle," Hilliard said. "What am I supposed to do with them?"

"Like the order says, you can take your cattle with you."

"Take them where? This is a small ranch. There's only my

wife, my boy, and me. And my boy's only eight years old. How are the three of us going to move five hundred cows? And where would we take them?"

"That's none of my concern," Dancer said. "My only concern is to see that you are off this property by noon tomorrow."

"And if I ain't off tomorrow?" Hilliard challenged.

"Then you'll have to dance with the demon," Dancer said.

"Dance with the demon? What does that mean?" Hilliard asked. It wasn't a term he had ever heard, but it had an ominous ring to it.

"You'll find out what it means when the music starts," Dancer said.

Hilliard sighed, then walked toward the house. His strides were measured and purposeful, and he didn't turn around as he walked away.

"Hi, darlin'," Cindy Hilliard said. "Dinner's ready. Have a seat and I'll bring you a plate."

Hilliard didn't say a word to his wife. Instead he got the double-barrel twelve-gauge shotgun down, broke it open, slid two shells into the chamber, then snapped it shut.

"Roy, what is it?" Cindy asked in a frightened tone of voice. "What are you doing? What's wrong?"

"Stay inside," Hilliard said as he started toward the door.

When he saw Hilliard go into the house with such purposeful strides, Dancer loosened the pistol in his holster and waited.

As Dancer knew he would, Hilliard came charging back out of the house, holding a shotgun.

"Get off my land you thieving son of a bitch!" Hilliard shouted, raising the shotgun.

The shotgun never reached his shoulder. Dancer's pistol was out in a heartbeat, and he fired one time. The impact of his bullet knocked Hilliard back against the wall of his house. The shotgun discharged with a roar, but the gun was pointing straight up, so no one was hit, though a moment later the buckshot came rattling back down against the roof of the house.

"Roy!" a woman screamed. Running out of the house, she knelt beside her husband, who was already dead. "Roy!" she cried again. She looked up at Dancer, who was still holding the smoking gun in his hand.

"You killed him!"

Dancer stared at her but said nothing.

"Why?" she asked. "Why?"

"Your husband didn't leave him no choice," Metzger said. "He come charging out of the house with that scattergun."

"What did you say to him? What set him off like that?"

"I'll tell you what I told your man," Dancer said. "The government's taking over your land. Be out of here by noon tomorrow."

"What? What are you talking about?"

"It's all in that piece of paper, there in your man's shirt pocket," Dancer said.

Cindy was just reaching for the paper when Roy Jr. came running up from the barn, where he had been doing his chores.

"Papa!" the boy shouted. Seeing his father dead and his mother distraught over the body, Roy Jr. grabbed the shotgun and pointed it at Dancer.

"Roy Jr., no!" Cindy said, reaching for the gun.

Because he had not expected that reaction from a mere boy, Dancer was beaten to the draw. Roy pulled the triggers, but because his father had already discharged both barrels, nothing happened.

Cindy took the shotgun and tossed it to one side. "Go," she said to Dancer and Metzger. "Please, just go away. Leave us alone."

"You have twenty-four hours," Dancer said, then looked over at Metzger and nodded. Then the two of them rode away.

Chapter 15

~~~~~~~~~~

ALTHOUGH WAGONS HAD BEEN MAKING REGU-
lar runs up to South Pass in the Sweetwater Mountains, this
morning a sizable train had formed up on Railroad Avenue.
Leading the train was a surrey in which Dupree, Libby,
Lulu, and Sue were riding in the facing seats at the back,
while a driver sat up front. The surrey and driver, like the
four freight wagons and their drivers lined up behind the surrey, belonged to the Gold Nugget Haulers.

Hawke came down to see them off, shaking hands with
Jay Dupree to wish him good luck and to say good-bye to
the women. Libby held his glance a little longer than the
others and smiled a knowing smile but otherwise made no
allusion to the "concert" they had played upon the bedsprings in Hawke's hotel room the night before.

Several men were gathered around the wagon train. Most
of them had just arrived in town and were eager to begin
their search for gold. Dupree stood up then, to address those
assembled.

"Gentlemen, how many of you will be going up to South
Pass?" he asked.

At least twenty men held up their hands.

"Well then, allow me a few minutes to introduce myself and these three beautiful young women. My name is Jay Dupree, and these ladies and I are going ahead of you to South Pass, to open an establishment for your relaxation and pleasure. Propriety forbids my getting too detailed as to *what* these ladies are, but I can certainly tell you *who* they are."

The men laughed at his inference.

Dupree held his hand out toward the women. "Stand up, ladies, one at a time, and let these gentlemen behold true beauty."

Lulu stood first, curtsied and blew kisses to the crowd.

"My friends, this is Lulu. Lulu is only nineteen years old, a New York debutante, and almost a virgin. As you can see, she is a fire-haired beauty. Oh, and in case you are interested, I can personally attest to the fact that she is a natural redhead."

Lulu assumed a shocked pose, and the men laughed loudly.

Lulu sat down and Sue stood.

"This is Sue, blond and beautiful. What you may not know is, at the age of fourteen, Sue was forced into marriage with a Persian sheik. She spent ten years in Persia in the sheik's palace, surrounded by luxury and attended to by a hundred servants. But she didn't love the sheik."

Sue made a sad, pouting expression and shook her head slowly.

"So, one night when all in the palace were asleep, Sue escaped, made her way to a seaport, and came to America. And now she is here with us, offering to red-blooded American men—for a price, of course—that which was once reserved for Persian royalty."

Sue sat down, and Libby stood.

"And finally, Libby St. Cyr. Libby's beauty speaks for itself, gentlemen. Libby is the daughter of a United States congressman from the state of North Carolina. For obvious reason, she has changed her last name to protect her father. And as some of you will find out, I'm sure, Libby is a wicked, wicked girl."

Smiling, Libby shook her head and pointed a finger at Dupree, making the "shame on you" sign.

"We will be calling our establishment the Golden Cage," Dupree went on. "Look for us when you come there, and remember, we are there for your pleasure."

The wagon master waited patiently until Libby had sat down again and Dupree was through talking before he called out.

"Mr. Dupree, we're all loaded up and ready to go whenever you are."

"We're ready, Mr. Clayton."

"Head 'em up! Move 'em out!" the wagon master called.

Clayton's command was followed by whistles, shouts, and the pistol pops of snapped whips as the train started forward. Rolling slowly up White Mountain Road, it was followed by what would be its symphony on the march, a cacophony of clopping hooves, clanking chains, squeaking wheels, creaking axles, and canvas snapping in the wind.

Hawke watched the train leave, then walked down to the livery to saddle his horse. Though back in town from Chicago for two weeks, he had not yet been out to Northumbria. He wasn't particularly looking forward to telling Dorchester that he'd been fired from his job as a pianist on board the transcontinental train, since Dorchester had gotten the job for him. On the other hand, he felt he owed it to him.

As Hawke dismounted in front of the house, a servant hurried to take the reins of his horse. At almost the same time, Pamela came out onto the porch.

"Hawke!" she called happily. "You're back!"

"And all in one piece, as you can see," Hawke replied.

"Come in, come in, Father will be so pleased to see you."

"Thanks."

Pamela met him halfway down the front steps. Putting her arm through his, she walked back up to the porch with him. She called to her father as they stepped into the foyer, and Dorchester came from his study to greet them.

"Well, Hawke, my good man, how was your trip?" Dorchester asked. Seeing his valet, he called out to him, "Mr. Wilson, do bring tea and biscuits to the drawing room, would you?" He glanced over at Hawke. "Or would you rather have coffee?"

"Tea will be fine."

"Then tea it is, Mr. Wilson."

"Yes, sir, Mr. Dorchester," Wilson replied.

In the study, the three sat in big leather chairs and, as before, Pamela prepared cigars for the two men.

"Thank you," Hawke said, accepting the cigar. He puffed as Pamela held a match to the end. She lit her father's cigar as well, and by the time they were surrounded by an aromatic cloud of smoke, Wilson entered, carrying a silver tray with a silver pot of steeping tea, three cups, and a plate of cookies.

"When will you be going back?" Dorchester asked, picking up one of the cookies.

"I beg your pardon?"

"To Chicago. You will be making another trip, won't you?"

"Uh, no," Hawke said. "I was fired."

"You were fired? Why, that's absurd! You play the piano more beautifully than anyone I've ever heard. Why would Union Pacific fire you?"

Hawke told the story of the drunken and disruptive cowboy, ending with what happened to him. To his surprise, Dorchester laughed.

"You threw him from the train?"

"Yes. I'm sorry, it was very rash of me, I admit. But at the time, it just seemed like the right thing to do."

Dorchester continued laughing, and he laughed so hard that tears came to his eyes.

"No, no, dear boy, do not apologize," he said, waving his finger back and forth. "How often I have wanted to do something exactly like that. Unfortunately, my very proper British upbringing has prevented me from giving in to those urges. But disabuse yourself of any idea that I can't take vicarious pleasure from someone else doing it."

"Yes, well, it did get me fired from the Union Pacific job," Hawke said. "And since you went out of your way to locate the job, I felt that I owed you an apology."

"Nonsense, my good man, you owe me nothing of the sort. As I say, I am deriving a great deal of pleasure from imagining the look on that boor's face as he found himself flying from the cars."

"So, what will you be doing now?" Pamela asked.

"I'm not sure."

"I hope you don't decide to play the piano at the Royal Flush," Dorchester said. "Their piano is so bad it would be a sin for someone with your talent to even try to play it. I've heard better music from rattling harness chain."

Hawke laughed. "That's a pretty good description of the piano, all right."

"And their piano player. Unless . . . good heavens, you *aren't* working there, are you?" he asked, now genuinely concerned.

"No, I'm not working there."

"Thank goodness for that."

"Father, why don't you ask Hawke to work for us?" Pamela said.

"Hello, that is a marvelous idea!" Dorchester said. "It has nothing to do with the piano, I'm afraid, but would you consider working for us?"

"Oh, I don't know, I don't think I would make much of a cowboy. I never was much of a farmer either, and I was raised on a farm."

"Well, actually, you wouldn't have to be a cowboy, as such," Dorchester said. "I would use you in more of a supervisory role."

"As foreman of the ranch," Pamela clarified.

"What about the foreman you have now?" Hawke asked. "How do you think that would sit with him?"

"Oh, that fellow wouldn't even know it," Dorchester said. "He left the ranch right after he heard that gold had been discovered up at South Pass. And, remember, as foreman, all the manual labor would be supplied by the hands who are under you."

"It is a tempting proposition," Hawke admitted.

Someone knocked on the door of the study, and Dorchester looked toward the door. A slim, gangly-looking cowboy stood there, holding his hat in his hand.

"Yes, Willie, what is it?" Dorchester asked.

"It's about the water in Sugar Creek,"

"Oh? What about the water in Sugar Creek?"

"There ain't none," Willie said stoically.

As Hawke, Dorchester, Pamela, and Willie rode toward Sugar Creek, Dorchester took delight in talking about his ranch.

"The first four years I was here, I was beginning to think that I had lost my mind in even contemplating a ranching venture. I had to deal with Indians, weather, and the fact that I was too far away from civilization to make it practical. Then the railroad arrived and I had a way of getting my beef to the market. Since then it has been wonderfully profitable."

Thousands of cattle milled about, some cropping grass some lying under shade trees, others sunning themselves in open fields. The range consisted of gently rolling grassland. To the southeast lay a low-lying ridge of hills, close enough that Hawke could see the vegetation on the slopes. To the north was another line of mountains, purpled by distance.

"That's the Sweetwater Range," Dorchester said, pointing toward the distant mountains. "Half of my cowboys are up there right now, hunting for gold. A couple of them have even told me that when they strike it rich, they are going to come back and buy Northumbria. But they hastened to add that they would offer me a job," he said with a chuckle.

Just ahead of them was a long, irregular line of bright green vegetation.

"That must be the creek," Hawke said.

"Yes. It was one of my earliest accomplishments," Dorchester replied. "The water actually flows from the Big Sandy, but the channel was clogged nearly shut with rocks and bank cave-ins and such. It took me two years to get it open and cleared out, but the result has been a steady, year-round supply of water. I can't imagine what would stop it."

"Perhaps a beaver dam," Hawke suggested. "I've seen beaver dams so large that they've shut down small rivers."

"Perhaps," Dorchester said, "though we don't have a history of problems with beaver."

When they reached the line of vegetation, they dismounted and walked up to the creek to look down into it.

"What in the world?" Pamela said aloud.

There was nothing where the creek had been but a few

disconnected puddles of water, slowly drying up under the sun. Not one trickle of water was flowing.

"Let's go upstream and see if we can find out what happened," Hawke suggested.

The four riders began following the dry stream bed along its meandering course.

"I hope Walter Louis doesn't think that I purposely shut down Sugar Creek," Dorchester said as they rode.

"Who is Walter Louis?"

"He owns a small farm just south of Northumbria, and he is totally dependent upon water from Sugar Creek. In fact, he has been very good about coming over to help my men keep the creek cleared of debris."

After a ride of about five miles, they reached a thick-growing patch of woods. Just on the other side of the woods they saw a large dam.

"What in the world?" Dorchester gasped. "When, and how, did that get here?"

"It's no beaver dam, that's for sure," Hawke said.

"Look at the size of it, Father. It had to take some time to build it." Pamela turned to Willie. "Why didn't we know about this before now?"

"Ma'am, we ain't run no stock on this here section of range since last summer," Willie replied. "We was about to move some beeves over when one of the men noticed that the creek had run dry."

"Is that dam on your property?" Hawke asked.

"No, it isn't," Dorchester admitted. "My property line ends there, with the edge of that copse."

"Who does own the property?

"It belongs to a man named Anthony Miller," Dorchester said.

"Perhaps we should talk to Miller," Hawke suggested.

Dorchester shook his head. "That's not possible, I'm

afraid," he said. "Miller is an absentee owner who lives in New York. In fact, that's what makes this whole thing so odd. This land isn't being used. We've exchanged a few letters as to whether or not I would be interested in leasing some grassland from him."

"Perhaps he's trying to sweeten the pot by adding water to the deal," Hawke suggested.

Dorchester shook his head. "No," he said. "I don't think so. I've only met Miller one time, and he was a very nice person. I can't see him doing something like this."

"Well, someone did," Hawke said. "Why don't we ride over and find out who."

Just beyond the patch of woods was a sign.

KEEP OUT
PROPERTY OF
SWEETWATER RAILROAD COMPANY

"Sweetwater Railroad Company?" Dorchester said. "Why, I've never heard of such an organization."

"What do we do now?" Pamela asked.

"We keep going," Dorchester replied. "Whether this land is owned by Mr. Miller or by some railroad that I've never heard of, they are guilty of stealing our water, and I intend to get to the bottom of it."

The four crossed the property line, then rode up to the dam and dismounted. They were surprised when a man dressed in a business suit suddenly showed up.

"Well, it looks as if we managed to attract attention from someone," Dorchester said.

Three other men came out to join the man wearing the suit. One man was carrying a rifle, a second had a shotgun, and the third, unarmed, wore new jeans and a clean shirt. Hawke recognized the man carrying the shotgun as Luke

Rawlings, who had come into the saloon yelling that he had discovered gold.

"You people are trespassing," the man in the business suit said.

"Who the devil are you?" Dorchester asked.

"I know who he is, Father," Pamela said. "His name is Addison Ford. He is Administrative Assistant to Secretary of Interior Columbus Delano."

Ford looked more closely at Pamela, then at Hawke.

"It's you!" he said in a disgruntled voice. "I recognize you two. You are the people from the train, the ones who forced us to move to another car."

"Yes," Pamela said.

Ford smiled. "Well, well, now isn't this a bit of sweet irony? You ran us out of the rail car, now I am running you off this property."

"Are you responsible for this dam?" Dorchester asked.

"I authorized it, yes," Ford said.

"And I designed it," the unarmed man in jeans said proudly. "My name is Jason White. I'm a civil engineer." White stepped forward and stuck his hand out, but Dorchester made no movement to take it.

"You are trespassing on property belonging to the Sweetwater Railroad Company," Ford said.

"Yes, I saw the sign. But I've never heard of the Sweetwater Railroad," Dorchester replied. "What is it?"

"The Sweetwater Railroad is a railroad that will be built from Green River to South Pass."

"My daughter said you were with the Department of Interior."

"That is right."

"Then I don't understand. What does the Department of Interior have to do with the Sweetwater Railroad? Since when did the U.S. government get in the business of building railroads?"

"The government isn't building it. It is being built by a private company. We are merely providing the incentive."

"The incentive?"

"According to the Railroad Land Grant Act of 1862, any approved railroad company is entitled to a four hundred foot right of way, plus ten square miles of property for every one mile of route."

"You mean the government gives land to people who build railroads?" Dorchester asked in surprise.

"How do you think the transcontinental railroad was built? Without the land incentive, it would never have been completed."

"Yes, well, I can't believe Miller sold his land to the government without first checking with me. He knew that I would have bought it if he had put it up for sale. And he knew that I would give him a fair price for it."

"I'm afraid Miller had no say in the matter," Ford said smugly.

"What do you mean he had no say in the matter?"

"We acquired his land by eminent domain."

"In other words, the government stole Mr. Miller's land," Dorchester said.

"It's not stolen. The land was acquired by a writ of eminent domain, with provisions, of course, for the landowners to apply for reimbursement."

"To apply? You mean they aren't automatically compensated?"

"No. But as I have explained to everyone whose land we have acquired, there are provisions in place for them to apply for, and receive, compensation. That is, if they meet the guidelines."

"Oh? And what is the government paying for prime land?"

"A dollar an acre," Ford replied.

"That is robbery."

"No, that is democracy in action," Addison Ford insisted.

"All right, so you have government authority to steal Miller's land," Dorchester said. He pointed to the dam. "Why in heavens name did you dam up Sugar Creek?"

"I'm sure you know how steam engines operate," Ford replied patronizingly. "They require water to generate steam. If the railroad is to succeed, it will have to have a ready and plentiful source of water."

"Why, you bloody rascal, you have not only stolen land, you have squeezed dry every drop of water from Sugar Creek! I have other sources of water, but those property owners below me are totally dependent upon Sugar Creek. What will happen to them?"

"I'm afraid that is really none of my concern," Ford said. "I am acting on government orders. If you have a problem with it, take it up with the United States Land Management officer."

"And who might that be?" Dorchester asked.

"Why, that would be Mr. White," Ford said, pointing to his son-in-law and laughing out loud.

"You haven't heard the last of this, you bloody bastard," Dorchester said, wagging his finger in Ford's face. "I don't roll over that easily."

"Gentlemen, I do believe I'm being threatened," Ford said.

The two armed men reacted to Ford's comment. The one with a rifle operated the lever, while the one who was holding the double-barreled shotgun came back on the hammers of both barrels.

"Luke Rawlings. What are you doing here guarding this dam?" Hawke asked. "I thought you had made a lot of money gold mining."

"It ain't none of your business what me 'n' Percy's doin' here," Luke replied. "The thing is, we are here, and we're telling you to leave."

"I don't think we're ready to leave yet."

Luke pointed his shotgun at Dorchester.

Hawke drew his pistol then and pointed it at Luke.

"Luke, you want to ease those hammers back down before someone gets hurt?" he asked.

"What are you doin' here, anyway? This is none of your affair," Luke said.

"I just made it my affair."

"Looks to me like you are a day late and a dollar short," Luke said.

"Not really," Hawke replied. "I have the advantage."

"Yeah? How is that?"

"Neither of you are pointing a gun at me. On the other hand, I am pointing my gun at you."

"Maybe not, but we are pointing them at your friend."

"My friend isn't armed—I am. And if you shoot him, I'll kill you. In fact, I will kill all four of you."

"What?" Ford suddenly shouted. "What are you talking about? You are going to shoot all four of us? Do you realize that you are threatening a representative of the United States government?"

"Mister, every man I killed during the war was a representative of the United States government in one way or another. Now, you tell your men there to lower their guns, or I'm going to start shooting."

"You two men put your guns down," Ford said in a frightened tone.

"I think he's bluffing," Luke said.

"I said put the guns down! Now!" Ford ordered, his voice nearly breaking.

The two men lay their weapons on the ground.

"Back away from them," Hawke ordered.

When neither of the two men moved, Hawke shot at Luke's foot, coming so close that he took a small nick from the sole of Luke's boot.

"What the hell!" the man shouted in sudden fear, dancing back from the impact of the round. He looked down at his boot and saw the little nick. "You just barely missed blowing off my toe," he said angrily.

"I didn't miss," Hawke said. "If I wanted to hit your toe, I would have. Now, back away, or the next one *will* take off a toe."

The two men backed away. Hawke kept waving them back until they were at least twenty yards from the guns.

"Mr. Dorchester," he said quietly. "Perhaps now would be a good time for us to leave."

"Yes," Dorchester said. "Yes, I do believe you are right."

Just before they crossed back onto Dorchester's land, a lone rider came out from behind a rock outcropping. He placed himself right in front of them.

"Father!" Pamela said with a gasp.

The rider was Ethan Dancer.

"You folks are trespassing on private property," Dancer said in a low, evil, hissing voice.

"We were checking on why the water stopped flowing," Dorchester replied.

"Next time you come onto this land, get permission," Dancer said.

"And if we don't?" Hawke asked, putting himself between Dancer and the others.

Dancer stared at Hawke for a moment. "You're the one they call Hawke, aren't you?"

"That would be Mr. Hawke to you," Hawke replied.

He held Dancer in a gaze that was fully as intense as it had been in the mirror on their first encounter. Dancer's face twitched a couple of times and he ran his finger across his scar. Why wasn't this man afraid of him? he wondered. Who was he? Was this someone he should know?

"Who the hell are you?" Dancer asked.

"I thought we had settled that. I'm Mr. Hawke."

"I wouldn't get too smart . . . Mister . . . Hawke."

"Yes, well, it's not very likely that you would," Hawke said.

Dancer's eyes narrowed for a second. He had the idea that he'd just been insulted, but he wasn't sure exactly how.

Despite the tension of the moment, Pamela couldn't hold back a chuckle.

Dancer pointed at Hawke. "One of these days, you're going to find yourself dancing with the demon." Slapping his legs against the side of his horse, Dancer rode off quickly.

When he was gone, Pamela shuddered. "What do you suppose he meant by dancing with the demon?" she asked.

"I've heard tell that's what he says to someone just a'fore he shoots 'em," Willie said.

"Oh!" Pamela said, putting her hand to her mouth and looking at Hawke with fear in her eyes. "Hawke! He just said you were going to dance with the demon."

"Ah, I wouldn't worry about it." He smiled. And to ease her fear, he joked, "My dance card is already full."

Chapter 16

IT TOOK FOUR DAYS FOR JAY DUPREE AND HIS LIT-tle wagon train to reach South Pass. Three of the wagons had precut lumber, windows, doors, and other building items, and the fourth had furnishings.

At the time of Dupree's arrival there were no permanent structures in the mining camp, so the fact that he had the building material was enough to attract notice. But what really got the attention of the prospectors in the camp were the three beautiful women riding in the surrey with him. Though less than six weeks old, the mining camp, which called itself South Pass City, had nearly a thousand residents. It was now the third largest settlement in Wyoming, but the three women with Jay Dupree made up the entire female population of the settlement.

The men flocked down to the edge of the road and walked alongside the convoy, keeping pace with it and looking on in awe. Libby, Lulu, and Sue smiled, waved, and blew kisses at the men.

The shelters were tents, though many of the tents, including the saloon, had wooden floors.

Jay drove until he reached what he considered a suitable location. There, he stopped, stood, and called back to his drivers, "We'll unload here!"

"What is all this?" one of the men from the gathered crowd shouted.

Jay held up his hands to call for quiet, then addressed the men who had crowded around.

"Gentlemen, I bring you greetings." He paused for a second, and with a broad smile continued. "But greetings are not all I bring. I bring you also three of the most beautiful women this side of the Mississippi River. Take a look at them, boys. Am I exaggerating?"

He made a sweeping gesture to draw attention to the three women with him, and the men cheered loudly and lustily.

"As you can clearly see by the beauty of these women, they are not your ordinary soiled doves. And you'll never find these girls keeping a crib, working in a bar, hustling drinks, or walking the streets. No sir. These ladies are beautiful, talented, intelligent, and gracious. Stand up, ladies."

The three women stood up, smiled, waved, blew kisses again, and flirted outrageously with the men in the crowd.

"I'm sure you understand that ladies of this quality do not come cheap. They are reserved for those of the most discriminating tastes, those who are knowledgeable enough to understand that something worth having is worth paying for. They are reserved for you. So, there you have it, gentlemen, the three lovely ladies I have brought to help me run the Golden Cage. As proprietor of the Golden Cage, I promise you a place to come to relax, have a few drinks from my specially selected stock of beer and blended whiskey, enjoy a good meal, and spend some very interesting private time with one of these beautiful women."

"What do you mean by very interesting private time?" someone called from the crowd. "I mean, you said they was

intelligent, but I ain't interested in any of 'em readin' no poetry to me, or anything like that."

The other men laughed.

"By private time, I mean just that. You, and the young lady
of your choice, will retire to her room. Whatever you do
there is strictly between you and the young lady. Now, propriety and common decency prevents me from spelling out
exactly what you can do there, but I guarantee you, they
won't be reading poetry."

Again the men laughed.

"Yeah, but what will we be doin'?" the man asked again.

"Mister, if you are in a private room with a beautiful
woman, and you can't figure out what to do, then perhaps
you have no business going in there with her in the first
place."

This time the laughter turned to hoots and howls. "Jimmy,
my boy, I tell you what," one of the men said. "You pay for
me, and I'll invite you to come along and watch and learn."

That elicited more laughter.

"Of course," Dupree continued, "none of this can happen
until we get our establishment built. I'm wondering if there
are any carpenters among you who would volunteer to build
it? Those who help will be given ten dollars credit toward
drinks, food, or women."

As Dupree knew there would be, more than a dozen men
rushed forward to offer their services.

"Thank you, gentlemen, thank you," Dupree said. "I think
you will find everything that you need to begin construction
in the wagons."

In Green River, nearly every business had closed down for
Roy Hilliard's funeral. Hilliard had been an exceptionally
popular man in the town. He was active in the Holy Spirit
Episcopal Church, a volunteer in the Green River Militia,

and a member of the Green River City Band. On the Fourth of July he had played a trumpet solo at the Green River Independence Day picnic.

Because of his popularity, the entire town turned out for his funeral, and the band, wearing black armbands, led the cortege from the church to the cemetery. Behind the band was the glass-sided hearse, brought by train from the St. Louis Carriage Company just two months earlier. Behind the hearse was a buggy, its wheels laced with black bunting. Cindy and Roy Jr. rode in the buggy. The rest of the town fell in behind and followed it to the cemetery.

Hawke attended the funeral, along with Dorchester and Pamela. In addition to Dorchester, there were several other ranchers present to pay their last respects to their friend.

When the hearse reached the cemetery, it stopped in front of an already opened grave, and the pall bearers—a mix of ranchers and townspeople—moved the black-lacquered coffin from the hearse to the grave, then lowered it by ropes. Cindy and Roy Jr. sat on folding chairs under a canopy. Father Cumbie, the vicar, stepped to the head of the grave and began reading from the *Book of Common Prayer.*

"'Man, that is born of a woman, hath but a short time to live, and is full of misery. He cometh up and is cut down, like a flower; he fleeth as it were a shadow, and never continueth in one stay.

"'In the midst of life we are in death; of whom may we seek for succour, but of thee, O Lord, who for our sins art justly displeased?

"'Yet, O Lord God most holy, O Lord most mighty, O holy and most merciful Savior, deliver us not into the pains of eternal death.'"

The vicar nodded at Cindy, and she and Roy Jr. stood up, then walked over to the mound of dirt alongside the grave.

Cindy picked up some dirt and put it in Roy's hand, then picked up a handful for herself.

The vicar continued, " 'For as much as it hath pleased Almighty God, in his wise providence, to take out of this world the soul of our deceased brother, we therefore commit his body to the ground; earth to earth, ashes to ashes, dust to dust; looking for the general Resurrection in the last day, and the life of the world to come, through our Lord Jesus Christ.' "

Cindy and Roy Jr. dropped dirt on the coffin, then, weeping, she turned away. Dorchester stepped up to her and, putting his arms around her, led her back to her chair.

Later, Dorchester brought her out to Northumbria for a meal and to relax after the funeral.

"I can't get the sight out of my mind, of Roy lying dead while that horror of a man stood over him with his gun in his hand," she said. "He was one of the most frightening creatures I've even seen." She made a motion across her face with her finger. "He was disfigured by a terrible scar."

Hawke, who had been quiet till then, looked up when he heard that. "Ethan Dancer," he said.

"Ethan Dancer?" Pamela said. "What was he doing out there? He's working for Bailey McPherson."

"That's a good question," Hawke said.

"What will you do now, Mrs. Hilliard?" Dorchester asked.

"I don't know. Go back to Pennsylvania, I suppose," Cindy answered. She shook her head. "I really don't know what else I could do."

"What about money?"

"I have enough money for railway tickets back home. Once I get there, I will find something to do, some way to raise Roy Jr."

"How about your cattle? How many head do you have?"

"We had five hundred head," Cindy said.

"Why, at thirty dollars a head, that's fifteen thousand dollars," Dorchester said. "That should be enough to keep you and your son quite comfortable for a while."

"I don't have them anymore. When they took our land, they said I had twenty-hours to move the herd. All I could think of was poor Roy lying there dead. I mean, to come through the hell of Andersonville, only to wind up like this." Cindy sighed. "Anyway, there was no way I could have moved the herd, even if I had tried. There was just simply no way it could be done."

Dorchester shook his head in sympathy. "That's too bad. If you could have gotten the herd here, I would have bought your cattle."

"Mrs. Hilliard, did they give you a piece of paper when they took your land?" Hawke asked.

"Yes. I wasn't even going to take it, but they said I would need it if I planned to apply for compensation."

"I'd like to see it, if you don't mind?"

"I don't mind," Cindy said. She looked through her handbag, took out the paper, and handed it to Hawke. He looked at it for a moment, thanked her and handed it back.

"Mr. Dorchester, could I speak to you in private for a moment?" Hawke asked.

"Yes, of course," Dorchester said. Then, to Cindy and Pamela, "Would you ladies excuse us?"

Dorchester and Hawke left the parlor and stood out in the hall, next to one of the suits of armor.

"Were you serious about buying the cattle if she had brought you the herd?"

"Yes. I wouldn't have paid the same price Mr. Hilliard would have gotten at the railhead, but I would have paid a fair price."

"What if the herd was delivered to you now? Would you still buy it?"

"Well, of course I would," Dorchester replied. "But how is the herd going to be delivered to me?"

"I'll bring it to you," Hawke said.

"What? You mean you would steal the herd?"

Hawke shook his head. "It wouldn't be stealing," he said. "The paper they served her said that she had to vacate the land, and she had to leave the fixed property there. But it specifically granted her the right to take all movable property, including her livestock. And there was no time limit."

"No time limit?"

Hawke shook his head. "It gives the property owner twenty-four hours to vacate the property, but it does not say when the livestock must be moved. Technically, even though the herd is still there, it belongs to her."

"So you think if you just ride up and ask for the herd, they'll turn it over to you?"

"I don't plan to ask for the herd," Hawke said. "I aim to take it."

"Oh, I don't know," Dorchester said. "That's far too dangerous. I would hate to think of you getting yourself killed trying to do something for me."

Hawke smiled. "Then let's say I'm doing it for Mrs. Hilliard. And I don't plan on getting myself killed."

Dorchester drummed his fingers on the helmet of the suit of armor for a moment as he studied Hawke.

"Do you really think you can get the herd here?"

"Yes," Hawke said. "I'll need a few men to help me, but if you would pay a bonus to anyone who volunteers, I will get the herd to you."

Dorchester smiled broadly. "Then, by Jove, let's do it."

Dorchester returned to the parlor. "Mrs. Hilliard, I am prepared to pay you $12,500 for your herd," he said.

"What?" Cindy gasped in surprise.

"I don't want to cheat you. You do understand, don't you,

that you could get more for them if you delivered them to the railhead?"

"Yes, I understand that, but I don't understand why you would make such an offer. I told you, I no longer have a herd."

"Not according to Hawke."

"What?"

"Tell her, Hawke."

"According to the paper that was served you, Mrs. Hilliard, that herd still belongs to you. It is on confiscated land, but it is still your herd."

"I thought he said twenty-four hours."

"Twenty-four hours for you to leave. That has nothing to do with your herd."

"That may be true," Cindy said. She sighed. "But true or false, the effect is the same. Thank you for offering to buy my herd, Mr. Dorchester, but I still have the same problem. I have no way of getting them to you."

"You let me worry about that," Dorchester said. "If you are agreeable to the deal, we'll go down to the bank and I'll write out a draft for the sale and buy them where they stand."

"I . . . I . . . Mr. Dorchester, I don't know how to thank you," she stammered.

"Don't thank just me," Dorchester said. "Mr. Hawke is the one who discovered the loophole in the contract. And he is the one who is going to deliver your herd to me."

"Oh!" Pamela gasped, putting her hand to her mouth. "But won't that be very risky?"

"Life is risky," Hawke said.

"Father, no. Don't let him go," Pamela pleaded.

"My dear, you have already observed this stalwart fellow in action. Do you think for one moment I could stop him from doing anything once he sets his mind to it?"

"No, I suppose not," Pamela agreed. She looked at Hawke. "But please, Hawke. Be careful."

* * *

Win Woodruff and Eddie Taylor had been cowboys at
Northumbria for three years, but four weeks ago they quit
their jobs. Buying picks, shovels, pans, and other supplies
they might need for prospecting, they went up to the Sweetwater Mountains to try their luck.

So far their luck had been bad.

It was late in the day and the two men were exhausted,
having spent the last three days breaking large rocks into
smaller rocks, looking for any sign of gold. At the moment,
Win was sitting on an old log smoking his pipe, while Eddie
was a few yards away, near the campfire he'd made.

"Ha!" Eddie said aloud. "You shoulda seen that, Win."

"I shoulda seen what?"

"I pissed this here grasshopper clean off a weed."

"If it's all the same to you, Eddie, I'd just as soon not
watch you take a piss."

"Well, it was just funny, that's all," Eddie said, buttoning
his pants as he came back over to the log. "I mean that little
grasshopper wrapped his arms and legs around that weed
and was hangin' on for dear life."

"Grasshoppers don't have arms."

"Uh-huh. This'n here did," Eddie insisted. Getting his
own pipe out, he began filling the bowl with tobacco.

"Eddie, you think Mr. Dorchester would take us back?"
Win asked.

"I don't know," Eddie answered. He looked up from his
pipe. "Why? Are you thinkin' about askin' 'im to take you
back?"

"Yeah, I am," Win admitted.

Eddie reached down to pick up a twig, then stuck it in the
fire and lit it. Using the burning twig, he lit his pipe. "How
long—" he started to ask, then took a couple of puffs until

the tobacco in the bowl caught. "How long you been thinkin' about this?"

"I don't know. At least for a week now."

"You don't say."

"Come on, Eddie. You can't tell me you ain't thought of it a few times your ownself," Win said.

Eddie sighed. "Yeah," he agreed. "I admit that I have thought of it."

"Well, what do you think? Do you think he'll take us back?"

"I don't know. But if I was a bettin' man, I'd say I reckon he probably would. He's a good man, even if he does talk funny."

"Well, I'll tell you the truth, I'm about ready to go back. I don't think there's any gold at all up here."

"Well, come on, Win, you know there has to be some gold, somewhere," Eddie said. "Hell, somebody found gold else there wouldn't be so many folks up here."

"Can you tell me one person who has found gold?"

"Luke Rawlings has found gold."

"I mean somebody other than Luke Rawlings and Percy Sheridan. And they don't count, 'cause they're the ones that found it in the first place."

"I know," Eddie said. "But they keep finding it regular. Sheridan come out the other day with a nugget that was as big as a walnut."

"Yeah, I know people say that, but—"

"I seen it, Win," Eddie said. "I mean, I seen that nugget with my own eyes."

"If they're findin' all that gold, how come they ain't up here all the time?" Win asked.

"What do you mean?"

"I just mean that most of the time they're gone," Win said. "Don't that strike you as peculiar?"

"I don't know. I guess I just never thought about it," Eddie said.

"So, you want to stay up here and keep looking, or what?" Win asked.

Eddie looked over at the pile of rubble that represented the rocks they had broken up in the last week.

"We sure ain't been broke out with luck, have we?" Eddie asked.

"So far we've 'bout broke our backs and we ain't come up with so much as one ounce," Win said, continuing to make his case. "We're runnin' low on food. Fact is, we ain't got nothin' left now but some jerky and a little coffee. And what are we going to do come winter if we ain't found nothin'? You may recall, Mr. Dorchester kept us on all last winter, even though there wasn't that much work to do. We had three hots and a cot. This tent's okay for the summer. But it won't do much for keepin' us warm in the winter."

"Yeah," Eddie finally said. "Yeah, you're right. As far as I'm concerned, we're just wastin' our time here. I say we go back and see if we can get our old jobs back."

"Good. I was hopin' you would come around to my way of thinkin'. Hey, how much money have we got left?"

"Fourteen dollars," Eddie answered. "Why?"

"Fourteen dollars is enough," he said. "What do you say that, before we go back and start punchin' cows again, we go down here to the Golden Cage and have us a little fun?"

"Doin' what?"

"Doin' what?" Win laughed. "I tell you what, don't worry about it. I'm willin' to bet you'll figure out what to do when we get there."

The Golden Cage had been put up in only six days, and it was clearly the most impressive establishment in South Pass City. That was the case even though a couple other wooden structures were now being erected. The Golden Cage was two stories high, with a second-story balcony that ran all the way across the front of the building. Below the balcony, at street level, was a fine wooden porch with a swing and a couple of rocking chairs.

For the first week after it was built, business was so good that Dupree thought he was going to have to bring in some more girls. But for the last couple of weeks business had been getting slower and slower.

At first Dupree wasn't sure why business was so bad. Then, as he began questioning the girls, he learned that the men were frustrated because they weren't finding any gold.

"None of them are?" Dupree asked.

"None that I've had anything to do with," Libby answered.

The other two girls gave the same response. So far, not one of them had heard a success story.

"Maybe they're just keeping quiet about it," Dupree suggested.

"No, it isn't that," Libby replied. "Listen, the one thing men like to do more than anything else when they are with a woman is brag. If any of them had found gold, we would have heard about it."

Dupree smiled. "You mean when a man is with one of you girls, he would rather brag than do *anything* else?"

It was a teasing comment, and the three girls laughed at its implication.

"All right," Libby said. "Bragging is the second thing he wants to do."

"Lookie here," Lulu said, looking through the front window. "We've got a couple of customers."

"In the middle of the day?" Dupree said. "That's odd."

"Get on out there and meet them, Jay," Libby said, pushing him. "We can't afford to lose them. As it stands now, we aren't doing enough business to keep the doors open."

"All right, all right, I'm going," Dupree said, stepping out onto the front porch. He smiled at the two men as they approached. He was smoking a cigar, and as he greeted them, he tapped off the ash at the end.

"Good afternoon, gentlemen. My name is Jay Dupree, and on behalf of myself and the young ladies of the Golden Cage, I welcome you."

"My name's Win Woodruff, this here is Eddie Taylor."

"This is our first time here," Eddie said.

"I see. And you are gold miners, are you?" Dupree asked.

"Ha," Eddie said. "I reckon you could say that, but we ain't been doin' a whole lot of what you would call gold minin' so far."

"Fact is, we ain't done no gold minin' at all," Win added. "Mostly what we been doin' is huntin'."

"But no findin'," Eddie said.

"Well, then it sounds to me like you two gentlemen need some relaxation," Dupree suggested. "Come on in and get acquainted with the girls. Maybe it will bring you a change of luck."

Inside, a dozen or so chairs and sofas were scattered about, along with several potted plants, mirrors on the walls, and a staircase rising to the second floor. Three girls were sitting in the parlor, but there were no customers anywhere to be seen.

Two of the girls got up and walked over to greet them.

"My name is Lulu," the one who stepped up to Eddie said.

"And I'm Sue. What are your names?"

"I'm Eddie, he's Win," Eddie said. He looked around. "Where at's all the men?"

"Oh, honey, don't tell me you like men better than you do women," Lulu asked, and she and Sue laughed.

"What?" Eddie replied in an almost explosive reaction.

"Hell no! What do you mean, do I like men better than women? Why would you ask me such a thing?"

Win laughed. "Don't get in such a huff. They was just teasin' you, that's all." Then, to the girls, he explained Eddie's question. "What he means is, how come you ain't got no customers?"

"Because they're all working their claims," Lulu replied. "We normally don't get anyone in the middle of the day. That means you fellas have us all to yourself."

"Well now," Win said with a big satisfied smile. "Ain't we the lucky ones?"

"Listen, you got a place to take a bath in this here whorehouse?" Eddie asked, rubbing the stubble on his chin. "It's been a while since I've had me a proper bath."

"Oooeee, tell me about it," Lulu said, pinching her nose and laughing. "Come on, I'll give you a bath."

"You'll give me a bath?" Eddie replied. "Well, I don't know about that."

"What do you mean you don't know about that?" Win asked. "Are you crazy?"

"Well, come on, Win, I ain't had nobody give me a bath since my mama done it when I was real young."

"I said you would figure out what to do when you got here," Win said, shaking his head. "I can see now that I was wrong."

"You mean he's a virgin?" Lulu asked Win.

Win nodded. "He's a virgin, all right, and about as green as they come."

"Well, then, I'll just have to teach him, won't I?" Lulu said in a husky voice. "And we'll start with the bath. Honey, I'll just bet you that your mama never gave you a bath like the one I'm going to give you."

"Why? What's different about it? A bath is a bath, ain't it?"

"Jesus, Eddie, you are one dumb turd, do you know that?" Win asked in exasperation.

"Shh, don't scold him. You have to be patient with virgins," Lulu said, chuckling. Then, to Eddie, she said, "Here's something your mama never did. I'll be naked while I'm giving you this bath."

"Oh," Eddie replied. Then, finally understanding the implications of what she'd just said, he smiled broadly. "Oh!"

"Honey, you could use a bath too, you know," Sue said to Win.

"That's fine with me," Win replied. "As long as I don't have to share a tub with Eddie."

The girls laughed as they led the two men away.

Chapter 17

ON THE DAY AFTER THE FUNERAL, EVERYONE IN town knew who was behind the Sweetwater Railroad Company, because a big sign went up on the front of Bailey McPherson's building:

SWEETWATER RAILROAD COMPANY
BAILEY MCPHERSON, PRESIDENT

Dorchester came down to the depot to see Cindy off on her trip back East. Cindy, with $12,500 safely tucked away in the false bottom of her trunk, expressed her thanks, then waved a tearful good-bye as she got on the train.

Dorchester said nothing when he first saw the sign, but as soon as the eastbound train left the station, he walked down the street, then into the Sweetwater Railroad Company's office.

A young woman was in the front office, seated at a desk behind the counter. When Dorchester entered, she said, "Yes, sir, may I help you?"

"I would like to talk to Miss McPherson."

"I believe Miss McPherson is busy now."

"Tell her to get unbusy."

"I beg your pardon?"

"Tell her Dorchester is here."

"Sir, I told you, she is—"

"Now!" Dorchester shouted, banging his fist so hard on the counter that it caused the windows in the building to rattle.

"It's all right, Mrs. White," Bailey said, appearing in the door then. "I'll talk to the gentleman." Bailey smiled at Dorchester, though the smile was obviously forced. "It's good to see you, Sir James," she said.

"Sir James?" the young woman repeated.

"Oh, yes, dear. Allow me to introduce you to our resident royalty," Bailey said. "This is Brigadier Sir James Spencer Dorchester, Earl of Preston, Viscount of Davencourt."

"You can dispense with all of that," Dorchester said with a dismissive wave of his hand. "I want to know what is going on with this railroad business."

"Oh, yes, exciting, isn't it? I'm building a railroad from here up to the Sweetwater. To South Pass."

"What in heaven's name for? There are no settlements between here and the Sweetwater. And even South Pass is a temporary settlement, until all this gold fever passes."

"Well then, perhaps the railroad will ensure that a real city develops there. Wouldn't that be exciting?"

"In the meantime you are taking land away from honest ranchers and farmers. Hilliard, Miller, who else will you be getting land from?"

"What a coincidence that you would ask," Bailey said. "You're coming in here will save us the trouble of serving you."

"Serving me?"

"Yes. I'm afraid we are going to be taking a five mile strip of land all along the Green River and up the Big Sandy. That means that from you we will be taking a total of, let me see . . . yes, here it is. One hundred and forty-four thousand acres."

"What?"

"I would advise you to move all your stock off that property," Bailey said.

"We'll see about this," Dorchester said angrily. "This is outrageous, and one way or another I'm going to stop you."

"I don't think so," Bailey said. "I have the law on my side."

Hawke was sitting at a table in the cookhouse, drinking coffee and examining a topographic map of the area between Green River and the Sweetwater Mountains. He looked up when two men came in and stepped up to the table, their hats in their hand.

"Are you the new foreman Willie told us about?" one of the men asked. "Are you Hawke?"

"I am," Hawke said. "What do you need?"

"Well, the thing is, Hawke, uh, Mr. Hawke, me 'n' Eddie Taylor . . ." He paused in mid-sentence and pointed to the man standing beside him. "This here is Eddie Taylor, I'm Win Woodruff. And the thing is, we used to cowboy here."

"And we was good hands too," Eddie said. "You can ask any of the other cowboys here and they'll tell you. We was good hands."

"But we quit to go hunt for gold," Win continued.

"Only we didn't find none," Eddie said.

" 'Cause I don't think there's none there," Win added.

Hawke stared at the two men. He knew that they wanted him to ask them to come back to work for the ranch, but he was determined to make them ask.

"So, uh . . ." Win said. He cleared his throat nervously. "Uh, so, we thought maybe . . ."

"Maybe we could get our old job back," Eddie put in quickly.

"When's the last time you two men had a good meal?" Hawke asked.

"Well, we had some jerky this mornin'," Eddie said.

"And yesterday," Win added. "And the day before that too."

"But now, a real sit down and eat kind of meal," Eddie said, "well, sir, that's been a good while."

"Have the cookie fix you a plate," Hawke said. "I can't be hiring cowboys who are so hungry they can't work."

Win and Eddie smiled broadly, then hurried over to the big wood-burning stove where the cook was already preparing supper. He gave them both a generous helping of some stew, left over from lunch. There was also half a pan of left-over biscuits, and the two men cleaned it out.

Bringing their food back to the table, they sat down and began eating, wolfing the food down ravenously. It wasn't until Win had cleaned his plate and eaten the last biscuit that he happened to glance across the table to the map Hawke was studying.

"That there map ain't exactly right," he said casually.

"What?"

"That map," Win said, pointing. "Accordin' to that map, this whole area here is flatland. But that ain't the way of it. Crowley's Ridge is there, but this here map don't show it."

"Do you know how to read a map?"

"Yeah," Win said. "'Afore I cowboyed, I worked some for the Union Pacific when they was buildin' the railroad. I had to read maps all the time, and sometimes even drawed 'em."

Hawke turned the map around. "Where is this ridge you were talking about?"

"Right here," Win said, "betwixt the Big Sandy and the Pacific rivers." He traced the location with his finger.

"Can you point out the location of the Hilliard ranch?" Hawke asked.

"Sure, it's right here," Win said.

"Just on the other side of Crowley's Ridge?"

"Yes."

"Damn," Hawke said with a sigh.

"What's wrong?"

"There are five hundred head of cattle up here," Hawke said, putting his hand on the Hilliard ranch, "that I need to get down here. I was trying to find the best route. But with this Crowley's Ridge in the way . . ." He let the sentence hang.

"Oh, you don't have to worry about that," Win said. "The Little Sandy River comes right through the middle of the ridge. There's a break there that's prob'ly a hundred yards wide or so. You could bring five hundred beeves through there easy. Me 'n' Eddie will help bring 'em down, won't we, Eddie?"

"Sure will," Eddie said, mumbling around a mouth full of biscuit.

"Thanks, I can use you."

"When you going to bring 'em down?"

"Tonight, just after dark."

Win looked surprised. "Tonight? After dark?"

"Yes."

"Uh, pardon my askin' you this, but why the hell would you want to move five hundred head of cattle at night?"

"It's probably safer that way."

"Safer? To move a herd at night? Through a narrow pass in a high ridge?"

"I thought you said it would be easy bringing them through the pass," Hawke said.

"Well, yeah, I did say that. But I was talkin' about bringin' 'em through in the daytime when you can see what the hell you are doin'."

"There's a full moon tonight," Hawke said. "It will be moon bright."

"Still in all, it's not like bringin' 'em through in the daylight. What do mean when you say you think it would be safer to bring 'em down in the dark?"

Hawke took the final swallow of his coffee and looked for a long, appraising moment at Win and Eddie.

"Safer, because there is less chance of us getting shot."

"Less chance of getting shot?" Win gasped. He held out his hand and shook his head. "Wait a minute, hold it. I ain't goin' to have nothin' to do with stealin' no cows. What's this all about, anyway? I've never knowed Mr. Dorchester to swing a wide loop."

"No," Dorchester said, "and I haven't started now."

None of them had heard Dorchester come into the dining hall. Now they all looked around at him.

"They're my cows, bought and paid for," he continued. "With a bill of sale. You boys are back, I see."

"Yes, sir. We just talked to Hawke, and he hired us back. I hope that's all right with you," Win said.

"Yes, of course it is all right," Dorchester said. "I'm happy to have you boys back. And are your saddlebags filled with gold?"

Win and Eddie shook their heads contritely.

"We didn't find nothin' up there," Win said.

"Not even so much as one little flake of yellow," Eddie added.

"Well, I'm glad you both have it out of your system and have come back. I was left pretty short-handed. I hope some of the others will come back as well."

"Like as not, they'll all be comin' back sooner or later," Win said. "Soon as they discover there ain't no gold up there, they'll come back wantin' to work."

"And I'll hire them."

"Mr. Dorchester, if we ain't stealin' them cows, why is it we're going to get 'em at night?" Win asked. "And what did Hawke mean when he said that we might get shot at?"

"Yeah," Eddie added. "I'm not all that anxious to get shot at."

Dorchester told them the story of two men riding up to confiscate Roy Hilliard's ranch. He told them how Roy tried to resist, how they shot him down and then served Mrs. Hilliard with the paper that said she no longer owned the land.

"They gave her twenty-four hours to get off her property and take her livestock with her."

"Twenty-four hours?" Eddie said. "And her just a woman? Now, just how the hell was she s'posed to do that? Excuse my language."

Dorchester shook his head. "No need to apologize, I feel the same way you do about it. So, I bought the cattle from Mrs. Hilliard."

"You bought the herd while it is still up there?" Eddie asked.

"Right," Dorchester said.

"So now you want that herd down here."

"Right again," Dorchester said.

"So, if you bought the herd, why don't you just go up and get it in the broad daylight?"

"There is a question of who actually owns it," Dorchester said. "I'm afraid that the Sweetwater Railroad Company believes they own the herd, and they probably have it guarded with orders to shoot anyone who attempts to take it."

"Excuse me for sayin' this, Mr. Dorchester, but that just don't make a whole lot of sense, you buyin' a herd that you ain't even got yet."

"Events may yet prove you right, Win," Dorchester said. "But Mr. Hawke assured me it could be done, so I am putting my trust in him."

"You still want to help me bring the herd down?" Hawke asked.

Win scratched his cheek and, after pausing for a moment, nodded in the affirmative. A broad smile spread across his face. "Always did want to try myself a little cattle rustling."

"This isn't exactly rustling," Dorchester said.

"Yeah, I know. But it's close enough. Count me in, Hawke."

"Me too," Eddie said.

"Thanks," Hawke said.

"Hawke, could I speak to you for a moment? Outside?" Dorchester asked.

"Sure," Hawke said.

"Hey, Cookie, you got 'ny coffee left?" Eddie asked, starting toward the kitchen. Win joined him as Hawke followed Dorchester out onto the front porch of the cook shack.

"Bailey McPherson is the Sweetwater Railroad," Dorchester said when Hawke joined him outside. "I spoke to her today."

"So she's the one responsible for taking Hilliard's and Miller's land?"

"Yes. And 144,000 acres of Northumbria."

"What?" Hawke gasped.

"That's what she said today, and she has government papers to back her up. In addition to that, the land she is taking will leave the rest of Northumbria isolated from water. And not only Northumbria, but the entire valley. And without water, my ranch, and everyone else's ranch—and farm in the entire valley—will be worthless."

"Are you going to fight it?"

"Yes, of course I'm going to fight it," Dorchester said. He took his hat off and ran his hand through his hair. "I just don't know how to fight it."

Chapter 18

UPSTAIRS IN HER ROOM AT THE GOLDEN CAGE, Lulu lit a candle. Then she poured some water from a pitcher into a basin and, taking the water with her, stepped around behind a screen.

Rob Dealey could hear the splash of water as Lulu began her ablutions. He looked at the bed. It was made, though somewhat crookedly.

Rob had come up to the Sweetwater Mountains with seven other men from the Northumbria. They had come, in the words of one of them, "bright eyed and bushy-tailed," to make their fortune in found gold.

But none of them had found gold, and now there were only three of them left. Micah McGee and Billy Pearson had left first, saying they were going back down to Texas. Eddie Taylor and Win Woodruff were the next to leave, pulling up a couple of days ago. They were going to go back to the ranch and see if they could get their old jobs back.

Well, that was good for them, he thought. They probably could get their old jobs back. But Rob he knew that he couldn't. He had been the foreman, and Dorchester told him on the day that he got paid out that he would not be able to return to his old job.

He was a fool to have left. As foreman, he was getting almost twice as much money as the others. And he had a position of respect. Now he grubbed around in the mud and the mire, searching for gold.

What a fool he was to have left, he thought again.

When Lulu stepped out from behind the screen a moment later, he was surprised to see that she was totally nude. And though he knew that most whores promised much more than they were able to deliver, in this case he was not disappointed. Lulu was all she promised and more. She was slender, except for the flare of her hips and the gentle rise of her relatively small but well-formed breasts. Without her clothes, she really did look like she was only nineteen. For a moment he felt a little uncomfortable with the idea of going to bed with a nineteen-year-old. He was thirty-two, considerably older than Lulu.

On the other hand, Lulu was a prostitute, and prostitutes were without history, therefore they were without age. There was no doubt in Rob's mind but that Lulu was much older than he was in some areas. Especially when it came to sexual experience. For in truth, his own sexual experiences had been few and relatively far between.

"Honey, you don't even have your clothes off yet," Lulu said, the expression in her voice indicating that she was puzzled by that fact.

"What's the hurry?" Rob replied. "We have all night, don't we?"

Lulu laughed. "Yes, we do," she agreed. "It's just that most men are so—" Lulu stopped in mid-sentence. It was as if she were embarrassed to continue the statement about "most" men. "But that's all right," she said. "You're different."

"Does it bother you that I am different?"

"No. I like it that you're different."

Rob sat on the edge of the bed. "Will you help me take off my boots?" He held out his left leg.

Smiling at him, Lulu swung a long, naked limb over his leg, pivoting as she did, so that she wound up facing away from him. Rob found the image of her bare behind intensely erotic as she struggled with his boot.

As soon as his boots were off, Lulu removed his clothes. After he was naked, she leaned into him, pressing her bare breasts against his chest, grinding her pelvis against his and pushing him down onto the bed as she did.

They lay on the bed exploring each other's bodies with their hands until, finally, Rob climbed on top. For the next few minutes there was only the sound of heavy breathing, a few groans of pleasure, and the symphony of creaking bedsprings.

Afterward they lay side by side, bathed in perspiration and coasting back down from their erotic high.

"Where are you going now?" Lulu asked.

"What do you mean, where am I going? I'm staying here all night."

"No, I don't mean that. I mean after tonight. When you give up looking for gold, where will you go?"

"Are you that certain that I'm going to give up?"

"You should."

"Oh? And why is that?"

"Because there is no gold here," Lulu said.

"I know that's what everyone is telling you," Rob said, "and I don't blame them. It's frustrating as hell to bust your ass out there day after day after day and not come up with even the tiniest bit of color. I'm frustrated too, but I'm not ready to give up yet."

"There is no gold," Lulu said again.

Rob chuckled. "Are you trying to get rid of us so you and the other girls can go out and start digging where we left off?"

"No," Lulu said. "Do you know Luke Rawlings and Percy Sheridan?"

"Sure," Rob said. "Everyone in the camp knows them. They are the two who discovered gold up here in the first place."

Lulu shook her head. "They didn't discover it here, they put it here."

"What do you mean, they put it here?"

"I think the word is called 'seeded.' They seeded several rocks with gold, then scattered them around."

"Well now, why the hell would they do something like that? That doesn't make any sense at all. It's not like they are trying to sell off claims or anything."

"I don't know why, but they did it," Lulu said. "They just did it."

"How do you know this?"

"Because Luke got drunk one night and told me," Lulu said. "He did more than just tell me, he bragged about it. And Percy did the same thing with Sue. They seeded the field up here. And all this time they've been laughing at all you men, behind your backs."

"I'll be damn," Rob said. "You know, I could almost believe it. Nobody has really found anything since we started. Nobody. I just can't understand why they would have done it, though. By the way, if you know this, why are you and the other girls staying here?"

"We're here because we know where the gold really is."

"You do? Where?" Rob asked.

"It's in your pocket, honey. And the pockets of every other man up here."

Rob laughed. "I guess I walked right into that one," he said.

Somewhere in the predawn darkness a calf bawled anxiously and its mother answered. In the distance a coyote sent up its long, lonesome wail, while out in the pond, frogs thrummed their night song. The moon was full and the night was alive with stars, from the very bright, shining lights, all the way down to those stars that weren't visible as individual bodies at all but whose glow added to the luminous powder that dusted the distant sky.

Around the milling shapes of shadows that made up the small herd rode four men: Eddie, Win, Willie, and Hawke.

"You ever drove a herd before, Mr. Hawke?" Willie, one of the cowboys who had stayed on at Northumbria, asked.

"No, I can't say as I have," Hawke replied.

"Well, sir, I know you're the boss 'n' all, so's I wouldn't want to speak out of turn or nothin', but iffen it was me, I'd start drivin' 'em toward the river now."

"Good idea, thanks. All right, let's start 'em toward the river," Hawke said.

"I'm surprised they don't have anybody out here watching the herd," Win said.

"They do," Hawke replied.

"What do you mean, they do? Have you seen anyone?"

"No," Hawke answered.

"Then what makes you think they've got anyone out here watchin'?"

"I can feel it," Hawke said.

The calf's call for his mother came again, this time with more insistence. The mother's answer had a degree of anxiousness to it.

"Sounds like one of the little fellers has wandered off," Eddie said. "Maybe I'd better go find it and get it back to its mama."

"Leave it," Hawke said. "We need to get out of here as quickly as we can."

"Ah, I don't mind," Eddie said, slapping his legs against the side of his horse and riding off, disappearing in the darkness.

Suddenly, from the darkness, came a gunshot.

"What the hell is Eddie doing?" Willie asked. "He'll spook the herd."

"I don't think that was Eddie," Hawke said.

"What do you mean?"

"I think we've got company."

They heard the sound of galloping hooves. From the darkness, Eddie's horse, its nostrils flared wide and its eyes wild with terror, came running by them, its saddle empty.

"My God, where's Eddie?" Willie asked.

Now, several gunshots erupted in the night, and the muzzle flashes lit up the herd.

"Jesus! What's happening? Who is it? They're all around us!" Win shouted in terror.

The cattle, spooked by the gunfire, started running. But Hawke noticed they were at least running in the right direction.

"Willie, Win, keep the herd running!" Hawke said, pulling his rifle from the scabbard.

"What are you doing? Where are you going?" Willie asked.

"I'm going to stop them, then I'm going to find Eddie."

"By yourself?"

"Stay with the herd!" Hawke shouted again, already starting back toward the sound of the guns.

The two cowboys were more than anxious to comply with

that order, and they fell in beside the herd, shooting and yelling, urging the cattle to run faster.

Hawke rode at a gallop to a nearby ridge, leaped from his horse and lay on his stomach on a flat rock.

He saw them then, four mounted men, moonlit and silhouetted against the star-bright sky. They were riding hard in pursuit of the herd, their right arms extended in front of them, pistols in their hands, firing toward the thundering herd.

Hawke fired at the one in the rear and saw him tumble from the saddle.

Because of the noise of the nearly stampeding herd and the sounds of the gunshots, the men did not realize that they were themselves under attack, nor did they know that one of their number had been shot.

Hawke fired a second time, again taking out the man riding at the rear. Not until he took out the second man did the two remaining riders realize what was happening—that they were no longer the hunters, but the hunted. Breaking off their chase, they turned and galloped away as fast as they could. Hawke threw a couple of long distance shots at them, purposely missing them now, because they no longer represented a threat. But he put the bullets close enough so they could hear them passing and keep running.

With the danger now gone, he rode back over the ground, looking for Eddie. He found him about a mile back, lying belly down. When Hawke got down to look at him, Eddie suddenly turned over, his gun in his hand,

"No, Eddie, it's me!" Hawke said.

Eddie lowered his gun.

"Where are you hit?" Hawke asked.

"In the ass," Eddie replied. "The sons of bitches shot me in the ass."

Hawke looked, and saw that the bullet had hit him in one cheek of his buttocks. He didn't see an exit wound.

"The bullet is still in there," Hawke said.

"In the ass," Eddie said again. "Can you think of a worse place to be shot?"

"Yeah," Hawke said. "Think where you would be if it had hit you in the front at about that same place."

"Oh," Eddie said. "Oh, yes, I see what you mean. Yeah, I guess I am lucky at that."

"Think you can sit a horse?" Hawke asked.

"I don't know what happened to my horse."

"We'll catch up with him. Right now you're going to ride double with me."

Hawke helped Eddie up onto his horse, putting him on just behind the saddle.

"Oh, damn, this hurts," Eddie said. "We're not going to be able to ride very fast if those guys come after us again."

"They won't be coming after us."

"They won't? How do you know?"

"Because I ran them off," Hawke answered without further elaboration.

Chapter 19

EDDIE TAYLOR'S HORSE KEPT GOING, ALL THE WAY back to Northumbria. Several of the hands recognized the riderless horse as Eddie's, and they were forming a group to go after him and the others when a rider some distance from the Big House spotted a herd on the move. Cautiously, he headed toward them. When he recognized the men, he quickly closed the distance. That was when he saw Eddie being pulled in a travois.

"When Eddie's horse come runnin' in all alone, we was some worried about you," the cowboy said.

"Hey, Tim, is my horse all right?" Eddie asked. "Was he shot?"

"No, he wasn't shot. He's fine. What happened to you?"

"Nothin'," Eddie said. "Nothin' happened to me."

Win laughed. "He got shot."

"What's so funny about gettin' shot?" Tim asked.

"Here," Win said, pointing to his own posterior. "He got shot here."

"I'll go back and tell the others you are all all right. They was gettin' ready to come after you."

"Don't you tell them nothin' 'bout where I got shot!" Eddie shouted as the cowboy headed back toward the Big House. "Do you hear me, Tim? Don't you tell them nothin'."

"They're back!" Tim told the others a few minutes later, galloping into the main compound to report. "I seen 'em. They're back, and they've got the herd with them!"

"What about Eddie?" Dorchester asked anxiously.

Tim smiled. "He's all right. He just got shot in the ass . . . uh, the rear end," he said, amending his comment in mid-sentence because Pamela was present.

"Eddie was shot? Then there was shooting," Dorchester said.

"I reckon there was, bein' as Eddie got hisself shot," Tim replied. "But I don't know much else about what happened. I figured I'd better get on back here and tell you folks 'fore you rode off."

"Yes, Tim, that was the right thing to do, and I appreciate it," Dorchester said.

"Where is Eddie now?" Pamela asked, concerned for the young cowboy.

Tim laughed. "He's lyin' belly down on a travois, with his ass stickin' up in the air."

Several of the cowboys laughed, and Tim, realizing what he had said, blushed and apologized to Pamela.

"I'm sorry, ma'am, didn't mean no disrespect."

"That's all right, Tim," she said. "Your characterization was most . . . descriptive."

"Phil," Dorchester called to one of his men. "Ride into town and get Dr. Urban, would you? Tell him we have a wounded man out here."

"Yes, sir," Phil said, starting toward the corral to saddle his horse.

"How about some of you other fellas comin' with me?" Tim said to the others. "Let's go out there and take the herd, so those boys can come on in. They've had a long night of it, I expect."

"Thanks, Tim," Dorchester said. "That's a good idea."

Half a dozen cowboys responded to Tim's suggestion, and a few minutes later they were saddled and on their way.

About fifteen minutes after the cowboys left to bring the herd in, Hawke, Willie, Win, and Eddie showed up. Eddie was on his stomach on a travois, and as Tim had pointed out, his bottom was sticking up in the air. The few cowboys who were still there laughed at the sight.

"What the hell are you laughing at?" Eddie shouted angrily. "How about I shoot some of you in the ass and see how you like it?"

"Take him in the house," Dorchester said. "Mr. Wilson will find a bedroom for him. I think he would be better off there than in the bunkhouse."

"Yes, sir," Win said. "That's real decent of you, Mr. Dorchester."

Win helped Eddie up, and then, with Win on one side and one of the cowboys on the other, they started walking him toward the house.

"Hawke, you want to tell me what happened?" Dorchester asked.

"Well, they had clearly decided to keep the herd for themselves," Hawke said, "because they had people out there guarding it. When we came after it, they opened fire on us."

"How did you manage to get the herd away?"

"When the shooting started, the herd stampeded," Hawke explained. "And fortunately, they were running in the right direction."

"There was four of 'em, Mr. Dorchester," Willie said. "Four of 'em come at us, and Hawke, here, turned 'em back all by his ownself."

* * *

Dr. Urban came out of the bedroom where Eddie had been taken. His sleeves were rolled up and his hands were bloody, so he washed them in a basin that Wilson had placed on the hall table.

"How is he, Doctor?" Dorchester asked.

"If the wound doesn't putrefy, he should be all right," the doctor said. "I managed to extract the bullet without doing too much more damage to the wound, and I poured alcohol on it. There are a couple of doctors in Europe who are very much of the belief that if a wound is sterilized, the patient will have a better chance of recovery. Of course, not everyone agrees, but it seems to make sense to me that if you can keep a wound clean, there is less chance for putrefication, or, as they call it, infection."

"Doctor, I thank you very much for coming out," Dorchester said.

"I'm going to leave a little laudanum. If the pain gets too bad, you can give him a few drops in a glass of water. But don't overdo it."

Dorchester followed the doctor to the door to tell him good-bye. Hawke, who had waited in the parlor until the doctor was finished, was ready to leave as well.

"Doc, if you don't mind a little company, I'll ride in with you," Hawke said.

"Hawke, no need for you to go into town," Dorchester said, surprised at hearing his announcement. "As the foreman, you have a place out here. In the Big House, actually."

"Thanks," Hawke said. "And I will take you up on it tomorrow night. But I've got to go back for my clothes and things, and the hotel room is paid for through the night."

"All right," Dorchester said. "I'll see you tomorrow."

Thinking to have a drink before turning in for the night, Hawke turned his horse out in the livery, then walked across the street to the saloon. As soon as he stepped through the door, he caught, out of the corner of his eye, a chair being brought down on him.

Hawke's reaction was quick enough to enable him to avoid the full brunt of the chair, but the legs caught him on the left shoulder, sending a stab of pain shooting down his side and his arm. It also knocked him down.

"Where at's your pocket knife now, you son of a bitch?" Metzger yelled at him. Metzger lifted the chair back over his head to finish Hawke off. As he stepped forward, though, Hawke rolled and, with a sweep of his foot, caught Metzger behind the leg, bringing him down.

Hawke scrambled quickly to his feet. Metzger started for the chair again, but Hawke kicked it away.

Metzger smiled, then lifted his fists. "All right," he said. "We'll do it your way. I'm goin' to enjoy this."

"Fight, fight!" someone shouted, and the bar patrons quickly gathered around for the impromptu entertainment.

Neither Hawke nor Metzger had been longtime residents of Green River, so neither had a large following of supporters. Metzger had been there long enough, however, to make himself genuinely disliked, so what support there was in the saloon was for Hawke. But among his supporters there was little confidence in his ability to prevail.

"Metzger's damn near twice as big as Hawke," one of the patrons said. "Like as not, he'll break Hawke's back."

"I don't know," one of the others said. "I've seen big 'uns go down before."

After the initial comments, a hush fell over the others as they watched the two combatants go after each other. Hawke and Metzger circled about, their fists doubled in front of them, each trying to test the mettle of the other. On the surface it clearly looked as if Metzger would have the advantage. He was bigger and stronger. But to the surprise of nearly everyone in the saloon, Hawke wasn't backing off, and they wanted to see how he would handle it. They knew he would have to depend on quickness and agility against Metzger's brute strength.

Metzger attacked first, a clublike swing that Hawke leaned away from and counterpunched with a quick jab. It was a good punch, catching Metzger flush on the jaw, but the big man just laughed it off. As the fight went on, it was clear that Hawke could hit Metzger almost at will, but since he was bobbing and weaving, he couldn't get set for a telling blow. And what blows he landed didn't seem to faze Metzger at all.

Then Metzger connected. It was only a glancing blow, but enough to send Hawke careening into one of the tables, which fell over with a crash, sending glasses and bottles banging and scattering about. Trying to capitalize on it, Metzger rushed toward Hawke to kick him, but Hawke managed to get out of the way, though not without knocking over another table.

Recovering from the glancing blow, and having avoided Metzger's rush, Hawke was able to return to his fight plan. He hit Metzger in the stomach several times, hoping to find a soft spot, but there didn't seem to be one there. When that didn't work, he started throwing long punches at Metzger's face, hoping to score there, but they seemed just as ineffectual as the others had been, until he saw a quick opening that allowed him to send a long left to Metzger's nose.

Hawke saw the nose go, and it began bleeding profusely. He tried to hit it again, but now Metzger protected it. For his part, Metzger threw great swinging blows at Hawke, barely missing him, and Hawke knew that if just one connected, he would be finished.

After four or five blows that failed to connect, Hawke noticed that Metzger was leaving an opening for a good right punch, if he could just slip one in across his shoulder. On Metzger's next swing, Hawke was ready, counterpunching with a solid right, straight at the place where he knew Metzger's nose would be. He hit it perfectly, and Metzger let out a bellow of pain.

Blood poured from his nose, across his lips and teeth, and into his beard. The broken, bloody nose was not only painful, it was making it difficult for Metzger to breathe. And that contributed to his getting tired, so tired that he no longer danced around, he stumbled. And his punches had lost nearly all of their power.

Hawke extended the three middle fingers of his right hand, stepped inside one of Metzger's ineffectual swings and thrust his fingertips into the man's solar plexus.

With a loud *oof*, Metzger doubled over, his hands on his stomach as he tried to regain his breath. Hawke sent a whistling punch into his Adam's apple, and the big man collapsed, writhing in agony and struggling to breathe.

Hawke stood over him for a few seconds, until he saw that Metzger wasn't going to get up, then he started toward the bar. Without being asked, Jake poured a drink and slid it in front of him.

"I have to tell you, for a while there I wouldn't have given a bucket of warm piss for your chances with that big son of a bitch. I'd say he has about fifty pounds on you. You sure aren't particular about who you pick fights with."

Hawke chuckled. "Well, if you had paid attention to the start of it, you would see that I didn't exactly start it."

"Yeah, I guess you're right at that. He didn't leave you a hell of a lot of choice."

After finally regaining his breath, Metzger slunk out of the saloon, leaving so quietly, few even noticed that he was gone. The excitement over, the saloon got back to normal; poker games were picked up where they left off, conversations resumed, and the piano player started pounding out an almost recognizable version of "Buffalo Gals."

Hawke winced at a couple of the sour notes, and when the piano player finished the song, walked over to him.

"May I show you something?" he asked.

He was glad to see that the expression on Aaron Peabody's face was more curious than challenging.

Leaning over the keyboard, Hawke played "Buffalo Gals," very quietly, so quietly that only the piano player and those closest to the piano could hear it. As he played each chord, he held his hands in place for a moment so Peabody could see what he was doing.

"I'll be damn," Peabody said. "Do you mind if I play it that way?"

"Be my guest," Hawke invited.

Peabody began, playing it as quietly as Hawke had. A couple of times he made mistakes, but Hawke corrected him.

"Damn!" Peabody said proudly. "Damn, this is good!"

He played "Buffalo Gals" a second time, this time using the chords Hawke taught him. The song was a hundred percent better, so much so that when he finished, there was a smattering of applause.

"Very good," Hawke said.

Aaron Peabody smiled broadly, then looking at the piano, frowned. "You know what? I think I'll ask my brother to get this thing tuned."

"No doubt it would help," Hawke agreed.

Before Hawke went to bed that night, he lit the lantern and walked over to the window to adjust it to catch the breeze. He saw, then, a sudden flash of light in the hayloft over the livery across the street. He knew he was seeing a muzzle flash even before he heard the gun report, and he was already pulling away from the window as a bullet crashed through the glass and slammed into the wall on the opposite side of the room.

Hawke reached up to extinguish the lantern, cursing himself for the foolish way he had exposed himself at the window. He knew better than to do that.

"What was that?" someone shouted from down on the street.

"A gunshot! Sounded like it came from over there by the—"

That was as far as the disembodied voice got before another shot crashed through the window of Hawke's room. If he thought the first shot had cleaned out all the glass, he was mistaken, for there was another shattering, tinkling sound of a bullet crashing through glass.

"Get off the street!"

Hawke heard the voice, and even from up in his room it was loud and authoritative. The words floated up from the street below. "Everyone, get inside!"

Hawke recognized Deputy Hagen's voice. On his hands and knees so as not to present a target, he crept up to the open window. Lifting his head up just far enough to look out, he saw Hagen walking down the middle of the street with his pistol in his hand.

"Hagen, no, the shooter is in the livery!" Hawke shouted. "Get out of his way!"

His warning was too late. A third volley was fired from the livery hayloft, and Hagen fell facedown in the muck of the street.

With pistol in hand, Hawke climbed out the window, scrambled to the edge of the porch and dropped down onto the street. He ran to Hagen's still form and bent down to check on the deputy. Hagen had been hit hard, and through the open wound in his chest, Hawke could hear the gurgling sound of his lungs sucking air and filling with blood.

Hagen opened his mouth to try and speak, but no words came. Blood poured out of his mouth, he gasped a couple of times, then he died.

At that moment another shot was fired from the livery. The bullet hit the ground close by and ricocheted away with a loud whine. Hawke fired back, shooting once into the dark maw of the hayloft. Leaving Hagen, he ran to the water trough nearest the livery and dived behind it as the assailant fired again. The bullet hit the trough with a loud popping sound.

Hawke could hear the water bubbling through the bullet hole in the trough even as he got up and ran toward the door of the livery. He shot two more times to keep the assailant back. When he reached the big, open, double doors, he ran inside.

Moving quietly through the barn, Hawke looked up at the hayloft just overhead, though it was too dark to see anything. Continuing to the rear, he saw a ladder and started to climb it when he heard someone jumping down into the corral out back.

There were several horses in the corral, and they started whinnying and stomping around, disturbed by the fact that someone had suddenly dropped into their midst. There was no back door to the stable, but there was a side door, and Hawke ran to it, then looked out into the corral. It was dark and the horses were milling about, so he couldn't see anyone.

Finally, he gave up and started back out front. By now several people had gathered in the street, most of them were standing around Hagen's body.

"Hold it, mister. Put your hands up!" a cold, angry voice said.

Hawke complied.

"It wasn't him, Sheriff," someone said. "I seen him goin' in after whoever was doin' the shootin'."

"Yeah, I seen it too," another said, and several more verified the claims of the first two.

"Sorry," the sheriff said, putting his pistol back in his holster. "Did you get him?"

Hawke shook his head. "He jumped down from the loft window into the corral out back," he said. "By the time I got back there, he got away."

"Did you see anything? Would you be able to identify him?"

"No," Hawke said. "It was too dark."

After moving through the corral, Metzger got through the back fence then jumped into a ditch.

"Shit!" he said aloud, realizing what he had dropped into. This was the corral drainage ditch, and it was filled with horse manure, liquefied by horse urine.

He climbed up to the edge of the ditch and looked back though the lowest rung of the fence to see if Hawke was still chasing him. He didn't see him anywhere, so he was pretty sure Hawke had given up the search.

Metzger cursed himself for not taking a rifle up to the hayloft with him. If he had used a rifle instead of his pistol, he thought, Hawke would be dead now.

Chapter 20

DORCHESTER CALLED A MEETING OF ALL THE ranchers whose land was affected by the Sweetwater Railroad. Hawke watched the ranchers, big and small, arriving for the meeting in various means of conveyances; buckboards, wagons, open stages, phaetons, country wagons, traps, or just on horseback. Vehicles and livestock filled the curved driveway as the ranchers went into the house and gathered in Dorchester's large parlor. By now all of them knew about the dam, and most had had some of their land confiscated by the act of eminent domain. Though Dorchester's 144,000 acres was by far the largest amount, the others were proportionately just as badly hurt.

"I think all of you know that Bailey McPherson is behind all this," Dorchester said shortly after he started the meeting.

"What I want to know is, how did she get the government to give her all that land?" one of the other ranch owners asked.

"Well, here," Dorchester said, "I've got a copy of the act. I'll read it to you."

He pulled some papers from an oversized brown envelope and began to read:

" 'Whereas gold has been discovered in the Sweetwater Mountains of Wyoming Territory, and whereas it is the responsibility of the United States government to provide for the safety of those who travel, be it therefore known that:

" 'An act to aid in the construction of a railroad and telegraph line as follows:

" 'Be it enacted that the Sweetwater Railroad Company, together with Addison Ford, a commissioner herein appointed by the Secretary of the Interior, are hereby authorized and empowered to lay out, locate, construct, furnish, maintain, and enjoy a continuous railroad and telegraph from Green River City, Wyoming Territory, north along such route as Commissioner Ford directors, in accordance with the route as laid out by survey, to the area known as South Pass in the Sweetwater Mountains.' "

Dorchester quit reading for a moment and looked up. "And now, here comes the part effects us."

He cleared his throat and continued. " 'That there be . . . granted to the said company, for the purpose of aiding in the construction of said railroad and telegraph line, and to secure the safe and speedy transportation of mails, troops, munitions of war, and public stores thereon, every alternate section of public land, designated by odd numbers, to the amount of five alternate sections per mile on each side of said railroad, on the line thereof, and within the limits of ten miles on each side of said road. Provided that all mineral lands shall be excepted from the operation of this act; but where the same shall contain timber, the timber thereon is hereby granted to said company.' "

"So, what does all that mumbo-jumbo mean?" one of the ranch owners asked.

"That means that Bailey McPherson can take all the land she wants, and there is very little we can do about it."

"Yeah, well, McPherson ain't hurtin' none, that's for sure. Fact is, she's not only get land give to her, she's buyin' land from those who will sell to her," one of the owners said.

"That's true," another agreed. "She's made me an offer for my land." He paused for a moment before he went on. "And I have to tell you boys, seein' as how I ain't got water no more, I think I'm goin' to take her up on it."

"What did she offer you, Tony?" Dorchester asked.

"She offered me to buy my stock at half the market price, give me a dollar an acre for my land."

"A dollar an acre?" Dorchester scoffed. "Why, Tony, your land's worth forty times that and you know it!"

"It's worth that with water," Tony agreed. "But without water, that dirt ain't doin' nothin' but holdin' the world together. If it weren't for the fact that she's letting me water my stock on her land, my cows would all be dyin'."

"You mean Bailey McPherson is letting your stock water on her range?" someone asked.

"Yeah," Tony answered. Then he added, "But she's takin' every third cow for payment."

"Every third cow? My God, that's what she's askin'?" one of the owners exclaimed. He shook his head. "And here I was, thinking about going to her, hat in hand, to see if I could work out a deal. But every third cow?"

"Tell me, Mr. Vincent, you do agree that keeping two-thirds of your herd is better than letting all of your cows die of thirst, don't you?" a woman asked.

Dorchester and his guests looked toward the door of the parlor. Bailey McPherson was standing there, smiling triumphantly at the group of landowners.

"What are you taking the cattle for?" Dorchester asked. "I

thought you were in the railroad business, not the cattle business."

"My dear Mr. Dorchester," Bailey said. "The entire purpose of the Railroad Land Grant Act is to provide a means of income to enable entrepreneurs to have the means to build the railroad. The cattle will help me do that. And of course, the railroad will benefit us all. Think how much easier it will be now to get your cattle to the railhead back in Green River, for shipment to the stockyards in Kansas City and Chicago."

As always, Dancer was with Bailey, and he looked around assembled men and women in the room until he spotted Hawke. Then, without taking his eyes off Hawke, Dancer walked over to a nearby table where a tray of cookies and several cups sat.

"Would you care for tea or coffee, sir?" Wilson offered, stepping toward the table.

Dancer paid no attention to him. Instead, he continued to stare at Hawke as he reached for a cup.

"Of course, sir, help yourself," Wilson said weakly as he stepped back away from the table.

Dancer poured himself a cup of coffee, then moved back to stand beside Bailey, all the while staring pointedly at Hawke.

"What do you mean when you say the railroad will help us with our cattle?" Tony Vincent asked. "By the time you are through here, none of us will have any cattle, or land, left."

Hawke walked over to the service table, all the while returning Dancer's stare. Wilson took one step toward the table but saw that, as before, his services were neither required nor wanted. He stepped back.

Hawke poured himself a cup of coffee, then returned to his seat, never breaking eye contact with Dancer.

"We needn't be enemies," Bailey said. "I'm sure we can

work something out. We could have already been discussing it, if I had been invited to the meeting. After all, this is a landowner's meeting, isn't it? Wouldn't the neighborly thing have been to invite me?" She looked pointedly at Dorchester.

"Of course you are welcome here, Miss McPherson," Dorchester said graciously. "It's just that since you aren't facing the same sort of problems the rest of us are, I thought you wouldn't be interested."

"Nonsense," Bailey replied. "If my good friends and neighbors are hurt, then so am I. I want us to find some way to resolve this, if we can."

"Do you have any suggestions, Miss McPherson?" one of the other ranchers asked.

"Yeah," another put in. "Can you tell us how to get our water back?"

"I think we might be able to come to some solution whereby I will open a sluice gate to allow a measured amount of water through. For a fee, of course."

"A fee? You intend to make us pay for the water that by rights is ours anyway?" someone asked angrily.

Bailey shook her head. "Oh, but it isn't yours anyway," she said. "The government was very specific about making certain that I had control of the water. All the water. Why, it is absolutely necessary for the operation of steam locomotives. But surely you already knew that."

"But still, to make us pay for water?" the rancher said. "No. I won't do that. I'll see my cattle die of thirst before I pay you one cent for water."

"Same here," another said. "I won't pay for one drop of water."

"Oh, gentlemen, I do wish you would change your minds," Bailey said. "I think you will find my rates quite reasonable."

When nobody answered, Bailey smiled again, then nodded.

"Yes," she said. "Well, I can see how this might come as a shock to you at first. But I'll give you gentlemen more time to discuss this. I'm sure that, as you think it over, you will realize that I am offering you a way out. The only way out," she added pointedly. "Perhaps it was best that I not attend this meeting after all. Do carry on," she said as she started toward the door.

Dancer set his cup down and left with her, backing out of the room so as not to break eye contact with Hawke.

Shortly after the last of Dorchester's guests left, a lone rider approached. Hawke could see someone was coming, but it was too dark to make out who.

Thinking it might be one of the landowners who forgot something, he called back into the house, "Mr. Dorchester, there's a rider coming."

Dorchester came out onto the porch while Hawke stepped into the shadows and drew his gun, just in case.

"Mr. Dorchester?" a voice called from the dark. "It's me, Rob Dealey."

"It's all right," Dorchester said, waving to Hawke that he could holster his gun. "It's my foreman. Or rather, the man who used to be my foreman." Then, to Rob, he called out, "Come on up, Mr. Dealey."

Rob rode all the way up to the house, dismounted, and tied his horse at the hitching post.

"I didn't expect to see you again," Dorchester said.

"No, sir, I don't reckon you did. And I didn't figure on comin' back, only I found out somethin' I figured you ought to know."

"Oh? And what's that?"

"There ain't no gold up there in the Sweetwaters."

Dorchester laughed. "Heavens, man, you didn't have to

tell me that. Eddie and Win have already come back with the report that they didn't find any gold."

"Yes, sir," Rob said. "Only it's more'n that. They didn't find no gold, I didn't find no gold, and there ain't nobody goin' to find no gold, 'cause there ain't no gold there."

"I can see how it might be frustrating if—"

"No sir!" Rob said again, more forcefully this time. "I ain't makin' myself clear. There ain't no gold there and there never was. Luke Rawlings and Percy Sheridan just put some color around to make it look like there was gold up there."

"Now, why in the blazes would they do something like that?" Dorchester asked. Then, as soon as he asked the question, he knew the answer.

"Bloody hell!" he said. "I see it all now. This has been a ruse to justify the railroad! There is no gold, and if you want to know what I think . . . there is no railroad and there never will be a railroad. This was just a way to get land."

"And water," Hawke said.

"Yes, and water. I can't believe I let myself be taken in like this. Now, half my land is gone and my cows are dying of thirst."

"I don't know what to do about the land," Hawke said, "but I can guarantee you that, after tonight, your cows won't be thirsty again."

"Why? What do you plan to do?"

"You're better off not knowing," Hawke said.

Jay Dupree, Libby, Lulu, and Sue returned to Green River with much less fanfare than there had been at their departure. When they left, they were riding in a carriage, complete with driver, followed by an entourage of four fully loaded freight wagons. They returned in a buckboard that Jay was driving, and they were alone; no freight wagons followed them.

The town was almost as crowded as it had been when they arrived the first time, only now the crowd was leaving.

Jay stopped the buckboard at the railroad station. "I'll get tickets back to Chicago," he said, climbing down. "You ladies wait here."

Libby was sitting on the front seat, Lulu and Sue were on the back. They began talking among themselves as they waited.

"Well, it was fun while it lasted," Lulu said.

"Yes," Sue said. "But I can't help but feel sorry for all those men who worked so hard, when all along there was nothing there."

"I feel sorry for them too," Libby said. "And for Jay. He lost a lot of money in this venture."

Jay returned to the buckboard.

"Did you get tickets?" Sue asked.

"Yes," Jay said. He climbed into the driver's seat and picked up the reins. "But because so many people are leaving, the earliest I could get all of us booked on the same train is seven days from now."

Chapter 21

~~~

THAT NIGHT, HAWKE TOOK THREE MEN WITH HIM:
Rob, Willie, and Win. When Eddie heard they were going,
he wanted to go as well, but he was still recovering from his
wound so he had to stay behind. When they reached the dam
at just after midnight, Hawke held up his hand to stop the
others. They dismounted and ground hobbled their horses.
Hawke took his saddlebags from his horse and draped them
over his shoulder.

"Let's go," he said, starting toward the dam.

Just a slice was missing from a nearly full moon, so the
five men had an excellent view of the stream, the dam, and
the sluice gates, only one of which was open. The gates that
would have allowed the creek to flow on down to the
Northumbria and beyond were closed.

Hawke and the others moved to within about twenty
yards, stopping behind a rock outcropping for a closer examination of the area.

"Looks like they don't have anyone watching it," Willie
said. "Hell, we could just walk right down there and open the
gates."

"Yeah," Hawke said. "And they'll have them closed again by morning. I aim to fix it so they can't close it again."

"Let's do it," Win said.

The three men moved cautiously down to the dam. There, Hawke took out three bundles of dynamite, each bundle containing four sticks. He gave one bundle to Rob, another to Willie, and kept the third bundle himself.

"Get the bundles right up under the dam if you can. That way you'll get the whole thing. But don't light them until we are all ready, and we'll light them together. Win, you keep a good lookout."

"All right," Win said.

"Let's go," Hawke ordered, moving toward the dam. He sent Willie to one end of the dam, and Rob to the other, while he planted his bundle in the middle. When he had his in position, he raised up and looked to the left and the right.

"Ready?" Hawke called.

"Ready," Rob answered.

"Ready," Willie said.

"Light the fuses, then get the hell away!" Hawke shouted.

He struck the match, cupped his hand around the flame to keep it from blowing out, and held it to the fuse. The end of the fuse glowed, then caught and began spitting off sparks.

Hawke turned away from it and ran back toward the rock outcropping, arriving at about the same time as Willie and Rob. Rob stuck his fingers in his ears as the four men waited.

Willie's charge went first, a flash of light, followed a second later by the heavy thump of the explosion. Then came Rob's, followed almost immediately by the dynamite Hawke had placed. Even from there they could feel the concussion of the blow. Then pieces of debris rained down from the sky, followed by the sound of rushing water as Sugar Creek began to flow again.

"Yahoo!" Win shouted. "Damn that was good."

"All right, boys, let's get back home," Hawke said. "We've done a good night's work here."

By the next day, everyone on Northumbria and the adjacent ranches knew that the water was flowing again. And shortly after they learned that the water was flowing, they also found out why. Hawke and the men who had ridden with him became the heroes of the valley.

"What am I paying you for?" Bailey railed at Dancer.

"To be your bodyguard," Dancer answered.

"No, I'm not paying you just to be my bodyguard. That's just what I tell everyone," Bailey said. "What I really pay you for is to make certain that things like what just happened don't happen."

"I wasn't there," Dancer replied. "If I had been there, it wouldn't have happened."

"You are supposed to be intimidating enough that nobody would dare do something like this," Bailey said. "Here you are, one of the most famous gunfighters in the West, but a bunch of cowboys have no more respect for you than to go out to the dam and blow it up."

"I wasn't there," Dancer said again.

"I know you weren't there, you ignorant baboon!" Bailey said loudly. "My point is, if people were afraid of you, they wouldn't do it. But you know what I think? I think you are afraid of that man Hawke."

"I am not afraid of him," Dancer said.

"Really? Well, you can't prove it by me."

Metzger stepped into the office during the argument between Dancer and Bailey. As soon as he realized what was going on, he stepped back outside, without having been seen. He knew, intuitively, that he didn't want to get caught up in the middle of a fight between Ethan Dancer and Bailey

McPherson. The best thing for him to do now, he decided, would be to go down to the saloon and have a drink or two until things calmed down.

A piano tuner had come from Cheyenne, and Hawke stood at the piano with Aaron Peabody as the instrument was tuned.

"You know, there's not a lot I can do with this," the tuner said. "The soundboard is warped, the strings are stretched out of shape. This piano is in terrible condition."

"I know," Peabody said. "But my brother says I don't play well enough to make it worth buying a new one. Maybe if you could get it closer into tune, my playing would improve enough to convince him."

"I'll do what I can," the tuner said. "As long as you don't expect miracles."

"You want to hear a miracle, you should hear this man play," Aaron said, nodding toward Hawke. "I mean, even with the piano like this, he made it sound real good the other day."

"If he made this piano sound like anything at all, it was a miracle," the tuner said as he continued to work.

When Metzger stepped into the saloon, he saw Hawke standing by the piano. Hawke's back was to him.

Damn! he thought. He would never get another chance like this. If he was ever going to do anything, he would have to do it right now.

"Hawke!" Metzger shouted. "Turn around and die, you son of a bitch!"

Turning slowly, Hawke saw that Metzger was pointing his gun at him.

"I missed you the other night," Metzger said. "But I ain't goin' to miss you now."

"So you *were* the one in livery stable?" Hawke said. "I thought as much."

"Yeah, that was me." Metzger smiled a crooked, evil

smile. "When you get to hell, tell my ol' pards Poke 'n' Gilley I said hello."

Metzger lifted his thumb from the handle of his pistol, preparatory to pulling back the hammer, but his thumb never reached the hammer. Hawke drew and fired. His bullet crashed into Metzger's forehead, then burst out through the back of his head. A little spray of blood glowed pink in the light of the overhead lanterns.

Metzger fell back onto a nearby table, breaking it and winding up at the bottom of the V that was formed by the two pieces. He was dead before he ever realized he was in danger.

"My God! How'd you do that?" Jake asked.

"How did I do what?" Hawke replied.

"How'd you kill him, when he already had the drop on you?"

"Simple," Hawke said. "While Metzger was thinking, I was acting."

"What do you mean he had his gun in his hand when Hawke shot him?" Dancer asked.

"'Cause I was there and I seen it," Booker Landers said.

"Nobody is that fast," Dancer said. "Nobody."

"This here fella is," Landers said. "I was lookin' right at him, and I tell you the truth, I didn't even see him draw. I mean, one second he was standin' there by the piano, and the next thing you know the gun was in his hand and he was already shootin' it. I don't know how he got it out so fast."

"Do you think he is faster than you, Mr. Dancer?" Bailey asked.

"No!" Dancer answered, slamming his fist on the counter in the office. "He's not faster than I am."

"You're sure?"

"I'm sure," Dancer said. "Don't worry about it. When the time comes, I will take care of him."

"Yes, I have every confidence that you will," Bailey said.

Chapter 22

AT ALMOST THE SAME TIME THE WATER STARTED
flowing again, the cowboys who had left the range to try
their hand at searching for gold began returning. At first they
came back in ones and twos, then small groups, then in
droves. Within two weeks South Pass City, which had for a
short time been the third largest settlement in Wyoming, was
all but deserted, the tents struck and its occupants moved
out. Now all that remained was a half-built saloon and the
magnificent structure that was once the Golden Cage.

The overnight businesses that had sprung up in Green
River—the outfitters, the Gold Nugget Haulers, and others—closed their doors. Now, three passenger carriages and
six freight wagons were lined up down at the depot, waiting
for flat cars to transport them to someplace more productive.

A buckboard, driven by Hawke, came into town by way of
White Mountain Road. Pamela was riding in it, and they fol-
lowed the road to Railroad Avenue, stopping in front of
Blum's Mercantile.

"I'll just be a few minutes," Pamela said as she climbed
down.

"No hurry," Hawke replied.

"Why, Mr. Hawke, we meet again," a woman's voice called from the boardwalk in front of the mercantile.

Looking toward the voice, Hawke saw Libby St. Cyr. He touched the brim of his hat. "Miss St. Cyr," he said.

"Aren't you going to introduce me to your lady friend?" Libby asked.

Hawke hesitated for a second, then decided that Pamela was the kind of person who probably would not take offense.

"Miss Dorchester, this is Miss St. Cyr," Hawke said. Then, to Libby, he added, "Miss Dorchester is the daughter of the owner of Northumbria."

"Oh, yes, I know all about the great ranch called Northumbria," Libby said. "I must say, it is an honor to meet you, Miss Dorchester."

"Are you just visiting?" Hawke asked. "I thought you, Jay, and the others, were up at South Pass."

Libby chuckled. "There is no South Pass anymore. Not since word got around that there is no gold and there never was. Everyone left, so we had no choice but to leave as well."

"I can see how that would be bad for your business."

"Her business?" Pamela asked. "What is her business?"

"She, uh . . . that is . . ." Hawke started to say.

"I'm a whore, Miss Dorchester," Libby said easily. "A very high-class whore, but a whore all the same."

"Oh my," Libby said. "You eschew the use of euphemisms, I see."

"You mean like, soiled dove?" Libby replied. She chuckled. "Yes, that is the colorful and perhaps even genteel way of referring to the profession. But it is also dissembling. No, Miss Dorchester, I take full responsibility for what I am."

"Well, I must say that I admire your candidness."

"Listen, how would you two like to have lunch with us?" Libby asked. "Jay can get the private dining room at the hotel."

"Oh, I—" Hawke started to say, but was interrupted by Pamela.

"Would love to," Pamela said.

"Great!" Libby replied. "Say, one o'clock at the hotel?"

"We'll be there."

Excusing herself, Libby walked on down the sidewalk with all the flounces in her dress fluttering in the morning breeze.

"I hope you don't mind my accepting the invitation," Pamela said after Libby was out of hearing.

"No, I don't mind," Hawke said. "Although I'm a little surprised that you did."

"Why are you surprised?"

"Well, because Libby . . . uh, that is I mean Miss St. Cyr, is . . ."

"Yes, I know, she is a whore. She was quite candid on that point, I believe."

Hawke smiled and nodded. "Yes, she was that, all right."

"Mr. Hawke, are you not aware of the fact that every woman has a burning curiosity about such things?"

"No, I guess I didn't know that," Hawke replied.

"I'm very much looking forward to our lunch."

The private dining room of the hotel was well-appointed, and a large table was set for six with gleaming china, sparkling crystal, and shining silver. Jay Dupree was a gracious host, and he paid particular attention to Pamela, hurrying over to hold the chair for her before anyone else could.

The conversation during the meal was animated.

"You never did come up to South Pass to play the piano for us," Libby said.

"That would have been hard for him to do, my dear," Jay said. "Since we didn't have a piano."

Libby laughed. "Now that you mention it, we didn't, did we?"

"I had plans to bring one up there, but we didn't stay long enough. As soon as everyone found out there wasn't any gold, they left."

"That's for sure," Sue said. "Why, that place emptied like a theater after a play."

"Here's what I still don't understand," Libby said. "Why did they go to all that trouble to make people think there was gold up there? I mean, nobody was selling claims or anything like that. It doesn't seem to make sense."

"Oh, it makes sense all right," Pamela said. "If you understand the real reason."

"What is the real reason?"

"Yes, I'd be interested in that as well," Jay added.

"It was all a means of getting land," Pamela said. "Bailey McPherson convinced Addison Ford that she would be building a railroad from Green River to South Pass, and Ford, acting for the federal government, began taking land away from the valley ranchers and giving it to her."

"How can he do that?" Jay asked.

Pamela explained about the Railroad Land Grant Act of 1862.

"I'm sure that it was a good thing when they were building the transcontinental railroad," she concluded. "But Bailey McPherson has used it to steal land. Now we know that she had no intention of ever building a railroad in the first place, but it's too late to do anything about it."

"Why don't you go to Addison Ford and tell him what has happened?" Libby asked.

"Ha! A lot of good that would do," Pamela said. "Ford is in it up to his bottom lip."

"You think so?"

"I know so."

"Yes, but now that there isn't going to be a railroad, won't the land be returned to the original owners?" Lulu asked.

Pamela shook her head. "I doubt it," she said. "It would take an act of Congress for the government to admit it made a mistake. At least we've got the water back now, thanks to Hawke and a few of our cowboys. And without the excuse of the railroad, I don't see how they can possibly rebuild the dam. So our cattle won't die of thirst, but they will have a lot less range to roam around in."

"Well, that's something, at least," Jay said, and paused as the waiter came in, carrying a tray with several small bowls.

"Ahh," Jay said. "Dessert."

"Desert?" Pamela said. "Oh, I'm so full, I don't think I could eat another thing."

"Oh, but you have to try their bread pudding," Lulu said. "It is simply wonderful."

"It does look good," Pamela admitted as she examined the bowl put before her.

Abruptly, Libby stood. "Would you people excuse me? I just realized, there are some things I need to do before we leave."

"Are you sure, my dear? Before dessert?" Jay asked.

"Yes, this is something that has to be done. Please excuse me."

"Of course," Jay said.

"Libby, I'll bring your pudding to your room," Lulu offered.

"Thanks," Libby called back as she left the dining room.

"Hmm," Jay said when she was gone. "That was strange. I wonder what she had to do that was so important?"

* * *

"Really, Pamela, your mother would be rolling over in her grave if she knew that you had lunch with doxies," Dorchester said.

"They aren't doxies, Father," Pamela insisted.

"Oh? Then, pray tell, what are they?"

"They are whores."

Dorchester laughed out loud. "Whores, you say? Well, is there any difference?"

"They seem to think so, don't they, Hawke?"

Hawke, who was in the parlor with them, laughed and held up his hands. "Wait a minute, you aren't going to get me into this."

"What do you mean, don't get you into this? You are the one who introduced me to them in the first place."

Dorchester laughed again. "I do believe she has you there, Hawke."

Wilson stuck his head in the room then and discreetly cleared his throat.

"Yes, Mr. Wilson."

"This telegram has just been delivered to you, sir," he said, holding out a piece of paper.

"My word, a telegram for me?"

"What is it, Father? Not bad news I hope," Pamela said anxiously.

"Did you give the delivery boy a gratuity?" Dorchester asked as he opened the envelope.

"I did, sir."

"Good, good."

Pamela and Hawke studied Dorchester's face as he read the telegram, trying to discern its contents.

"Good Lord, can this be true?"

"What is it, Father?" Pamela asked again.

Dorchester began to read aloud. " 'Effective this day all land unjustly seized by the government is hereby returned to the original owner, stop. U.S. Marshals are being sent to Green River to place under arrest the perpetrators of this fraud stop. Signed Congressman Thomas Ashby of North Carolina stop.'"

"Oh, Father, that is wonderful!" Pamela said.

"Yes," Dorchester said. "It is, isn't it?" He looked at the telegram. "But to think our salvation would come from a congressman from North Carolina. How very odd."

At about the time Dorchester was reading the telegram, Rob Dealey was stepping into the Royal Flush saloon. The livelihood of every patron in the saloon depended upon ranching in one way or the other, and though they did not yet know that the land was being returned, they did know about the water. And the return of a steady supply of water was very important to them. Because of that, Rob was greeted with a cheer.

"Jake," one of the men said. "Rob's first drink is on me."

"No, sir," Jake said. "His first drink is on the house. The second drink is on you."

"And the third is on me," another patron said.

"Hey, Rob, tell us all about it."

"Tell you about what?"

"How you and some of the other fellas rode out to the dam and just . . . *boom*!" he said animatedly. "Just blew it up!"

"Well, Hawke is the one that took us out there," Rob said.

"Hawke?"

"Yeah, he's the foreman now."

"I thought you was the foreman."

"I was, but I'm not 'ny more," Rob said sheepishly. "I'm just lucky that Mr. Dorchester took me back at all. I mean, bein' as I took off on him to look for gold."

"The gold that wasn't there," someone said, laughing.

"Yeah, well, it ain't that funny when you spend more'n a

month lookin' for somethin' that wasn't never there in the first place," Rob said.

"So, you was tellin' us about blowing up the dam," someone said.

"Yes, tell us how you blew up the dam."

Rob turned with a big smile on his face, but the smile evaporated when he saw who had asked. Ethan Dancer was standing by the front door, having just come in.

"It, uh . . . was nothing," Rob said. He turned back to the bar.

"Oh, I don't think it was nothing," Dancer said, taunting him. "I've been hearing all over town about how a bunch of . . . brave men . . . blew up Miss McPherson's dam and got the water back. You were one of those brave men, weren't you?"

"I, uh . . . was one of the men who did it," Rob said. He was very nervous now; he didn't like the way this was going. "I wouldn't say that it was all that brave."

"You do know, don't you, that I work for Miss McPherson?"

"I, uh, heard that, yes," Rob said.

"So, you can understand why I'm not taking it all that kindly that a brave man like you would blow up her dam."

"I told you, I'm not a brave man," Rob said, swallowing his humiliation in order not to push the situation any further.

"Oh, but surely you are a brave man," Dancer said. "You are either brave, or you are a coward. Which is it?"

By now everyone in the saloon realized what was going on, and they began drifting away from Rob, even those who a moment earlier had wanted to stand next to him and buy him drinks.

Rob looked into the mirror behind the bar and saw the people drifting to the left and the right, like the parting of the sea. His hand shaking in fear now, he lifted the glass to his lips and took a drink.

"You haven't answered my question, cowboy," Dancer said. "Are you brave? Or are you a coward?"

"I don't know," Rob mumbled. He felt his stomach in his throat, and his knees were so weak that he had to put his hands on the bar to keep from collapsing. He was getting in deeper, and he didn't know how to get out.

"You know what I think?" Dancer said. "I think you are a brave man. Yes, sir, it takes a brave man to do what you done. Bartender, give this brave man another drink, on me."

"Thank you, no, I've had enough to drink," Rob said. "I don't want to go back out to the ranch drunk."

"Are you turning down my generous offer?" Dancer asked.

"Mr. Dancer, I don't think it's that," Jake said. "He never has been much of a drinker."

Dancer didn't say anything to Jake, but he held up his hand in a way that told Jake to stay out of it.

"Turn around, brave man," Dancer said to Rob. "Turn around and tell me to my face that you don't want to accept a drink from me."

"I reckon I'll have another drink at that," Rob said.

Jake's hand was shaking nearly as badly as Rob's now, but he managed to get the drink poured, then set it in front of Rob.

"Thanks," Rob said. He tossed the drink down.

"Why did you thank the bartender?" Dancer asked. "I'm the one that bought you the drink. Turn around and tell me thanks."

"No, don't do it, Rob. Don't turn around," Jake whispered.

"I've got to, Jake," Rob answered. "If I don't, I'll never be able to hold my head up in this town again."

Slowly, carefully, Rob turned around to face Dancer, who was about twenty feet from him. His jacket was pushed back to expose his pistol.

"You know where this is going now, don't you, cowboy? I mean, you aren't really all that dumb, are you?"

Rob took a deep breath. "It's not going anywhere," he said.

"Oh, but I think it is. You are a brave man, after all. I mean, we did decide that, didn't we?"

"Look, let me buy you a drink and let's call it even."

"Uh-uh," Dancer said, shaking his head. "I don't think we can do that now. I think it's time for you to dance with the demon."

"No," Rob said, holding up his left hand, palm out, as a signal to stop. "No, I've heard about you, how ever' time you invite someone to dance with the demon, they die. Well, I ain't goin' to dance with the demon."

"I think you will," Dancer said.

"No, I ain't, I tell you."

Dancer drew and fired, doing it so quickly that it caught everyone in the saloon by surprise. By the time they realized what had happened, Dancer's gun was already back in his holster.

His bullet had had hit Rob's left earlobe. With a shout of pain, Rob slapped his left hand over his ear. When he pulled it back, he saw little pieces of his earlobe in the palm of his hand.

"You son of a bitch!" he shouted angrily. "You shot my ear!"

"Are you ready to dance with the demon?" Dancer asked.

"No!"

Dancer shot again, this time taking off the lobe of his right ear.

"I'm just going to keep carving off pieces of your ears until you draw," Dancer said.

With a scream of fury, fear, and pain, Rob made a frantic grab for his pistol.

Dancer drew and shot him in the heart. By the time Rob hit the floor, dead, Dancer had already reholstered his pistol.

Chapter 23

DANCER LEFT THE SALOON, UNCHALLENGED, AND started toward the boardinghouse where he had a room. As he walked by the office of the Sweetwater Railroad, he was surprised to see a lantern burning inside.

Pulling his pistol, he pushed the door open and stepped into the building. The front room was dark, except for a bar of light that splashed through a partially open door leading into the back room.

Dancer moved quietly toward the door, wondering who was here. He stopped when he heard voices.

"How do you know this?" The voice belonged to Addison Ford.

"I pay the Western Union operator generously, to bring me copies of any telegram he thinks might interest me." This voice belonged to Bailey McPherson. "And according to one he just brought me, U.S. Marshals will be here by tomorrow to arrest the perpetrators of the Sweetwater Railroad Company scheme."

"The perpetrators?"

"Yes. You and me."

"Wait a minute," Addison said. "I'm not the perpetrator here. You are!"

"Try telling that to the U.S. Marshals when they get here tomorrow," Bailey said. "At any rate, you'll be on your own. I'm heading for California on the very next train."

Surprised to hear that Bailey was leaving, Dancer pushed the door open and stepped into the room. His sudden appearance surprised both Bailey and Addison Ford.

"Ethan! What are you doing here?" Bailey asked.

"I just killed Dorchester's foreman," Dancer blurted out.

"What? You killed Hawke?"

"No, I told you, I killed Dorchester's foreman. His name was Rob Dealey."

"You ignorant baboon, Dealey isn't Dorchester's foreman. Hawke is."

"I'm getting tired of you calling me a baboon," Dancer said, his eyes snapping angrily.

"All right, all right, I'm sorry," Bailey said, backing down. She knew she couldn't afford to get crosswise with him now. "It doesn't make any difference anyway. None of it does."

Dancer looked around the room and saw that the safe was open. In addition, he saw that she had been putting bound stacks of money into a carpetbag.

"What are you doing?" Dancer asked. "Why are you going to California?"

"If you heard me say that I'm going to California, then you also know why. Our scheme has been found out. The government has taken back the land."

"How did they find out?"

"I don't know, and I don't plan to stay around long enough to find out." Bailey took a packet of money from the carpetbag and handed it to him. "I won't be needing your services any longer. I don't owe this to you, but you can consider it a tip for a job well done."

"That's it?" Dancer said, his voice dripping with venom. "You are just going to give me one single stack of money and think that squares us?"

Bailey looked up at Dancer, surprised by his reaction. "That's one thousand dollars."

"And I'm supposed to be satisfied with one thousand dollars?"

"Mr. Dancer, what did you think, that you were my partner?"

Dancer nodded. "Yeah," he said. "Something like that."

Bailey began laughing hysterically.

"You actually expected that I could be partners with someone like you? Why, you are barely human, you grotesque creature. Now, get out of here, take the money I offered you while it is still on the table. And don't come back."

Addison laughed.

"Why, look at you," he said. "She practically has you quaking in your boots. I can't believe that I have been frightened of you all this time."

To the degree that Dancer's distorted face could even show expression, it registered shock and confusion, then cold, calculated anger. But neither Bailey nor Addison were astute enough observers to notice the subtle change in Dancer's demeanor. And that was too bad for them, because if they had noticed, it might have saved their lives.

"It's time," Dancer said.

"Time for what?" Bailey said.

"It's time for you to dance with the demon."

"Dance with the demon?" Ford said. He laughed. "What the hell is that supposed to mean?" Still laughing, he looked over at Bailey, but the expression on her face was one of horror, and that, he could recognize.

"No," Bailey said quietly, pleadingly. She held her hands

out in front of her. "Ethan, no, listen, I was just frustrated by events. I wasn't really going to cut you out. I didn't mean—"

Dancer drew and fired, his bullet punching through Bailey's left breast. Ford watched the black hole appear then pump blood as she fell. He was so mesmerized by it that he never even saw the shot that killed him.

"The sheriff isn't here, Jake," Aaron Peabody said, coming back in to the saloon. "So I brought the deputy."

Deputy Wells came in behind Peabody. A young man, until Hagen was killed he'd been one of the wagon drivers for the Gold Nugget Haulers.

Deputy Wells looked down at Rob Dealy's body, covered now by a sheet.

"Who done it?" he asked.

"Ethan Dancer."

Wells nodded, and licked his lips. He continued to stare down at the body, but had not yet removed the sheet.

"Was it a fair fight?" he asked.

"What do you mean was it fair?"

"Who drew first?"

"Take the sheet off and look at him, then ask that question," Jake said.

"What does that have to do with it?"

"Take the sheet off and look at him," Jake said again.

Looking around nervously, Wells squatted down beside the body and pulled the sheet back. He saw the bullet hole in Rob's chest.

"He was shot dead center from the front. That looks fair to me," Wells said.

"Look at his ears," Jake ordered.

Wells looked at the ears and noticed, for the first time, Rob's shredded earlobes.

"What the hell?" he said. "How did that happen?"

"Dancer shot both of his earlobes off, forcing him to draw."

"So, uh . . . this fella did draw first?" Wells asked.

"You dumb shit! Didn't you hear what I just told you? Dancer forced him to draw."

"I see. Where is Dancer now?"

"I seen him when he left," one of the patrons said. "He went into Bailey McPherson's office."

"Is he still there?" Wells asked.

"I ain't seen him leave."

Wells stood there for a moment, then took the star off his shirt and lay it on the bar.

"What are you doing?" Jake asked.

"Look, I'm a wagon driver," Wells said. "I just took this job after Hagen got hisself killed 'cause, what with there bein' no gold, they didn't need wagon drivers no more."

"Yes, but you did take the job. You are the deputy."

"Not no more I ain't," he said. "I ain't goin' up against Dancer. If any of you boys want to do it, well, there's the badge."

Nobody moved toward it.

"I didn't think so," Wells said. He sighed. "I need a drink."

"I think somebody needs to ride out to Northumbria and get Hawke," Jake said.

When Luke Rawlings and Percy Sheridan went into the Sweetwater Railroad office, they saw Dancer standing over the bodies of Bailey McPherson and Addison Ford.

"Holy shit!" Luke said.

"Did you do this?" Perry asked.

"What are you doing here?" Dancer asked.

"Uh, we was just down to the saloon," Luke said. "They're all up in the air 'bout Dealy gettin' kilt, and they've sent someone out to Northumbria to get Hawke."

"Yeah, on account of the sheriff ain't in town, and the deputy don't want nothin' to do with you," Percy added.

"Only he ain't the deputy no more. He quit."

Dancer reached down into the carpetbag and took out two packets of paper currency.

"There's one thousand dollars in each of these packets," Dancer said.

"A thousand dollars?" Perry said. "I've never seen that much money in one place in my life."

"U.S. Marshals are coming into town tomorrow," Dancer said. "We need to get out of town."

"Why we?" Luke asked. "After all this, you'll be the one they'll be looking for."

"You want this money or not?"

Luke hesitated.

"Damn, Luke, a thousand dollars," Percy said, rubbing the back of his hand across his mouth.

"What good is a thousand dollars if you're dead?" Luke asked.

"Have it your way," Dancer said. He started to return the money to the carpetbag.

"No, wait," Luke said. "All right, I'll go."

"My horse is in the stable," Dancer said. "Get him saddled and meet me down behind the Chinese laundry."

Luke lay on top of a flat rock, looking back along the trail over which they had just come. He saw the single rider following them.

"Is he still there?" Dancer asked.

"Yeah," Luke growled. "I believe that son of a bitch could track a fish through water."

"I'll say this for that son of a bitch," Percy said. "Once he gets his teeth into you, he don't give up easy, does he? We've tried ever' trick in the book to shake him off our tail and he's still there."

"We'll lose him," Dancer said. "Or kill him, one or the other."

"Dancer, why don't you just go down there and brace that son of a bitch? Hell, I know you're faster'n he is," Luke said.

"How do you know that?" Dancer asked.

"Well, 'cause you are. Ain't you?"

"I might be," Dancer said. "But who is to say that if I went down there to challenge him, he would give me a fair fight? Hell, if I got out in the open he could kill me with a long gun, long before I ever even got close to him."

"Yeah, I reckon you're right," Luke said. "Well, as steady as he stays on our tail, let's get to movin'. I don't mind tellin' you, I don't like havin' him that close."

"Don't worry, I've got an idea," Dancer said. "I've got an idea that, for all the good he is at tracking, he doesn't know this country. And if he stays on our tail for another five miles, we'll have him right where we want him."

Hawke had never been here before, but he'd been in dozens of places just like this. And if he had to make a guess, he would say that this was a dead end canyon. He stopped at the mouth of the canyon and took a drink from his canteen while he studied it.

Maybe it wasn't a dead end, he thought. Maybe there was a way out. Or maybe they knew it was dead end and wanted to go into it anyway. Why would they do that? he asked himself. Then he answered his own question. They figured they would set up an ambush then draw him in.

Pulling his long gun out of the saddle holster, Hawke started walking into the canyon, leading his horse. The horse's hooves fell sharply on the stone floor and echoed loudly back from the canyon walls. The canyon made a forty-five degree turn to the left just in front of him, so he stopped. Just before he got to the turn, he slapped his horse on the rump and sent it on through.

The canyon exploded with the sound of gunfire as the three men he was trailing opened up on what they thought would be their pursuer. Instead, their bullets whizzed harmlessly over the empty saddle of the riderless horse, raised sparks as they hit the rocky ground, then whined off into empty space, echoing and reechoing in a cacophony of whines and shrieks.

From his position just around the corner from the turn, Hawke located two of his ambushers. They were about a third of the way up the north wall of the canyon, squeezed in between the wall itself and a rock outcropping that provided them with cover. Or so they thought.

The firing stopped and, after a few seconds of dying echoes, the canyon grew silent.

"Where the hell is he?" one of the ambushers yelled, and Hawke could hear the last two words repeated in echo down through the canyon. ". . . is he, is he, is he?"

He studied the rock face of the wall behind the spot where he had located two of them, then began firing. His rifle boomed loudly, the thunder of the detonating cartridges picking up resonance through the canyon and doubling and redoubling in intensity. He wasn't trying to aim at the two men, but instead was taking advantage of the position they'd chosen. He fired several rounds, knowing that the bullets were splattering against the rock wall behind them, fragmenting into deadly, whizzing, flying missles of death. He emptied his rifle, and, as the echoes thundered back through the canyon, began reloading.

"Dancer!" a strained voice called. "Dancer!"

"What is it?" another voice answered, this one from the other side of the narrow draw, halfway up the opposite wall.

"Dancer, we're both killed."

"What?"

There was no answer.

"Luke!"

Silence.

"Percy!"

More silence.

"Percy, Luke, are you all right?"

There was no answer.

Hawke changed positions and searched the opposite canyon wall. There was silence for a long time, and then, as Hawke knew he would, Dancer began to get anxious. He popped up to have a look around.

"Dancer!" Hawke shouted, and the echo repeated the name. *"Dancer, Dancer, Dancer."*

"What do you want? . . . *want, want, want?"*

"We're playing my game now, Dancer," Hawke said. "Have you ever heard of a place called Devil's Den at Gettysburg?"

"Yeah, I've heard of it," Dancer called back, his words echoing and reechoing. "What about it?"

"I killed twenty-one men there, Dancer. In a place just like this."

In fact, Hawke wasn't sure how many he had killed at Devil's Den, but he'd said twenty-one because he knew it would rattle Dancer.

Dancer fired. Hawke smiled. He could tell by the sound of the report that it was a pistol. Dancer had been so sure of the effect of the three-on-one ambush that he hadn't even taken his rifle with him.

Hawke raised his rifle and shot at the wall just behind Dancer, creating the same effect he had with Percy and Luke. He fired several rounds—not to kill, but merely to give a demonstration of what he could do. The shots echoed and reechoed through the canyon, sounding almost as if a full army was firing.

"Son of a bitch!" Dancer shouted.

"I can take you out of there just the way I did Luke and Percy," Hawke said. "Or I can let you wait up there until you run out of water. You didn't take your canteens with you, did you?"

Hawke was running a bluff. He couldn't see well enough to determine whether Dancer had his canteen. He would bet, however, that if Dancer had thought he could ambush and kill him quickly, then he hadn't taken his canteen with him. It was actually a double bluff, because when Hawke sent his own horse through he had not removed his canteen and taken it with him either.

There was no response from Dancer, so Hawke waited a few minutes, then fired two more times. The booms sounded like a cannon blast, and he heard the whine of the bullets, followed once more by a curse.

"By now you've probably figured out that I can make one bullet do the work of about ten," Hawke said. "If I have to shoot again, I'm going to put the bullets where they can do the most damage . . . same as I did with the Luke and Percy. You've got five seconds to give yourself up, or die."

Hawke raised his rifle.

"No, wait! . . . *wait, wait, wait!*" The terrified word echoed through the canyon. "I'm comin' down! . . . *down, down, down!*"

"Throw your weapon down first."

Hawke heard and saw a pistol clattering down the side of the canyon. A moment later he saw Dancer coming down.

"I can't keep my hands up in the air now," Dancer said. "I need 'em in order to climb down."

"Come on down, I'm watching you."

It took almost five minutes for Dancer to work his way all

the way down the side of the rock wall. When he finally reached the canyon floor, he turned toward Hawke.

"Don't you want to try?" Dancer said.

"I beg your pardon?"

"Don't you want to see which one of us is the fastest?"

"I'm not particularly interested," Hawke said. "Right now I've got the gun and you don't."

"Answer a question for me, will you?" Dancer said.

"What?"

"Have you reloaded?"

"Reloaded?"

Smiling, Dancer reached behind him and pulled out a pistol he had secreted in his wristband. He pointed it at Hawke.

"That's a Spencer," Dancer said. "Seven shots. I counted 'em. You ain't got no bullets left, boy. It's time for you to dance with the demon."

Hawke pulled the trigger and the rifle roared. He hit Dancer high, in the center of his chest, and Dancer went down, his holdout gun falling beside him.

"You tricked me," Dancer gasped. "You reloaded."

Hawke cocked the rifle and pointed it at Dancer's face. Dancer closed his eyes and winced, waiting for the impact of the bullet.

"No," Hawke said. "You tricked yourself. You counted the echoes."

He pulled the trigger and Dancer jumped as the hammer fell on an empty chamber.

"I'll be damned," Dancer said.

Hawke dismounted at the depot, tied his horse off, and went inside.

"Hawke!" Jay Dupree called. "You've come to see us off! How delightful."

Squealing in delight, each of the three women gave Hawke a hug.

"Ladies, isn't that nice that he has come to see us off? We've been run out of a few towns before, but we don't often have people coming down to bid us a fond farewell."

Hawke laughed.

"I hear that you quit your job out at Northumbria," Libby said.

"Yeah, I did."

"I would have thought you might stay on out there."

"Why?"

"Well, it's a beautiful place, it has a fine piano that you could play anytime you want, and Mr. Dorchester has a beautiful daughter."

"I thank you for your interest," Hawke said, "but I've got what you might call the wandering disease. I can't stay settled in any one place too long. Besides, I wasn't that good a foreman. Willie is a lot better than I was. I talked Dorchester into giving him the job."

"You could do worse than marry a wealthy woman," Libby said, "And she could do a lot worse than marrying you."

"Are you playing matchmaker now, my dear?" Jay asked.

"I was trying to," Libby admitted. "Evidently, not very successfully."

There was a distant whistle as the train approached town.

"All right, ladies, grab your things," Jay said.

"Libby, could I speak to you for just a moment?" Hawke asked.

"Sure," she said, walking away with him.

"Libby, don't you miss the train!" Jay shouted.

"Don't worry, I won't."

"It was you, wasn't it?" Hawke said when he had her alone.

"What? What was me?"

"When we had lunch that day, you excused yourself early, remember? You sent a telegram, didn't you? To your father, the North Carolina congressman."

Libby looked back toward the Jay and the other two women. "They don't know," she said.

"What do you mean, they don't know? When Jay introduced all of you, he said you were a congressman's daughter. I didn't believe it until Dorchester got the telegram saying that all the land would be returned."

"Look, Lulu is not a New York debutante and Sue is not a Russian princess. Jay allowed us to make up our own stories. I just happened to choose one that is true. And what better way to keep it a secret?"

Hawke laughed and shook his finger. "Somehow, there is a woman's logic there. I'm just not sure I see it."

"Don't try to figure it out," she said, laughing as well. "It will give you a headache."

"Come, I'll walk you to the train."

The eastbound train pulled alongside the depot platform and came to a clanking, squealing, hissing halt. Hawke walked outside with Libby then waited until all were aboard. Once the train got underway, he left.

As he mounted his horse to ride away from town, he heard a distant roll of thunder. Looking to the west, he saw a dark bank of clouds building up, but knew the rain wouldn't get there. The Wind River Range would steal what moisture the clouds had, but at least it would make the ride a little cooler.